A RICH FULL DEATH

by the same author

ff

MICHAEL DIBDIN

A Rich Full Death

faber and faber
LONDON · BOSTON

To Sybil

First published in Great Britain in 1986 by
Jonathan Cape Limited, London
This paperback edition first published in 1988 by
Faber and Faber Limited
3 Queen Square London WC1N 3AU

Printed in Great Britain by
Clays Ltd, St Ives plc
All rights reserved

© Michael Dibdin, 1986

A CIP record for this book is
available from the British Library

ISBN 0-571-15045-4

6 8 10 9 7 5

'The poem's origin probably lies in . . . a painting in the Pitti Palace in Florence, then supposed to be del Sarto's portrait of himself and his wife; it is now known to be two portraits joined together, is no longer attributed to del Sarto, is not thought to depict the painter or his wife, and has been relegated to storage.'

Editor's note to Browning's
'Andrea del Sarto' (Yale edition)

Contents

BOOK ONE

Up at a Villa – Down in the City

I

My dear Prescott,
You will no doubt be surprised to receive another letter so soon,
but I have news which cannot await my monthly packet. Prepare
yourself for a shock, for I have sad and dramatic tidings: Isabel
Eakin, née Allen, is no more, having passed away yesterday
evening under tragic circumstances – of which more in a
moment. What a piece of my life – of both our lives – falls into
oblivion with her! Death must always diminish the survivors, but
when I consider how intimate a part of my life Isabel once was, I
feel half-dead myself at the thought of all she has taken with her
to the grave.

How vividly I recall those long summer afternoons we spent
together – you and I and she, and that freckly cousin whose
name and face and indeed everything except her freckles I
presently forget. Is it really fifteen years ago? Mighty fine young
fellows we thought ourselves then, as I remember; with the
bloom of college still fresh on us, like hothouse peaches. I forget
exactly how or when we discovered that there were mysteries of
which our professors had said nothing (and perhaps had nothing
to say), such as the miraculous transformation of scrawny little
Isabel – previously the butt of much boyish torment on my part –
into a fascinating and powerful figure with capacities of her own
for inflicting torment.

I was in love with her, of course. Was I the only one? Own
up, Prescott – were you not just as assiduous as I at inventing
pretexts for calling at the Allens' house as often as possible? Strange to think that we stood, without knowing it, at
one of the great crossroads of Life: we might have married her,
either of us, and then everything would have been utterly
different.

Well, well, all that is over now – separated by a desert of sterile years from the comfortable pastures of the Present. For what *did* happen? You launched yourself energetically on your academic career, married a woman who would loyally support you, and won fresh laurels with every year that passed – modestly at first, but set already on course to your present Parnassian position: a Professor yourself, author of a standard text on ethics – and all this at the age of forty!

I also achieved much – in my dreams. If plans, projects, or proposals counted for aught, I should be numbered among the greatest men of our age! What was I not going to write? An epic poem in twelve books on the War of Independence; *Washington*, a tragedy in five acts; a three-volume novel about a young man's picaresque travels through every state of the union, combining Smollett's dash and colour with the sentimental depths of Young Werther. I was, as you see, going to do much; so much that in the end I did nothing. Not content, like you, to reach for graspable gains, I have remained empty-handed.

And then, to cap so much failure and frustration, came Isabel's refusal – definitive and irrevocable – of my belated proposal of marriage. I am loath to speak ill of the dead, but she erred – of that I am convinced. At all events, after that I could stand no more: the very streets of Boston sickened me, the air seemed contagious and every face mean, stupid and provincial. I set out for the Old World with a heart as full of high expectations as any of our founding fathers making the journey to the New. Expectations which have been fulfilled, for here I have found minds to my measure, kindred spirits, and a fresh start.

Apart from fleeting appearances in my dreams, I had neither seen nor heard of Isabel for over twelve years when suddenly, in the course of a second-rate ball at the Baths of Lucca last summer, I found myself face to face with her. And when I say her, I mean with that lithe bewitching figure I had last seen amid the apple trees and dappled sunlit vistas of the Allens' garden – that superb type of American womanhood: vivacious, proud, high-spirited. The long years between had left no mark on her whatever. But then was that not the keynote she perpetually sounded: of one who, whatever befell, remained untouched?

If so, it was an illusion which was most cruelly dispelled last night. Poor child, to end thus!

First, though, let us leaven these sad tidings with some happier ones. Congratulate me, Prescott, for I awake this morning the confirmed acquaintance of Elizabeth Barrett Browning and her husband! Nor shall I stray entirely from my darker theme, for by a bizarre coincidence – if indeed it is no more than that – the circumstances are connected with the terrible details of Isabel's death.

Yesterday I was invited to dine by James Jackson Jarves, the Ruskinist – I have already recounted how I made his acquaintance apropos the Primitive altarpiece in Sansepolcro he wanted for his collection. That came to nothing, unfortunately, the monks proving too grasping, but the connection between us has remained, and one result was an invitation to Sunday dinner, where I was one of a dozen guests picked from the cream of the Anglo-American community here. (Jarves's Wednesday dinners are even more select, but I cannot hope for so much as yet.)

At all events, the gathering was an occasion to remember, and not only as a milestone in my standing here. Nevertheless, I was once again disappointed, at heart. How can I explain? It was all very worthy, the conversation was enlightening and cultivated – and yet, and yet! Where was the spark? The question may seem gratuitous, yet it is one which occurs to me with more and more force the longer I stay in this city where one is confronted on every side by evidence of the genius of the Past; where such figures as Giotto, as Dante, as Michelangelo, are as it were one's daily bread. Where are the names today that might be heard in such company?

On my way home from Jarves's I encountered a man who, in his own estimation at least, is such a one. I mean Mr Hiram Powers, who rejoices in the happy position of being able to sell copies of his 'Greek Slavegirl' for – one hears – some four thousand dollars apiece. Success, I am happy to report, has not had the slightest adverse effect on his character: he has always believed himself to be assured of a place among the immortals and the acclaim of two continents has done nothing to shake this opinion. He is, no doubt, a genius – but whether it be his mid-Western manners or the fawning adulatory throng which surrounds him, I cannot delight in his company. In short, he

13

does not inspire me – although his studio has been a fruitful source of social encounters.

As I was strolling back through the fast-gathering dusk, then, who should I spy ahead of me in the street but just this same Yankee stonecutter. Where was I going? Home; and he? Off to take coffee with the Brownings, who are close friends of his – you may perhaps have seen her pretty sonnet on his Greek slave-piece. Powers's casual words electrified me, for I have had my sights on Mr and Mrs Browning for some time, although well aware of the challenge; for they are difficult of access – a very social Alp; remote, elevated, and somewhat chilly.

I neither batted an eyelid nor faltered in my step, however; merely remarking as we proceeded down the street together that I had lately gone – after hours, being privileged by a personal contact, for the press of tourists during the day is a horrible example of Democracy in action, making it impossible for any to appreciate what all would enjoy – I had gone, I said, to view the 'Medici Venus', which I had long considered the acme of artistic perfection. Indeed – I continued – its inimitable qualities might well cause me, were I a sculptor, to throw away my chisel in sheer despair.

Now I must explain that my reasons for advancing this banal opinion were by no means purely aesthetic. I happen to know that Mr Powers has an exceedingly low opinion of the Venus, which he is fond of comparing to its disadvantage with his own work. Nor did I succeed in altering his views during our brief walk, but my companion became so warm on the subject that he was still holding forth when we arrived at the wedge-shaped palace where the Brownings live, secreted from the world like a monastic order of two. Loth to interrupt the coruscating flow of my companion's ideas, I took it upon myself to ring the bell; and there I still was when Mr Robert Browning came in person to open the door, leaving him little alternative but to admit me too. I was in the seventh heaven! To be permitted to worship at the feet of the poetess of the age is a favour eagerly sought after by all who live in or pass through Florence. But though many are called, few are chosen, and to be numbered among that elect band – well, I need not labour the point.

It proved, however, to be with *Mr* Browning that I was most particularly taken – surprisingly, since the object of reverence is of course his wife, to whose genius he ministers in the role of sacristan. And yet, for whatever reason I cannot tell, he struck me almost more forcefully than she. No doubt the fact that I had not expected anything in that direction heightened the effect. Certainly there was nothing whatever remarkable or 'interesting' about his appearance. An honest robust no-nonsense English gentleman is all one would take him for: about my own height, with a silvery-grey beard and dark, straight, neatly trimmed hair. Everything about him, indeed, is scrupulously neat and tidy; completely lacking in any hint of eccentricity or cheap artistic affectations of the sort that Powers, for example, is by no means innocent of. But neither is there any suggestion of fussiness or lack of manly vitality. On the contrary, Mr Browning's manner is forthright, virile and energetic in the extreme; his voice vibrant and full of expression; while his gestures seem more Italian than English, being large, frequent and emphatic. In short, a man's man – a woman's too, if I am any judge.

As for his wife, what can I say that has not already been said? It is like trying to say a fresh thing about Florence itself. I will therefore restrict myself to confirming the veracity of the many published accounts – and add my impertinent two cents' worth to the effect that they are a mighty odd couple. Him I have already described; now picture, if you please, a woman of more than a certain age, swaddled in rugs and propped up in an armchair too large for her, for all the world like an outsize doll; fearfully tiny and pale, with a shrill squeaky voice and features pinched with age and suffering, sickly, drained of all vigour, her general pallor accentuated by the thick black ringlets hanging about her face like funeral drapes.

Such is Elizabeth Barrett Browning – a creature seemingly more akin to one of the ectoplasmic apparitions she so fervently believes in than to any woman of flesh and blood. On her undoubted poetic gifts, on the spirituality which observers have described as shining from her face as light from a lamp, I do not presume to comment. My unspoken question was rather, granted all the genius and spirituality in the world, what the devil can be in it for a man like him? To drag out his days in that dim shadowy shrine of a drawing-room, heavy with tapestries and old Florentine furniture and a bust of Dante glaring at you from the sideboard?

15

There I was, at any event, and it felt enough that I *was* there, planted squarely atop the Matterhorn and coolly surveying the view in this fashion.

About eight o'clock, as Mr Browning was in the middle of one of his seemingly inexhaustible supply of lively anecdotes, a servant entered to inform him that someone was at the door with a message. Browning went to investigate. After several minutes he returned looking rather flustered, excused himself, and said that he had unexpectedly to go out. When his wife quite naturally enquired as to the reason for this, Browning muttered something about a man named DeVere.

Now I know a Cecil DeVere, and I therefore innocently asked if the man in question were he. To my surprise, Mr Browning shot me a look of – I don't know exactly what, but no very warm or happy emotion – and replied that it might be, he was not sure. Mr Powers saved the situation by remarking that his wife and brood of children would be expecting him, and that he too must be going. For a moment it occurred to me take Browning's 'No, please don't leave on my account' at its face value, and remain *à deux* with Elizabeth Barrett Browning! But it crossed my mind that this might be a trifle forward, and jeopardise my chances of future invitations to the Guidi palace. I therefore took an elaborate leave of the poetess, with fervent expressions of hope that we might meet again very shortly – to which, it seemed to me, she replied with genuine warmth! – and walked out with the other men.

At the door, I suggested to Mr Browning that we walk together to Cecil DeVere's house, which lies on the river bank along my natural route home. With an appearance of some confusion, he declined, explaining that the meeting was not at DeVere's house itself but at a suburban villa. As luck would have it, a cab came along at that moment, returning to the rank opposite the Pitti palace – for the Brownings' residence is in the most fashionable part of town, just opposite that of the Grand Duke himself – and Mr Browning immediately hailed it.

I did not hear the direction which he gave to the cab-driver – indeed, I fancy he deliberately moderated his voice to prevent my doing so. In which case he missed his object, for the man bawled it out in the strident tones of his profession, together with many expressions of his unwillingness to go so far outside the walls at that time of night. Imagine my feelings when I learned that the address to which Mr Robert Browning had been suddenly and secretly summoned was none other than the villa in which Isabel and her husband had been living for the past five months!

Literally open-mouthed I watched Browning overcome the cabbie's scruples by liberal recourse to the persuasive powers of coin of the realm. He then took a very perfunctory leave of me, and mounted, shooing the urchin who had delivered the message in ahead of him. As soon as I had recovered my wits I ran down the street to the cab-rank and engaged the solitary vehicle I found standing there, and a few minutes later was also on my way towards the remote villa on Bellosguardo hill.

II

It was not until we passed through the Roman Gate and outside the protecting circlet of the walls that I realised how violent the wind had become. It was a northerly – the dreaded *tramontana* which sweeps down on Italy like the barbarian hordes of old, and against which poor Florence's only defence is that massive and high circuit of stone designed to keep out the French, Germans, Milanese, and all the other bloodthirsty bands which once roamed this land, but whose only function nowadays is as a wind-break. Once we got outside the blast hurled itself at the cab like an animate and malignant force, pawing the vehicle about like a cat toying with a mortally-wounded mouse. The clouds had all been stripped from the sky, and the light of the full moon revealed the landscape of cypresses and olives in varying intensities of luminous grey.

As the cab crawled up the steep hillside I tried to explain to my satisfaction just what Cecil DeVere could be doing summoning Robert Browning to a rendezvous at the Eakins' villa at eight o'clock on a Sunday night. DeVere, I should explain, is a young Englishman of the languid aristocratic type, who is nominally Her Britannic Majesty's Consul at Spezia, a small port on the Tuscan coast. This post is in fact a perfect sinecure, and the fortunate DeVere visits the town only in those summer months when the heat drives everyone out of Florence. For the remainder of the year he lives here in the most complete idleness, devoting his energies to his wardrobe, his collection of ancient coins and medallions, and the social round of receptions, balls and afternoon drives in the Cascine gardens. He is a pleasant enough fellow, whose extensive range of contacts I found more useful during my early years here than I do now that I have established myself. None of which went any way at all towards explaining the mystery.

If the wind had seemed strong on the slopes of the hill, the effect at the top, more than two hundred feet above the river valley, was truly indescribable. More than once I feared that the cab would be overturned, and in fact when we reached the gates of the villa – which stood wide open – the driver roundly refused to go any further. Rather than waste precious time arguing I alighted and proceeded on foot.

The villa which Joseph Eakin has made his this winter, for the sum of one hundred dollars a month, is the largest and finest of all those which stand on the celebrated hill of Bellosguardo. It is in the classic Tuscan style, being modelled on the huge Medici villa at Artimino – a plain but elegantly-proportioned block of pale yellow rendered stone, with a superb swirl of steps up from the carriage sweep to the *piano nobile*, and rooms high and spacious within, set in several acres of walled park. The formal gardens at the rear of the house culminate in the famous belvedere, from which Florence has been indifferently painted so many times.

As there was no sign of life in the keeper's lodge I walked, or rather staggered, up the driveway into the teeth of that appalling wind. I just had time to observe that there were lights on the first floor of the house, and that the four-wheeler I had seen Browning hire was standing in the sweep, when another carriage came dashing up the drive. I stepped hastily into the shadows of the undergrowth, from which point of vantage I watched the conveyance draw up and four men emerge. Two of them I knew by their uniform to be constables of the Grand Duke's police force, while a third elderly man I recognised as the gate-keeper; the remaining individual, a slight well-dressed gentleman, I could not identify. All four disappeared into the villa through the low door beneath the sweeping double stair-way, which gives access to the servants' quarters on the ground floor.

I was now in something of a quandary, since my position was irregular, to say the least. I was not concerned about Mr Eakin's wrath, for I had established the friendliest of relations with him and Isabel, and had been a frequent visitor at the villa, where a distinctly transatlantic freedom and ease prevails. But it was now clear that the police were involved, and I had no wish to become embroiled with them until I had a clearer idea of what was afoot. I therefore decided to circle around the side of the villa to the gardens I have already spoken of, and try to see how matters stood before declaring my own presence.

Until now I had been in the lee of the house, and therefore to some extent sheltered, although such a wind has a way of finding you out wherever you are. But the garden faces north, towards the Apennines, and here the thing itself raged – a darkness whole, mobile and massive as a stormy ocean. I had only the most general impression of shapes and shades, of the outlines of the garden I knew so well, which seemed to have been shuffled like a pack of playing cards. The place was full of surprises: everything seemed larger or smaller, nearer or more distant, than I expected it to be. I pressed forward, however, towards one shape less dark than the rest, more constant, detaching itself from the blurry confusion of background forms with growing insistence; lighter and more agitated than the rest, swinging to and fro – long, luminous, white.

Steel yourself for a shock, my dear fellow, for it was poor Isabel I saw there, hanging by her neck from a tree!

The next instant my attention was seized by something I caught sight of moving on the ground beneath – something low, dark and bulky. At first I thought it was some animal – a dog, or a wild boar – and it was with a distinct thrill that I realised a moment later that the form was human, and then recognised Mr Browning!

His behaviour was bizarre, to say the least. Seemingly oblivious of the terrific figure which the wind tugged and buffeted this way and that in the luminous darkness above his head, he had crouched down and was devoting all his attention to a wrought-iron garden table which stood close by. So far as I could tell from my position some ten feet off, this item appeared to be as devoid of interest as other examples of its very common type; but there was Mr Browning, in the middle of a howling gale, that pathetic corpse swaying inches above his head, examining the claw-shaped feet of the thing with a degree of concentration worthy of an antiquary inspecting the latest Etruscan relic to come to light.

The next moment, to my utter astonishment, he began poking his fingers into the soil, and then holding them up in the moonlight to study the effect!

Just then my attention was attracted by a movement to my left, towards the house, and I quickly took cover as the two policemen who had arrived in the carriage walked towards us. They remained quite unaware of my presence, although they passed by no more than a few feet away, and I was able to watch them go up to Mr Browning, tap him on the shoulder, and direct him with gestures to return to the villa – any attempt at speech was quite out of the question in that wind. The two then set about freeing the tree of its awful burden.

It was evident that any future developments would take place at the house rather than in the garden, so I hastily made my way back around the side of the villa to the front, through the low door beneath the steps and into a warren of passages and corridors which eventually led me to the cavernous kitchens. Here I found a little group consisting of the gate-keeper, Isabel's maid, and the fourth man I had seen arrive in the carriage, who now introduced himself as Commissioner of Police Antonio Talenti.

'You are Signor Eakin?' he enquired.

I hastened to disabuse him.

'And what are you doing here?' demanded the official, once I had identified myself.

I explained that I had called in hopes of seeing Mr or Mrs Eakin, who were old friends of mine – this story would not have borne much scrutiny, but as luck would have it the door flew open at that very moment, admitting the two policemen carrying the body, and the anomalies of my presence were forgotten.

The corpse was incongruously deposited on the nearest table, which happened to be one of the marble-topped kind used for rolling out noodles; water dripped monotonously from the sodden garments to the stone floor.

Poor Isabel! I said just now that she was one who seemed to have the gift of effortlessly shrugging off the droop and pall of reality – yet here she was, unceremoniously laid out, a nightmare vision; the face horribly discoloured, the eyes and tongue protruding. It was an obscenely compelling spectacle: there was no looking at it, and no looking away. It had to be covered, and as there was nothing suitable to hand Beatrice was sent to search out a sheet.

Meanwhile the door to the garden – at which the wind was heaving to get in – flew open once more, and Mr Browning appeared. He barely glanced at us – did not see me, I am sure. He had eyes for only one thing: Isabel's corpse.

The police official, with an ironical display of politeness which was not lost on his subordinates, begged this newcomer to have the goodness to identify himself. In view of the tyrannical way the authorities here comport themselves, he was treating Browning with consideration. I was therefore the more impressed with the insolence Mr Browning showed in ignoring the fellow, as if utterly unaware of his existence. He crossed to the table where the corpse lay, and examined with admirable coolness the loop of rope embedded in the bare white flesh of the neck, and then each of the poor dead white hands in turn.

The constables were moving to recall Browning to the realities of the situation, when Beatrice returned and quite effectively did so by covering the piteous figure with the sheet she had procured. Deprived of the sole object of his attention, Mr Browning looked around like one emerging from a spiritualist trance.

'Mr Booth! Are you here too?' he murmured vaguely.

'Aha! So you two know each other, eh?' the police official demanded triumphantly, as if this fact were a crime. It was no doubt a justifiable impatience with the fellow's overbearing manner which made Browning reply, 'Certainly we do; and what of it?' – although of course the extent to which we 'knew' each other at this time was fairly limited. Nevertheless it was quite a feather in my cap to hear Mr Robert Browning roundly declare me to be his companion in this unequivocal manner!

Ignoring the question, Talenti seated himself at the head of a long wooden table in the centre of the room. His constables stood guard at either side, and the rest of us remained grouped uneasily together, like schoolboys before the master. And so the interrogation began.

The first point to be established related to the whereabouts of Mr Joseph Eakin: he had left Florence that morning to visit an elderly aunt of his who lives in Siena, and was not expected to return until the following day. That this was in no way remarkable, I was able to confirm from my own knowledge. The aunt suffers from some suitably genteel ailment, and – there being some question of an inheritance – Joseph Eakin has gone fortnightly to commiserate with her throughout his stay here.

In the absence of her husband Mrs Eakin had no plans either to entertain or be entertained, and she had accordingly dismissed all the servants except her own maid until the following morning. Beatrice had been retained to dress her mistress and to prepare a light luncheon, after which she had been given the rest of the day off, with instructions to return about supper time.

From that moment on, it at first appeared, Isabel had been alone in the villa. Shortly afterwards, however, a very important clue emerged in the testimony of the gate-keeper, who deposed that an unknown woman had called at the villa at about four o'clock, leaving about twenty minutes later – and despite the strenuous cross-questioning of the police official, he would in no way be shaken from this testimony. He had opened the gates to let her in, he said, and closed them again after her departure. There had been no other visitors.

This, therefore, brought us to twenty past four or thereabouts. Commissioner Talenti had astutely remarked that the victim's clothing was extremely damp. As I have already observed, there had been but one fall of rain all day, as brief as it was intense, and this was over by five o'clock. Before that the weather was unnaturally close and still for the time of year, afterwards it grew increasingly windy, but with no further precipitation. It therefore seems clear that Isabel could not have died later than five o'clock – a mere forty minutes after her mysterious visitor left.

The rest is quickly told. Returning at half past seven, Beatrice found the house deserted and the lamps guttering in the wind blowing in through the large glass doors which lay open on to the steps leading to the garden. As she went to close them, the girl caught sight of a strange white form apparently hovering several feet above the ground in the moonlit garden. As always with old houses, there are rumours that the villa is haunted – in this case by a beauteous maiden murdered long ago by a jealous lover, or some such nonsense. Directly the maid caught sight of the white shape glimmering in the garden she naturally assumed it to be the apparition, and fled to the gate-keeper's lodge. The old man, a sturdy old Tuscan peasant who would bargain with the devil himself, returned alone to investigate, discovered Isabel's body hanging from the tree, and went to fetch the authorities.

And Beatrice? She, left alone once more, began to realise the problems that her mistress's death was likely to cause her. Isabel Eakin was a foreigner; where foreigners are involved there are always complications; these are not likely to be diminished when the foreigner in question is young, beautiful and has met a violent death. The remedy, clearly, was to fight fire with fire – bring in another foreigner to deal with these problems in the high-handed foreign way. And so she sent a lad from a nearby farm to summon Mr Browning.

Yes, indeed! I too sat bolt upright and wide awake at this astonishing intelligence. So did the police official.

'We are so fortunate as to have several thousand foreigners here in Florence,' he commented, with a flicker of a smile. 'Why, out of so many, did you send for this one?'

A pointing finger reduced Mr Browning to the status of an inanimate courtroom exhibit.

And now, for the first time, Beatrice faltered – fatally. Thus far everything had been said calmly, smoothly, naturally; with some understandable confusion in places, but no sense whatever of embarrassment or difficulty. Yet now her eyes roved restlessly about, determinedly avoiding Mr Browning's – who for his part was looking at the girl with unusual intensity.

'I don't know,' she murmured at last.

'Don't know?'

Talenti had dropped his teasing manner.

'Do you think I can be fobbed off with such stuff, my girl? If you can't do better than that, I'll have you locked up in the Bargello until you do know. But first I'll give you one more chance. Why did you send for this man?'

Browning made to speak, but the official peremptorily silenced him. The maid started to weep. At length she spoke, almost inaudibly.

'He was a friend.'

'Oh, he was, was he? Your friend?'

I glanced at Browning, who sat strained forward, the image of a man in an agony of suspense.

'A friend of the family,' Beatrice replied between sobs.

'But what are you saying, you stupid girl?' the gate-keeper suddenly burst out. 'What friend of the family? I see everyone who comes to this house. For example, I know *you* well enough,'

24

he said, turning to me. 'But as for this man' – pointing at Browning 'I've never seen him before in my life!'

The police official stared bleakly at Beatrice.

'So, you have lied. That much is sure. Do you know the penalty for lying to the authorities?' He paused, terribly, for a moment. 'Now then, for the third and last time I ask you – why did you send for this man?'

The poor girl looked at Browning, and then at the policeman, and then back at Browning. I had not noticed before – one doesn't, of course, with servants – how beautiful she was, with very distinct features, a full figure, and long raven-black hair. Finally she spoke, in a wavering voice.

'He was a friend . . . of the signora'.

And she nodded at the table where Isabel's body lay stretched out.

The mocking little smile appeared for an instant on Talenti's features, and was gone.

'I see,' he replied blandly. 'Well, Signor Browning – what have you to say?'

After a long silence Browning asked if he could speak to the official alone, and to my surprise – and disappointment – this was granted. Browning then quickly scribbled a note, which he handed to me with the following words: 'Mr Booth, I implore you, as one gentleman to another, to deliver this to my wife as soon as possible. Will you do so much for me? It will prevent much needless suffering. But say nothing of what has happened here, I beseech you! I am, of course, completely innocent – as will very soon be established.'

I expressed my wholehearted belief in this, and promised to deliver his note immediately. Then, having supplied my address to the police, I reluctantly left the villa.

On my way home I tried to make some sense of what I had witnessed, and in particular of Browning's declaration that he was completely innocent – which very naturally provoked the thought 'innocent of *what*?' Of any relationship with the deceased woman? Then why should Beatrice so plainly have tried to conceal this fact? Why struggle to conceal from the police – with all the dangers this entailed – a relationship which did not exist?

No, surely what Mr Browning must have meant is that there

25

was a connection between him and Isabel, but that it was not a guilty one. The fact remains, however, that it looks bad – and this impression is not diminished by the fact that he is evidently striving to conceal the whole affair from his wife. This was confirmed by his note, which I took the liberty of reading before handing it in – falsehoods were in the air, after all, and I felt justified in knowing just exactly which one I might be taking responsibility for spreading. 'I have been detained longer than expected – do not wait up for me – will explain all tomorrow' was the gist of the thing. Fortunately I was spared any need to tell untruths myself, merely handing Browning's note to the servant and continuing home to bed.

I slept badly, tormented by doubts, questions, hopes and fears, and was awakened at six o'clock by the characteristic Florentine din of a bullock-cart passing by underneath my window. It is now almost nine, and with the sunlight streaming into the room last night seems little more real than a bad dream – it suddenly occurs to me that the answers to all the mysteries I have so laboriously described may well be known by now. I shall therefore lay down my pen and go and seek them out, in hopes of concluding this letter in a more satisfactory fashion than with a mere series of question marks.

III

Has it ever happened to you, while going through old papers, to hit upon some youthful journal or memorandum, full of shallow certainties and easy courage? If so, you will be familiar with the mixture of contempt and pity which I now feel on scanning the above lines – the difference being that these were penned not six-and-thirty hours ago!

Judge from this the intensity of the changes that have taken place in so short a time: truly I may say that most of the things I thought yesterday have been unceremoniously seized and stood on their heads, leaving my own in a state of utter bewilderment. Believe it or not, Prescott, I find myself in the extraordinary situation of aiding and abetting Mr Robert Browning in an attempt to pervert the course of justice!

But this is not the way to set about it. 'First things first' must be my motto, if I am to make any sense of all.

By Monday morning, then, as I mentioned, the storm had quite blown over, leaving a clear sky and crisp sunshot air – one of those splendid days, harbingers of spring, that make one feel like crying out aloud 'The South! The South!' Needless to say, I restrained any such impulse, but nevertheless my heart was high as I strode through the streets of Florence. Poor Isabel's death seemed a distant memory, a horror of the night, and my grief had become almost an abstraction. Nature's compensation for the loss of our loved ones is a renewed sense of our own vitality. 'Alas, that she is gone!' I sighed, and back came answer, 'Rejoice, that you remain!' At such a moment, on such a day, simply being alive is reason enough to exult; and I exulted.

The streets of Florence are a spectacle of which one never tires, but that morning every scene produced an effect overwhelmingly rich and deep and full of life. The profusion of anecdote and incident which assails the eye here may be partly explained by the way in which the aristocrat here lives cheek by jowl with the pauper, the merchant with the artisan. There is no 'good' quarter, with the result that you see more in the time it takes to stroll the length of one average street than you will in a week elsewhere; and all bizarrely juxtaposed with the greatest non-chalance: grave burghers in fur-lined capes discussing the real unpublished news of the city in discreet murmurs; a locksmith at work on a creaky old door; a brace of counterfeit Madonnas set out in the street, awaiting the framer's art; a ringing laugh, a cutting jibe, a sullen retort; chickens being throttled, plucked and suspended on strings; a peasant woman carefully sprinkling water to freshen her horde of green vegetables; meat being hoisted in a basket on a rope towards an inaccessible window from which a face peers anxiously down; a distinguished-looking gentleman complaining loudly that the watch he has been sold keeps stopping dead at five to five every day; a priest scurrying along on some urgent mission of life or death; a soldier with a prisoner in guard; a girl with big grave eyes who leaves her work for a moment to watch you pass.

And when at length you reach the river, and the huddling mediaeval walls fall back to reveal San Donato hill with the monastery, and the great reach of glinting water bridged by the quaint old Ponte Vecchio (which is apparently to be pulled down any day now) and the snow-capped mountains in the distance – well, to my unphilosophical eye it all seems a quite sufficient justification in itself for the existence of the world.

Once beyond the river, however, this mood of unreflecting joy waned, deserting me altogether as I approached the Guidi palace. I had set off thither without much thought of the difficulties of my enterprise, but as I drew nearer to my goal these became only too evident. What did I think I was about, setting off thus blithely to pay a morning call on Mr Robert Browning? Even assuming that this gentleman was prepared to receive me at such an hour, it would almost certainly be impossible for us to discuss what had happened the previous night, since his wife was bound to be present. Moreover, I realised, it was more than likely that I featured in whatever story Browning had dreamed up to account for his late return home – the servant to whom I had handed in the note had recognised me, and this would have had to be explained. To blunder in and attempt to improvise my part in this domestic comedy was to risk my entire standing here. At one stroke I might become a social leper, persona non grata wherever I turned, the man to whom no one would ever again be at home!

On the other hand, the fact remained that I absolutely had to know the outcome of Browning's interrogation and the police enquiries into Isabel's death; and since an approach through a third party might equally give rise to embarrassing questions my informant could only be Mr Browning himself.

The only solution which occurred to me was to wait until Mr Browning left home, and then approach him in the street. I accordingly made my way to a small café on the other side of the Rome road, ordered a large dish of coffee and settled down to read the morning paper – keeping a careful watch on everyone who emerged from the Palazzo Guidi.

I had not been there very long when I became aware that I was not the only person thus employed: in the doorway of a church opposite stood a man lounging in a painfully self-conscious fashion, whom I recognised with a shock as one of the policemen who had been at the villa the night before!

For a moment I assumed that the fellow was spying on *me*, but I soon realised that his attention too was fixed on the building opposite. This naturally redoubled my curiosity, but I was obliged to contain myself in patience for the best part of an hour before I spied the stocky figure of Robert Browning emerge from the cave-like entrance to his lair into the strong sunlight and deeper shadows of Via Maggio.

I had devoted some thought to what the police agent might do at this juncture, and what my best course would be if – as indeed proved to be the case – he were to follow Browning. To have two of us dogging the poet's footsteps was manifestly absurd, yet now Browning had emerged I did not wish to risk losing him. I therefore crossed the road and dashed down a side-street opposite, past mangy cats and beggar brats – for though the Brownings face the Grand-Duke's palace, the alleyways behind are plebeian in the extreme – to the next street, where I turned right and continued my headlong course, lungs bursting – thank heaven they are fully mended now, and can support this kind of exercise! – as far as the Trinity bridge. Thanks to my exertions, however, I arrived at the bridge before Mr Browning, and was leaning over a parapet contemplating the turbid waters of the Arno when he passed by – at which moment I turned and greeted him with as convincing a show of natural surprise as I was capable of.

'You are followed,' I told him, indicating with a nod the spy who had just hove in sight at the end of the bridge, struggling to keep up with the foreigner's brisk pace.

A look of deep dismay crossed Browning's features.

'Have you time for a coffee?' I enquired without pause. 'I would like to hear how last night's little drama ended.'

'All the time in the world,' he replied.

And indeed all his earlier haste, his sense of purpose and bustle, had quite evaporated. Where had he been headed so urgently, I could not help wondering, that he would not go now he knew himself to be watched?

We strolled up Via Tornabuoni as far as the famous Doney's, where somewhat to my disappointment – for I naturally had no wish to make any secret of my familiarity with Elizabeth Barrett Browning's husband – he insisted on taking a table in a small room at the rear of the premises, where the scions of noble Tuscan families fallen on hard times come to read the news-sheet and drink coffee strained from grounds that have served already for the brew of rich barbarians. In the end, however, it all worked out as well, or even better, for some half dozen of my friends saw us pass through the main saloon together, and then retire to the intimacy of the back room to pursue matters we did not wish to have overheard.

On our way from the bridge I had mentioned to Browning that there seemed to be no word of Isabel's death in the news-sheet, and asked if he knew what conclusions the police had arrived at concerning her death. He said that he had no idea, beyond the fact that they were trying to trace the mysterious woman who had called at the villa at four o'clock, on the theory that her visit might in some way have occasioned this tragic and unnecessary act of self-destruction.

As soon as we were seated and had been served I pressed my companion more closely. What of his questioning by the police, for example?

'Bah! A formality,' replied Browning dismissively. 'I quickly explained the situation to the official, who apologised profusely for having detained me. The whole incident was an absurd misunderstanding and nothing more.'

I could not help feeling that the presence of the police spy rather gave the lie to these bland assurances, but I merely asked my companion how this 'misunderstanding' had arisen.

He gave me a pained look.

'The authorities have accepted my explanation, Mr Booth,' he replied in a distinctly frosty tone. 'I must beg you please to do the same.'

'I shall be happy to,' I cried, expectantly.

But Mr Browning did not continue. After a long moment's silence, he added: 'I mean, to accept that the explanation I gave the police last night was accepted by them.' Another silence, longer than the last, fell. Then, relenting slightly, he went on: 'I can assure you, however, that what Mrs Eakin's maid said was utterly and completely untrue. No relations of any nature ever existed between her mistress and me. You have my word for that.'

'I never doubted it for an instant,' I hastened to affirm. 'But that being so, have you any idea why the girl should have made such an absurd claim?'

It seemed that I had once again unwittingly touched a raw nerve.

'Mr Booth, I hoped that I had already made it clear that I do not wish to be subjected to a second interrogation on this matter, which I can assure you has no bearing whatsoever on the principal issue at stake here: namely, the murder of Isabel Eakin.'

So curious had I been to learn why any reference to the maid's testimony should embarrass Mr Robert Browning to such a very marked degree, that it was not for a moment that I realised exactly what he had just said. When I did, I repeated the word in a cry of anguish.

'Murder?'

Browning hissed urgently to silence me, and looked anxiously around the room. But none of the other people there, being Italian, had taken the slightest notice of the word.

'Please forgive me!' he said. 'I had not meant to tell you so brutally. But the fact remains, I fear, that Isabel Eakin did not take her own life. She was killed – cold-bloodedly murdered.'

31

It cost me a long and bitter effort to master the waves of horror that threatened to overwhelm me at the repetition of that ghastly word! Isabel's death was still a fresh wound; to have it dressed thus!

'But how on earth can you know that?' I demanded, when I could at length express myself with some degree of equanimity.

Browning looked at me with keen appreciation.

'An interesting question, Mr Booth. You go straight to the heart of the matter, I see. The answer is simple. I am a collector of life's ephemera – an amateur of the odd. I am interested in exceptions, not because they prove a rule, but for themselves; because they exist, and sometimes – more often than you might think! – they disprove one. In a word, I notice. Always have, nothing to be done – the thing's a disease with me. Now last night, up at the villa, I happened to notice some very odd things. And instead of pushing them to one side, as so many tiresome irregularities, I let them tell me their tale. What they told me was – that Mrs Eakin did not take her own life.'

I lit a cigar in an attempt to calm my nerves.

' "Things"? What things?' I demanded somewhat testily.

Browning drank his coffee off in a single gulp and settled back at his ease.

'It is difficult to know where to start,' he said. 'From the very beginning, the whole business seemed wrong, and the closer I looked the more wrong it seemed. Why should an elegant young lady choose to hang herself in the depths of a cold and windy garden when she has an entire house and more convenient methods of self-destruction at her disposal? Or, if that question seems frivolous, where did she get the rope, and what became of the knife that was used to cut it? How is it that this rope is green with damp mould, so that it marks the hands of anyone who touches it, but the victim's hands are spotless? These and other oddities worried me; I felt the thing was impossible. And when I saw the feet of the table Mrs Eakin is supposed to have jumped from I knew I was right – it *was* impossible.'

I recalled the strange scene I had observed the night before: Mr Browning crouching down beneath the swinging corpse to examine the clawed feet of the garden table. I also recalled that he did not know that I had been there.

'The feet of the table?' I queried cautiously. 'Why – what was so odd about them, then?'

'Nothing – apart from the fact that I could see them. Just think for a moment! That table was standing on soft earth, yet the feet had not sunk into it to even the smallest degree. That makes nonsense of the idea that Mrs Eakin had ever climbed up on it, tied one end of the rope round her neck, the other to the tree, and then jumped off the table to hang herself. That is what we are expected to believe, but it is patent nonsense.'

'Then what *did* happen?' I burst out impatiently.

'This is what I set myself to reason out last night in the garden. Let us work back from what we know. Mrs Eakin is found dead, hanging from a tree. If she did not hang herself then plainly someone else must have hanged her there, and used some support such as the table to do so. Now just imagine for a moment that you were standing on a table to attach a heavy weight to the branch of a tree, Mr Booth. Would you position the table directly underneath, or to one side?'

'Directly underneath, evidently.'

'Which is precisely what our murderer did. But then he realised that if the table were left there it would give the game away, for he wanted to disguise his crime as suicide – and you cannot very well hang yourself with your feet resting on a table. So he moved it back clear of the body – *setting it down lightly on the ground*. To have thought to force the feet down into the ground would have been an act of genius.'

'It is surely no less an act of genius to have read the whole story from such obscure indications, as clearly as though you had been present when it happened!' I cried in unfeigned admiration.

To my surprise, Mr Browning betrayed the pleasure my praise had given him by blushing.

'That is not all,' he continued. 'By dint of exploring the surface of the soil with my fingers I soon found – directly underneath the body, as I expected – the deep impressions left by the table when it bore the weight of both Mrs Eakin and the person who killed her, thus confirming my theory as to the manner in which she met her death. I might well have discovered some further clues, but unfortunately the policemen arrived and that was the end of that.'

I repeated my compliments.

33

'But I cannot by any means understand how the police can persist in viewing the case as one of suicide, as they apparently do, in the face of such overwhelming evidence to the contrary,' I commented. 'How did they refute your arguments?'

'They are not aware of them.'

'But do you mean to tell me ... '

'I gave them every chance! I did not change or falsify the record in any way. They saw what I saw – or had their chance to, at least. Is it my fault they looked the other way? Am I to be blamed for their limitations? Why should I do their thinking for them?'

I said nothing, stunned by this outburst.

'Let them do their worse – or their best!' Browning continued. 'As a free-born Englishman, I thank heaven that I have no more reason to be afraid of such petty Dogberrys than I have of the tuppenny-ha'penny tyrant who pays their wages.'

'But if Mrs Eakin has been murdered ... ' I protested, allowing this reference to the Grand-Duke Leopold II to pass without comment.

'There is no "if" about it, Mr Booth. She *was* murdered – and I intend to make every effort to identify the person responsible.'

IV

'You? Alone?'
  'If need be!'
  Then an idea seemed to strike him.
  'That is, unless you would be prepared to assist me. Clearly I cannot drag anyone else into this business, but as fate has already made us confederates . . . '
  As I set all this down now I see clearly for the first time what he meant by this. The reason Mr Browning does not want to involve anyone else in the matter can only be because it is connected – in some way I do not as yet understand – to various private concerns of his which he does not want known. I am thus his 'confederate' in the sense that I am aware, however vaguely, of the existence of this secret. Might not his appeal for my assistance have been prompted at least in part by his need to assure himself that I could be trusted to keep it?
  My first thought, however, was that to take matters into our own hands in the way Mr Browning appeared to be proposing was to risk putting ourselves in the wrong not only morally but also legally. If he believed that murder had been done, his clear duty was to communicate this belief – together with his reasons for holding it – to the proper authorities, who could achieve far more than two private individuals such as ourselves.
  'Ah, but that is just the point, don't you see? *Could* they? In my London, Mr Booth, or your Boston, there would be no question. But here the matter is very different. Crime is rare in Tuscany, violent crime almost unknown. The police here are recruited, trained and employed for purposes of simple repression. Breaking heads is their style, not teasing out the truth. They don't want the truth; it's the very last thing they want, for their government is a lie, built of lies, and dependent on force for its survival.
  'But even leaving that out of account, let us not forget that it is

35

a hundred to one that the criminal, like the victim, is a foreigner. Now, where does that leave the police? You know how it is here in Florence: the English and Italian communities are like oil and water; there is no friction, but neither do they mix. What do the Tuscan police know of us exiles? Consider what happened last night, for instance – the official became suspicious of me over a trifle, whilst remaining blissfully ignorant that you were lying to him.'

'What?' I bleated weakly.

'Why, your story of having come up to the villa to visit Mr Eakin, when all their friends knew that Mr Eakin had gone to Siena. Besides, even if he had been at home, in our little community one does not pay social calls at that hour of the evening. But how is a Tuscan police officer to know that, you see? How can he judge what people like us say or conceal, do or leave undone? How can he spot the revelatory fact, the inconsistent detail? In a word, how can he discriminate? Where all is strange nothing is remarkable. No, if I have not informed the Grand-Duke's constables of my suspicions, it is precisely because I believe that the best hope of catching Mrs Eakin's murderer lies not with them but with us. At present he thinks that his attempt to mask his crime has been successful: the authorities have given out that Mrs Eakin died by her own hand. Let him go on thinking that no crime is suspected; he will be off his guard and so easier to take. What *were* you doing there, by the way?'

Once again I was caught completely unawares, and would no doubt have had to admit to Browning that I had been following him, had not our colloquy been interrupted at that moment by the appearance of the police agent. Having observed us enter Doney's, the spy had presumably set down to mark the entrance and await our reappearance; after some time he had become suspicious, and had determined to search the premises to ensure that we had not given him the slip.

As soon as he caught sight of us the man wished for nothing better than to beat a hasty retreat. But he was not so lucky. Mr Browning rose to his feet and in stentorian tones bade him approach. With a reluctance almost comically marked, the fellow obeyed.

'Return to your masters,' Browning pronounced in the most

icily correct Italian, 'and inform them that in the event of this harassment not ceasing instantly I shall contact Her Majesty's Minister Plenipotentiary to the Court of Tuscany and ask him to raise the matter with the Grand Duke in person. Is that clear?'

The man muttered something inaudible, and went.

'I begin to despair of the Italians, Mr Booth,' Browning commented. 'What has become of the flame that once burned so bright? Speak to them like dogs and like dogs they obey.'

It seemed to me to be very convenient for Mr Browning that this was the case, and that the English diplomatic corps in Florence are all friends of his – but I said nothing. Instead I enquired what action we were to take to identify Isabel's murderer, if the police were not to be informed.

'There is one suspect whose guilt or innocence must of course be established before we waste time looking elsewhere,' Browning told me. 'I refer of course to Mr Joseph Eakin.'

'Eakin?' I exclaimed. 'But he was in Siena! Everyone knows that, as you yourself just pointed out.'

'Not so. I pointed out that everyone knew he had gone to Siena. It is not at all the same thing. How do we know he did not come back, murder his wife, and return to Siena later the same evening? It is but a few hours' journey on the new railroad.'

I must admit that I was not unduly distressed to learn that Mr Joseph Eakin was the object of Mr Browning's suspicions. Although I have hitherto been at proper pains to conceal the fact, my opinion of Isabel's choice of husband – when at long last she *did* choose – was by no means of the highest. 'Pique!' you will say, and evidently the rejected suitor must always find it difficult to approve of his successful rival. But even discounting any personal animus, there were grounds for thinking – and I was by no means the only one of Isabel's friends to do so – that her choice of Joseph Eakin had been motivated to some extent at least by – how shall I put it? – expediency.

They made such an incongruous pair that when I spied them together for the first time, at that ball I told you of, I took him to be some species of uninteresting relative: an uncle, or something of the kind, brought along to act as chaperon. So forceful was this impression that even when I overheard Isabel being presented to someone as Mrs Eakin I did not immediately realise that she was *married* to the fellow.

What led polite opinion here to speak of Mr and Mrs Eakin in terms of the proverbial chalk and cheese was not solely his age (although I'll lay he wasn't born this century), nor even the fact that he hails from Philadelphia, but rather his marked, his so painfully evident and unashamed fascination with Money.

Not – as with *her* – the spending of it on a million madcap projects and celebrations of every nature – no, Mr Joseph Eakin is one of Mammon's truest and purest believers, worshipping Cash not obliquely, as a means of exchange, but for itself. Despite the fortune he has amassed by the manufacture of some product without which the human race is either unable or unwilling to do, he is meticulous in counting his change when buying a cup of coffee, while 'How much did that cost?' is the question most frequently on his lips.

In short, then, I had no reason to love Mr Joseph Eakin, and so when Mr Browning asked me if I would be prepared to go to Siena that afternoon and make some discreet enquiries concerning Mr Eakin's whereabouts at the time of Isabel's death, I found myself quite agreeably disposed to the idea.

'You are intimate with the Eakins' circle,' Mr Browning explained, 'and can easily find some pretext for asking the necessary questions without giving offence. Besides, I can ill spare the time, for there are one or two urgent matters which I must follow up here in Florence.'

Well, to be brief, I agreed, and it was with no small thrill that I handed Mr Robert Browning my card, and received in return his assurance of a personal visit the following afternoon to hear the results of my enquiries! That interview in Doney's had left me more impressed than ever with his masterful manner, his sharp intelligence and knowledge of human nature, and that piquant and quirky manner of expressing himself – which I have endeavoured to set down verbatim in so far as I can recall it.

Indeed, there is even the glimmer of a notion stirring somewhere in the back of my mind . . .

But of that another time, if at all, for I am grown as cautious as an old fox. Enough to say that I went that very morning to the English bookshop, which is but two steps from Doney's, and asked if they could supply me with any of his works. I knew vaguely that he had written plays, though I had never read any of them – or indeed seen a single copy. I was therefore both surprised and delighted when the assistant cried 'But of course!', and returned in a few moments carrying an armful of volumes which I seized avidly – only to discover that their author, although indeed of the genus Browning, was not the rare Robert but rather the common Elizabeth Barrett variety. I tried to explain the mistake, but the assistant was now engaged in selling someone a modern prose version of Dante's *Inferno*, and merely waved me towards the shelves at the back of the shop, where after much searching I eventually unearthed – like uncut raw diamond – a single volume of verses by Mr Robert Browning, entitled *Dramatic Romances and Lyrics*, of which I promptly possessed myself.

As the weather bid fair to continue fine, I decided to eschew the advantages of modern civilisation – in the form of the railroad, the first in Italy, which the Englishman Stephenson has built the Duke – and drive to Siena along the old highway, not yet fallen into complete disuse, through the Chianti hills.

The road is of some forty miles, but steep in places, and the horse attached to the gig I had hired proved as weak as hireling beasts usually are. Moreover I was late leaving, having a number of matters to attend to in town, and compounded this by making a detour out by way of Bellosguardo and then stopping at an inn on the road for a country repast of bean soup, tough bread and roasted songbirds washed down with black wine, accompanied by the howling of a mad dog and the sullen prattle of the peasantry. The result was that by the time I reached Siena it was growing late, and I drove directly out to the villa where Mr Eakin's ailing relative lives, on the hills to the west of the city.

If chronic invalidism should ever prove to be your lot, Siena has much to recommend it. Florence may have had its day, but that era seems almost contemporary with our own compared to that of its ancient rival. Here life and hope and striving are notions so long extinct that the Siennese turn up their noses at the mere words. The only really well-bred thing to do here is to expire gracefully, like the city itself, by exquisite degrees; which is precisely what Joseph Eakin's aunt, along with many others of her sex and nation, is single-mindedly engaged in doing.

I was received not by this lady herself, who was 'indisposed', but by a youngish man whose relationship to her – as indeed his name, race and other details – remained nebulous. I introduced myself as a friend of Mr Eakin's, who had been the subject of a bizarre and disturbing experience which I hoped my visit could resolve. I had been strolling past the Cathedral in Florence (I said) at about five o'clock on Sunday afternoon, when I caught sight of my old friend Joseph Eakin walking towards me. Much surprised – for I had believed him to be in Siena for the weekend – I hastened to greet him. To my astonishment and chagrin he had cut me dead, walking on without so much as pausing in his stride, as though I were a complete and utter stranger! I was quite naturally astounded and hurt by this behaviour, but above all anxious to learn the reason for it. Had I unwittingly done or said something to offend him? Had some-one been spreading malicious gossip? Having learned that he *was* now in Siena, I was come thither in hopes of finding him and resolving this misunderstanding.

The young man replied with slightly insolent politeness, in an accent I could not quite place, that Mr Eakin had unfortunately returned to Florence by the midday train. However, he assured me that I must have been mistaken, since he could vouch for the fact that on the afternoon in question Joseph Eakin had not been in Florence, but sitting in the very room in which we were presently talking – a gesture indicated the chair which had supported the plutocratic posterior during this period.

This seemed final, but to ensure that there was no mistake I pressed the point. Was my informant really quite certain? The resemblance had been quite astonishing; I scarcely thought it possible that I could have been mistaken. Was it not possible that Mr Eakin had absented himself for a few hours and returned to Florence? But the young man was not to be shaken: Eakin had spent the whole of Sunday afternoon at the villa, first with his aunt and subsequently with her personal doctor, one McPherson.

There was nothing more to be done that evening, so I put up at an inn which *Murray's Guide* accurately described as 'very indifferent', where I fell asleep over Mr Browning's verses – this implies no criticism of the latter, which pleased me, but I was exhausted from my long drive and all the shocks these last days had sprung upon me.

This morning I was up betimes, and in an hour was on the road back to Florence, having verified Mr Eakin's alibi by applying to Doctor Alistair McPherson: a lean sliver of upright Aberdeen morality as out of place in these accommodating climes as an Italian cupola astride a Presbyterian kirk. Here was a man whose every feature proclaimed his utter probity, and when he assured me that he had been with Joseph Eakin at the hour in question, then I knew that Mr Browning's convenient theory would no longer serve.

The weather at this time of the year is notoriously capricious, and by the time I arrived back in Florence early this afternoon the wind was rising and the sky streaky with clouds. As I drove at a snail's pace through the town, where twice as many carriages as in Boston are crammed into streets that are less than half the size, I heard myself hailed, looked around, and saw none other than the man who had formed a shadowy third with Browning and me the night before – Cecil DeVere, instantly recognisable amid the mob of slouch-hatted locals with cloaks draped operatically over their shoulders.

He was going home, and although it was out of my way I offered him a lift, which he was glad to accept. As we drove along we talked about poor Isabel's death, and I was surprised to discover that this event seemed to have hit DeVere very hard – he spoke of it in a manner unusually agitated for one normally so suave, and then abruptly changed the subject, as though the matter was too painful, and told me a very interesting story.

It seemed that the previous morning he had driven up to the villa at Bellosguardo to offer his condolences to Mr Eakin. As the latter had not yet returned from Siena, DeVere left his card and was leaving, when he noticed someone prowling about the garden in a suspicious skulking manner at the very spot where Isabel's body had been found!

DeVere promptly walked out and around the side of the villa to investigate. When he reached the garden, however, the mysterious figure had disappeared, despite the fact that the only two other ways out – the gate at the end of the garden, and the large glass doors leading into the villa – both proved to be locked.

I was careful not to betray to DeVere my extreme interest in this incident, and changed the subject in my turn, asking my passenger when he had last seen Mr and Mrs Browning. He appeared utterly bewildered by my remark.

'The Brownings?' DeVere replied. 'Why, I hardly know them – and don't really care to know them better. All Literature and Liberalism, from what I hear, and each in rather more substantial quantity than appeals to me, to be perfectly honest.'

All this, as you may imagine, has done nothing to diminish my impatience to see Mr Browning again – I expect him at any moment.

But what do you make of it all? Could Isabel's death really have been murder, as Mr Browning claims? Or is there some detail we have overlooked, or some other way of arranging the known facts which would make matters look quite different? The police should surely be trusted in these affairs, and they apparently see no evidence of foul play.

And supposing they are wrong, whom are we to suspect now that Joseph Eakin's innocence is proven? Where can we begin to look? What about the mysterious woman who called at the villa shortly before Isabel's death? But could a woman have done such a deed?

And what of DeVere's name, which keeps cropping up in this affair with the most inexplicable frequency? Yes – might not the solution to our problems lie in that direction?

The bell! It is he!

Ever yrs affectionately,

Robert N. Booth

V

Dear Prescott,

It is over! Thank God, we have come out of it safely, and if so terrible an affair can be said to have ended well, then this has. This has ended, and another has begun – one as full of light as that was of darkness, as rich in promise and the hope of worthy achievement as that was heavy with terror and despair and sinful sordid squalor. You may imagine which I had rather make my theme – but the bad news must be told first, for as I close that door the other opens. But guard this letter well, Prescott! It is intended for no eyes but yours, for it contains secrets which must be buried with those they concern, as you will appreciate once you have read it.

I ended my last letter just as Robert Browning called on me following my return from Siena. Subsequent events have necessarily coloured my view of much of what was said at that meeting, but nothing can dim or diminish the memory of my feelings when at four o'clock precisely my door-bell mixed its humble strains with the majestic chimes of Santa Maria Novella and – was it real? was I dreaming? No! – there was Mr Robert Browning, in person, walking in at *my* door, standing on *my* carpet, looking down from *my* windows and commenting on the scene in the square below! I could hardly believe my eyes.

Sitting, it must be said, looking remarkably subdued; and considerably readier to comment on the scene in the piazza, where the little steam-tram was hissing and clanging off on its way to Prato, than to tell me what had happened. That something *had* happened became ever more painfully apparent, in direct proportion to Browning's evident unwillingness to broach the subject.

Meanwhile I filled the gaping silence by describing my expedition to Siena, reporting my conversations with Doctor

43

McPherson and the fragile aunt's gigolo, and concluding with a statement to the effect that Mr Joseph Eakin's innocence had apparently been established beyond any doubt.

At this, without the slightest warning, Mr Browning threw his head back and broke into deafening peals of laughter, which then abruptly subsided again, leaving for all trace the smallest of ironical smiles – like the gentle swell of the ocean when the storm has blown over.

'I don't need you to tell me that, Mr Booth,' he said quietly. 'No, no – I found that out the hard way!'

And at length the whole story emerged.

That day – we are speaking of last Monday, following our conversation at Doney's and my departure to Siena – had initially seemed auspicious for Mr Browning. First of all, a stroke of fortune had enabled him to succeed where the police remained baffled, and identify the woman who had called on Isabel shortly before her death – or rather, she had identified herself, for it was none other than Miss Isa Blagden, the doyenne and mainstay of our little community here, and one of the Brownings' closest friends.

She lives in a villa on Bellosguardo hill not far from the one the Eakins' were renting, and had in a very short time become intimate with Isabel, partly perhaps by the accident of sharing the same Christian name (as do Mr Browning and I, it just occurs to me; may that augur well!). She had therefore hastened to share with the Brownings her horror at the tragedy which has shocked us all so deeply, and communicate to them the particularly ghastly thrill with which she had learned that she had been the last person to see poor Isabel alive.

'She had called at the villa,' Browning explained, 'as dearest Isa always does everything – on a sheer wild whim of kindness, and with as little thought of formality as the bird that comes to perch on your window-sill – and found Mrs Eakin all alone in the house. Instead of relishing the prospect of company, however, as one might have expected, her hostess seemed oddly *distraite* and ill at ease – indeed I gathered that her reception had been what a nature less sweet than Isa's might have simply called rude. After twenty minutes of desultory and inconsequential chat, therefore, Isa left Mrs Eakin to the solitude which she seemed so anxious to resume.

44

'Nothing they said appears to shed any light whatever on what happened so soon afterwards – but one very important point did nevertheless emerge. Isa repeated several times that Mrs Eakin appeared to be very nervous, starting and looking out of the window at every sound. One way in which this nervousness apparently betrayed itself was by her continual fingering of a gold locket she was wearing.'

The significance of this point can hardly be overstated, for when Isabel's body was laid out on the table in the kitchen no such locket had been visible.

'I had an opportunity to question the maid, Beatrice, about this,' Browning went on. 'She at first absolutely denied that her mistress had ever possessed such a piece of jewellery, but when I showed her I knew she was lying she changed her story quite dramatically. There *was* such a locket – and, significantly, it was not kept with the rest of Mrs Eakin's jewellery, but hidden in a chest containing items of clothing. Beatrice, sensing some intrigue, had examined it one day, and found that it opened, and that the inside was inscribed with the initials O.V.A.'

This seemed indeed to be an important clue, although its utility is unfortunately considerably diminished by the fact that these initials do not seem to correspond with any name that either Browning or I know of here in Florence. At all events, in an attempt to solve the other puzzle – namely, what had become of this locket – Browning decided to go and search the garden of the villa once more.

Once again, he was in luck, for he found – not the locket, but something so infinitely more damning that it put all thought of the locket out of his head: a folding pocket-knife, engraved with the name Joseph Ernest Eakin!

'While I was examining this object with a degree of excited attention which you may well imagine,' Browning continued, 'my attention was attracted by the appearance of Mr Eakin himself, who enquired heatedly who the devil I was and what I was doing in his garden. In other circumstances I might have been flustered or embarrassed at being thus surprised by the object of my suspicions, and on his own land. But not after finding that knife! With no great effort to be conciliatory I identified myself and explained that there were several unusual circumstances surrounding his wife's death, and I should be grateful if he could help to throw some light on them.

'Mr Eakin's eyes narrowed – suspiciously, I thought – as he enquired frigidly what those circumstances might be. I then attempted to explain them, as I did to you yesterday in Doney's. But – well, some of the points appear to have little enough weight, taken in isolation, while the matter of the table, which ties and binds all together, is really quite tricky to expound clearly and simply to such a totally unsympathetic listener. In short, it no doubt all sounded rather confused and impertinent, and enabled Eakin to make a cutting remark at my expense. This stung me, so to clinch the matter I produced the knife I had just found and challenged the man to deny that it was his.

'It did not for a moment enter my head that he would be able to brazen it out: his name was on the handle and I had found it lying where his wife had been found hanged from a piece of rope cut with a knife. Imagine my dismay, then, when he took the thing from me, examined it long and coolly, gave it back with an untrembling hand, looked me straight in the eye and declared in a level tone that he had never seen it before in his life!

'Well, it was a superb opportunity to put me in my place, and Mr Eakin did not allow it to go to waste. With a highly effective combination of wounded dignity and scrupulously controlled rage, he proceeded to remind me that the subject under discussion was the death of his wife, whom he had loved dearly, and of whose loss he had been informed only that morning. "Your feelings for your wife, Mr Browning, are famous," he went on, while I stood there biting my lip. "Please try to remember that even ordinary mortals, their hands soiled by commerce, may be capable of feelings which are none the less real and painful because they lack your skill in expressing them. I neither know nor care where you obtained that knife, or what your object was in trying to discountenance me with it, or in telling me these absurd tales of tables and holes in the ground. I will say only this – my wife's death is my personal tragedy, and if you wish to play the amateur police detective I suggest you avoid doing so at others' expense. I bid you good morning, Mr Browning, and goodbye." With which he turned on his heel and strode back to the house, while I slunk off the premises like a poacher.'

The idea of that horrible Philistine upstart Eakin thus scoring an easy victory over a man such as Robert Browning was so distressing that I doubly regretted the impossibility of bringing his wife's murder home to him. Certainly in a just world he *ought* to have done it – or to have hanged for it at any rate!

But meanwhile Mr Browning, with that restless mental energy which characterises him, had already moved on to confront a new complication.

'We agree, then, that Joseph Eakin did not murder his wife,' he said, rising from the divan to stand in front of me.

I nodded.

'Then who, pray, tried to make it seem that he had?'

'What do you mean?'

'Why man, the knife! If it is not Eakin's, it must have been placed where I found it with the intention of incriminating him.'

'But why should anyone do that when it has been given out that Isabel died by her own hand?'

'It may have been so given out,' Browning retorted, 'but remember that at least one person knows better. The murderer is not fooled by his own stratagems, and must at least be worried that the police may also see through them, in time. This knife, I take it, represented his insurance policy against that eventuality. If the suicide verdict held, no harm had been done; if it fell through, suspicion would be diverted in the most natural direction, towards the victim's husband.'

'But how did he get the knife, then? Where does it come from, if it is not Eakin's?'

For all answer Browning handed me the article in question.

'Open it,' he said.

I tried to do so – without success.

'I cannot.'

'No more could I. See, here is the thumb-nail I splintered in the attempt. Plainly the thing is brand-new, bought from a cutler's shop the same day I found it. It has never been used, never been opened. It was taken straight to an engraver, and Eakin's name placed on the handle – if you examine the lettering closely you will observe several flakes of metal scalloped up by the burin and not yet dislodged.'

I was extremely impressed with this further demonstration of Mr Browning's intellect; the operations of his mind, combining as they do an unparalleled grasp of reality in all its raw and unrefined quiddity, with a soaring reach and synthetic power to meld all into ideas of the very largest and grandest carry, are a delight and an inspiration. But there was still one further question in my mind.

'All this is wonderful, and I have no doubt that you are quite correct in your assessment of the murderer's motives. But I fail to understand how this knife could constitute evidence against Mr Eakin, given that it is not his.'

'It couldn't, of course, from the moment that it emerged that he had an unshakeable alibi. But suppose he had not had one. Who would then have believed his protestations that the knife was not his? You know how the police proceed here – they find some scrap of evidence against some likely suspect, and then obtain a confession by recourse to methods into which no one enquires too closely.'

I remembered that Cecil DeVere had told me while we drove together through the streets of Florence that afternoon that he had seen someone skulking about the garden of the villa on the Monday morning, at the very spot where, a few hours later, Browning had found the knife. When I mentioned this, Browning's response was immediate and enthusiastic.

'Splendid! Let us go and see this man DeVere immediately – I have an appointment, but it can wait.'

But I was forced to disappoint him.

'Unfortunately DeVere will not be at home. I recall him telling me he was going out.'

'Very well, then – tomorrow morning, without fail! There is no time to lose.'

As though these words had prompted a thought in his mind, Browning consulted his watch and announced that he had to be going. I was genuinely disappointed that he was not staying longer – but he explained that his wife's chronic consumptive condition had become aggravated again, and that he had to return to look after her.

'You are not a friend of Cecil DeVere, then?' I remarked casually as we walked to the door.

Browning replied with an air of slight puzzlement, 'DeVere? No – I have met the man, I believe. That's all. Why do you ask?'

'I was curious as to why you used his name to explain the

message which arrived for you on Sunday night – the summons from Isabel's maid?'

I was very aware that I was treading on delicate ground here – as was confirmed when Browning flushed at this allusion to his mendacity.

'Did I?' he queried.

'Use DeVere's name? Certainly.'

Browning looked utterly blank.

'Mr Booth, you may believe this or not, as you choose – and I should hardly blame you if you do not – but the fact of the matter is that I have not the slightest recollection of having mentioned Mr DeVere – whom, as I say, I hardly know – nor the remotest notion why I should have done so!'

This response was so hopelessly inadequate that I did not doubt its veracity for a second; a man as gifted as Robert Browning, had he wished to lie, could certainly have invented a more satisfactory explanation than this ingenuous shrug of the shoulders. The mystery, however, remained.

We arranged to meet the following morning at nine o'clock, at the south end of the Ponte Vecchio – DeVere's house lies hard by this venerable structure. Then, with a second glance at his watch, Mr Browning left.

It may have been that excessive interest in the time that did it, or perhaps I remembered how he had strangely contradicted himself in the reasons he had given for having to leave a few minutes before. As soon as he had gone, at all events, I rushed to the window and looked out. What I saw so intrigued me that I ran back to the hall, grabbed my cloak and hat, and hurried downstairs after him.

VI

When I got out into the darkening streets Browning was already lost to sight, but I hurried off in the direction I had seen him go, towards the Cathedral. It had been this that had caught my attention, for Casa Guidi is in the district the Florentines call the Oltrarno, south of the river; wherever Browning was so urgently bound, it was not there.

He was not going home, then – at least not directly. And yet he had justified his abrupt departure with talk of his wife's illness. I had noticed at the time, but without remarking its significance, that this rather failed to tally with his mention of an 'appointment' he was prepared to postpone in order to see DeVere. There was no reason to suppose that the Brownings' marriage was upon such terms that husband and wife were in the habit of making appointments to see each other.

At this point you may be forgiven for thinking that the atmosphere of continual mystery and intrigue I had been breathing since Isabel's death had quite turned my head, so that I saw riddles in everything. Might Browning not be going quite simply to an appointment with a doctor, or a pharmacist, or lawyer, on any ordinary everyday business, before returning to his wife's side? That indeed was what I asked myself as I hurried along over the great treacherous gleaming flagstones of the street, which was emptying earlier than usual owing to the onset of a light drizzle. All I found by way of justification for my impulse was that I was surrounded by so many mysteries that the possibility of finally resolving even one of them was not to be missed.

By the time I reached the Cathedral I had almost despaired of catching up with Browning, who is an almost aggressively brisk walker – one of those you fancy might actually tear themselves to pieces were they tied to a chair for twenty-four hours together, so necessary to their spiritual and intellectual economy does the relief that walking affords them seem to be. I was in fact on the point of giving up the chase when I suddenly caught sight of him, buying something from a street-trader. I approached, taking good care that he did not spot me, and waited until he had concluded his purchase. I then made a slight detour past the huckster's stall, and discovered that his principal stock-in-trade appeared to consist of embroidered lace handkerchiefs.

Browning had meanwhile got ahead of me again, striding away down Via De' Calzaioli. We were now heading south, and I thought that he must be going home after all, having picked up a little keepsake for his wife. The street runs straight into the very centre of Florence: a mess of mediaeval squalor grown like congestion in a lung upon the clear grid of the ancient Roman city. This area is a maze of the narrowest and crookedest alleys you will ever see, lined with that typical Florentine assortment of wretched tumbledown tenements with more inhabitants than a dog has fleas; ancient palaces whose rock-like walls seem to ooze the memories of evil deeds; quaint churches, half-amalgamated with the rest, preserving primitive frescoes as faded as the piety of their parishioners; the truncated stumps of the tall towers built by proud Guelf or Ghibelline to pour scorn and boiling pitch on their opponents; and little squares, like clearings in the forest, where men lounge and smoke cigars, children play noisy games, women gossip and make eyes, appear and disappear at windows.

When we left the Piazza del Duomo Browning was some hundred yards ahead of me, a lead which by dint of breaking almost into a run I had gradually reduced to half that distance. I dared not approach closer, after the incident of the police spy, for if he had noticed my presence he must have become suspicious. Thus I was obliged to hang back to some extent, and when Browning suddenly turned left into a side-street I was some fifty yards behind him.

I increased my pace directly, and on reaching the corner was just in time to see him cross into the next street. I could tell by the sound of his footsteps that he had turned neither right nor left, but continued straight on, and I hastened on through the gloom towards the feeble oil-lamp at the next street-corner.

When I reached it I paused: all was still. The only sound was the steady hush of the rain, which had grown more persistent.

The next street, named after Dante Aligheri, whose house stands there, was too long for Browning to have reached the other end before I gained the corner where I now stood. He must therefore have entered one of the buildings in it. But which? There was no way of telling, save by keeping watch until such time as he might emerge – which is what I determined to do.

I was counting on his reappearing almost immediately. 'He has gone to call on a friend on his way home,' I thought. 'He will stay but a few minutes – is not his wife ill and anxiously awaiting his return?'

So I reasoned; but I was mistaken. I crouched in a doorway for more than three quarters of an hour, but in vain; of Mr Browning there was no further sign. Meanwhile the rain grew ever heavier, until my clothes were quite soaked. In the end, cold and dispirited, I abandoned my vigil.

Perhaps you think that I was foolish to risk my health like that – despite the fact that my lungs are quite mended now, and I feel younger and healthier than ever – to risk it for nothing, for a mere whim of curiosity, an unseemly nosiness about matters that are none of my business. And so before going on to describe what happened the next day, let me explain; let me give you the good news I spoke of at the beginning of this letter, since without it you will be unable to understand even what I do – never mind these other mysteries.

First, though, you must understand *me* more deeply – must understand, above all, that I have been one who, while still young, knew – *knew*, mind! – that he had been born to excel greatly.

At what, I could not say – nor did it seem important. I dabbled in writing, because I could write, but often it seemed to me that my soul might worship more aptly at some other altar. Music moved me very greatly, and Art – but as I could never tell a crotchet from a minim, or draw a passable likeness, I stuck to words, over which, though poor things, I had at least some power. It mattered little what I achieved: that was for the future, of which I knew only that it would be glorious. For the moment it was enough, and more than enough, just gloriously to *be*; to feel, think, plan, dream . . .

Oh Prescott, those days! I walked, I talked, I sang and danced and laughed and wept with spirits! The rhythms of the Universe sometimes whispered, at others roared through me, at the behest of rules so ancient and all-embracing that it is absurd to speak of rules at all, as of something that might be broken.

Such, then, is what I was at five, at ten, at fifteen. Much, though by no means all, survived, surprisingly intact, into my twenties – a mere decade ago! It might be a century. But then the rot set in: slowly at first, and by fits and starts, I began to have doubts. What had I achieved? True, my room was full of paper – as full of paper as my life was empty of anything else, for I had sold my soul and kept my end of the bargain – but was all that paper covered in my scribbles worth any more than it had been blank, fresh from the stationers at a dollar a ream? Was it not rather worth *less*? I had spoiled it, and added nothing. That was the terrible truth which, over the course of several years, I gradually came to admit to myself.

Note the point – it was not the world's judgment which sank me, but my own. I was quite prepared to be ignored, despised, rejected by my contemporaries. It was, indeed, almost a requirement; for what, after all, did they know? Was true greatness ever recognised or rewarded? Their contempt would, all other things being equal, have set the seal upon my belief in my stature and assured my ultimate triumph – posthumous, if necessary. I was ready even for that. But the wound I had now was internal, and mortal: a slow draining-away of that youthful faith, drop by drop, until nothing remained.

When this knowledge truly came home to me, and had settled down, coiled like a foul worm in my breast – well, my friend, just try and imagine (you won't succeed, but try) that one day you gradually came to the realisation that instead of being the eminent and well-respected Professor of Intellectual and Moral Philosophy at Tuft's University, Medford, Massachusetts, you were in fact the inmate of quite another kind of institution! In short, that you were, and had long been, a pitiful lunatic – but one for whom there was apparently some reason to hope, since your delusions were now happily beginning to lose their force, and there was every prospect that you would soon be able to grasp for the first time the realities of your position! What a joyful awakening that would be, eh Prescott?

It was in much the same spirit that I gradually awakened from *my* delirium – to what? A world stripped bare of any inducement to endure its puerile crudities a moment longer. And when you consider that this was also the period when my health collapsed and when Isabel finally tired of teasing me – well, all in all I think it is a wonder I did not put an end to my miserable existence there and then.

Instead, I drifted to Europe, and round Europe, until I came to rest with all the other flotsam and jetsam of every nationality in this pleasant backwater. Florence is the right place for us weightless men: a burned-out city with a past too massy for its present, and no future at all. We gravitate towards it as naturally as waste paper and dead leaves end up in an angle of wall, whirling about in a miniature tornado of febrile energy – hollowly gay, exhausting itself in a restless round, changing nothing and itself unchanged.

Oh, I know that from where you sit at your daily grind in dull joyless New England, it must seem a splendid and an enviable thing, this exile existence of mine – a continual dream of Art, Romance and Pleasure in a land where the good life's to be had at prices which even a Joseph Eakin can find little to complain about; where I have my dinner sent up from the trattoria with a flask of Montepulciano, and a valet in to cook my eggs and make my coffee in the morning, and a girl to clean and wash, and can walk or ride or drive out any day to see what's best and costs nothing: the most beautiful landscapes in the world; and not mind Fra Somebody's frescoes, but choose instead to study – what luxury! – that lizard there upon the sun-hot wall, so absolutely still and weighty you'd swear him incapable of movement, a toy worked in gold and bronze by Cellini, except if you blink he's gone! All this, Prescott, and much more, upon the miserable pittance my father sends, thinking it not quite enough to live on (as would be true in Boston) so that I'll be obliged sooner or later to turn my hand to some earnest trade – and in the meantime he's done his duty by his feckless idle off-spring.

But after a while these marvels pall, as marvels will – is this not why literary visions of hell are so much more convincing than those of paradise? And what's your exile life then but a heap of motley moments pasted at random into a commonplace book: some good, some bad, all meaningless, devoid of any

54

sense of purpose, neither redeemed nor threatened by the informing touch of the Real.

And then one day I had my insight! I had been reading Vasari's *Lives of the Artists* – reading it *here* in the city where Vasari was born, and which he never ceased to regard – like the majority of his fellow-citizens – as the centre and cynosure of the world; reading it amid the surviving works of those giants of whom he writes with the same easy yet undiminishing familiarity as Homer of his heroes. And as I came to know this second-rate dauber, who walked with the Great and was transfigured, something stirred in the back of my own brain. Like Vasari, I was not Great – that bitter lesson had been learned. But had Greatness therefore been abolished? Because I had fallen short, did the goal cease to exist? And were there not others, more worthy than I, who would grasp that torch handed down through the ages? All that I had to do, then, was to find one of these men who have that Power, to stand close to him, and draw off a portion of that Greatness from him, as Buonarroti's Adam draws Life itself from his Creator's finger.

But first I had to find the man! No easy task, and one of which I have often despaired. He had, first, to be truly Great – for, having duped myself for dreary years, I have no wish now to become another's dupe. First, then, the threshing, to tell wheat from chaff – nor could I make the task easier by following the crowd to one of the idols of the age such as Mr Powers, for I had no wish to worship from afar, one of a throng. My Great Man would be mine alone! *My* glory would lie in my having recognised *his* before it became a mere commonplace, parroted in every review.

And now at last I think my efforts are all rewarded, Prescott, and I almost dare to say that I have found my man! I shall speak no more of this for the moment – though I expect to talk of nothing else for the remainder of my life – for first I must conclude my account of this bad business by describing the dramatic developments which ensued the following morning. But can you now understand my interest in every detail of Browning's life, in every one of his words and deeds, however obscure or apparently trivial? For what particle of Greatness is not itself Great, and which of its meanest features is unworthy of our attention?

55

VII

When I awoke the next morning the weather had changed
completely. The sky weighed down like a cauldron lid upon the
city, which on such a day can appear the most dreary, inhospit-
able, depressing place on earth. All its picturesque charms
wither and shrivel away to nothing, illusions foisted on us by our
desire to escape the realities of our own bleak age. Seen with
such a cold eye, what are all these palaces and towers and walls
and gates but the grim relics of a history that was anything but
gay, if the truth be known. It is on such days that the exile asks
himself for the hundredth time just what on earth he is doing
here, ekeing out a tenuous unreal existence in the shadow of
these massive monuments to Power and Wealth and Privilege
and Will: these grim memorials to the mighty Dead, who so
terribly outnumber – outeverything! – us.

The streets, glimpsed from my window, presented a prospect
which was uninviting in the extreme. The rain had turned hard
and punchy, coming down in squally showers beaten into every
corner by a nasty wind which roamed the streets like a mob in
search of victims. It found few enough, for sensible folk stayed at
home, and listened to it howling in the chimney. But I could not,
alas, and so, bundled up in every protection against the elements
I could lay my hands on, I set off across town towards the Ponte
Vecchio.

Having noted that Mr Browning is extremely particular about
punctuality, I had taken care to pay him the politeness of kings
myself, and was therefore both surprised and mildly annoyed
when there was no sign of him by the time the nearby churches
had finished ringing nine o'clock. I was still puzzling over his
non-appearance when my attention was drawn by a crowd of
men in the standard Florentine garb of slouch hats, short cloaks
and cigars, clustered around a doorway to my right.

As Mr Jarves has said, Florence is a city where you may see

ten men watching an eleventh buy two oranges from a street-trader with a degree of lively interest which an American crowd might bestow upon one of Mr Barnum's raree-shows. But the natives' aversion to foul weather is even more marked than their curiosity, and for a crowd to collect on such a day as that the spectacle, I felt, must possess some greater intrinsic interest than orange-trading. After another five minutes' fruitless wait, I therefore walked over to investigate.

When I reached the fringes of the crowd I heard my name called, looked up – for the voice had come from above – and found Robert Browning waving at me from a window of the house before which the onlookers had gathered. The next moment he disappeared, but I shouldered my way through the crowd, which parted reluctantly to let me through, and when I reached the doorway Browning was there to lead me past the police constable on guard into the dry empty echoing spaces of the vestibule.

His eyes glittered with a hard intense brilliance.

'It is all over!' he hissed excitedly. 'Come!'

We mounted the shallow slab-like steps to the first floor, three at a time. I asked what had happened, but my companion would say only that he wished me to see for myself.

Another policeman guarded the door to DeVere's apartments, and once again Browning's word was enough to gain us entrance, and I could not help remarking on this astonishing volte-face in the authorities' attitude to my companion. A few days before he had been the object of a police interrogation, his house was watched and he himself followed by a police agent – for all the world like a man under suspicion. Yet here he was, a foreigner with no official standing, ordering the local constables about like one of their own officers! How on earth had he effected this miraculous transformation?

'Commissioner Talenti has pestered me no more since I called his bluff by challenging that ruffian in Doney's – he wouldn't dare!' Browning explained. 'As for my status here, it is the result of a little bluffing of my own. I was on my way to keep our appointment when I noticed the crowd outside the house. The police had just been called, but by feigning to be a friend of DeVere's I was able to gain entrance on the pretext of repre-senting his interests until an official from the embassy arrives.

He is expected at any moment. But there is just time, I hope, for you to see what there is to be seen.'

We had entered the main room, a noble salon overlooking the river. Now when I say 'the river', you are not to imagine some stately body of calmly-proceeding water such as the Thames, the Seine, or for that matter our own Charles. The Arno is quite another type of beast: a moody Latin, either thrashing about in spate and threatening to inundate the city (as it did to such disastrous effect in '44); or more usually a drab and uninspiring waste of murky water, thick with all the filth of the city and the rank ooze of the tanneries and cloth finishers upstream, split into a maze of tiny channels winding through the banks of silt, torn-up trees and rubble washed down from the mountains. A damned ditch, Dante called it – and such it remains to this day.

The glass doors on to the balcony stood open, and Browning led me outside. The first thing I noticed was that the railing was broken in half, the right-hand section leaning out over the river at a crazy angle. I approached the edge of the terrace with care, and looked down. On a mud-flat below the house a small group of men were standing in a circle around a formless heap covered with a blanket. I saw several policemen, as well as some of the poor fellows called sandmen, who scrape a living sieving for that commodity in the same way the Californians do for gold. As for the sinister object in their midst, Browning informed me that it was the lifeless body of Cecil DeVere.

Although the subsequent examination of the body indicated that death had occurred at some time during the night, the corpse had lain undiscovered until shortly after eight o'clock, when one of those same sandmen had come upon it in the course of his work, and raised the alarm. Knowing what I now know, I have no compunction in pointing out the irony: the vain DeVere had once held forth to me at some length upon Beau Brummel's definition of elegance, which was also his: dressing in such a way as not to excite attention. By this criterion his toilet had remained impeccable to the last, for his body had lain there for several hours not twenty yards from the busiest bridge in Florence, without being noticed by anyone.

But my immediate considerations were quite different, for you must remember how vital DeVere had been to our hopes of solving the murder of Isabel Eakin. Now those hopes appeared to have been extinguished for ever. I asked Browning if it was yet known how DeVere had come to fall to his death. He pointed to the broken railing.

'That rail has apparently been defective for some time, and DeVere had repeatedly spoken of having it repaired. The authorities' view would seem to be that he has now paid the price of his procrastination.'

Browning's voice was bland – too much so.

'And is that view also yours?' I queried.

For all answer, he turned away and led me back inside.

The living-room bore all the marks of its late occupier's good taste and long purse. Tapestries, pictures, statuary, old books and musical instruments, primitive crucifixes, classical antiquities and suchlike abounded on every side. In the centre of the room, beneath the inevitable chandelier, stood a highly-polished inlaid walnut table, at which I had sat with other guests a score of times, sipping the excellent aleatico dessert wine which DeVere obtained from a local marquis for whom he had done some favour – the story of which invariably circulated with the decanter, for DeVere was one of those who never seem to know when they have told a tale before.

Upon the table lay two very different objects. The more immediately striking was a golden locket in the shape of a heart. It was open, revealing an incised inscription consisting of the letters O, V, and A, almost hidden amidst a profusion of curlicues and tendrils, like the figure in a carpet. Beside the locket lay an object as different from it in every respect as can well be imagined – yet if anything even more interesting. It was a dirty, crumpled, torn scrap of cheap paper, bearing the name Joseph Ernest Eakin in a well-formed flowing hand.

At that moment we heard a sound of footsteps and voices on the stairs, and to my astonishment Browning picked up the scrap of paper and put it in his pocket. The next instant the door was opened, and in walked a group of three men, headed by the dapper melancholy little figure of Antonio Talenti.

The worst of it was that he did not even seem particularly surprised to find us there, merely nodding familiarly at my companion in a way that seemed to say, 'Ah, so you're in this, are you? I thought as much'. For some reason I found this infinitely more disturbing than any amount of histrionics.

Browning, however, was no whit abashed – on the contrary! Totally ignoring the policeman, he greeted the other two men – the British chargé d'affaires, Mr Scarlett, and one of his assistants – and explained our presence there. Having thus established the free and easy terms on which he stood with the diplomats, he then turned to the Italian and greeted him elaborately, as though remarking his existence for the first time.

'I'm so glad to see that you are putting your considerable talents' – emphasising the word humorously – 'to some worthwhile use at last,' he continued. 'It is of the highest importance that no mistake is made in this matter. Mr DeVere was of course an accredited representative of the British Crown, and should any irregularity occur our Lord Palmerston is quite capable of sending a gun-boat up the Arno, shelling the Pitti Palace, and then sending the Grand Duke a bill for the costs of the operation. Thank heavens that such an awful responsibility rests in hands no less sure than yours, Signor Talenti.'

With which he made a slight bow, and with a 'Come, Mr Booth!' swept me from the room. And all with that vital piece of evidence burning a hole in his pocket the while! What a man!

Outside in the street one of the frequent showers was in full spate, and it was clear that in a few moments we would be as effectively soaked as if someone had thrown a bucket of water over us. It was imperative to seek shelter at the first opportunity, which as it happened was afforded by the porch of a nearby church. Here we stood shivering for several minutes, at which point, the downpour showing no signs of moderating, Browning suggested that we go inside and sit down.

I was surprised to notice Mr Browning make the sign of the cross as we entered, and remarked that I had had no idea he was a Catholic.

'I am not,' he replied, 'but the church is, and I like to respect the forms. Do you know that story of the English aristocrat on the Grand Tour, who found himself in a church in Venice during Mass? At the elevation of the host the entire congregation knelt, all except our staunch Protestant. "Kneel down!" hissed the man beside him. "I do not believe in the Real Presence," returned the Englishman. "No more do I," the Venetian retorted immediately, "but either kneel down or get out of the church!" That's the spirit! But perhaps I shock your principles,

Mr Booth. You Bostonians can be very strict, I believe.'

'You cannot shock my principles, for I have none,' I returned, without thinking.

Browning shot me a look of horror. 'No principles! Ah, then you must be a prodigy indeed! A man without principles – what a terrifying idea! Let us thank God it can be nothing more. But all you mean, of course, is that you have no fixed principles in regard to the forms of religious observance – or, perhaps, that they are none of my business – and thus I am rightly punished for my inquisitiveness.'

One of the ideas which had flitted, fugitive-like, through my mind since meeting Robert Browning was that I might one day write a memoir of the man – put my humble talents to some good use and become his Boswell! This being the case, I realise that I must become adept at fishing out his ideas as they casually arise in the stream of conversation, and stretching them out in cold black ink at the earliest possible opportunity, all nice and fresh. How else, I would like to know, are collections of aphorisms, *obiter dicta*, etc., assembled?

While we are on the subject, another volume I have thought of publishing one day is a small manual entitled *The Whole Art and Secret of Conversational Success*. It would certainly make my fortune overnight, for the method it would elaborate has contributed in no small measure to my rapid ascent into the better strata of society here. The entire work would consist of but two words: Ask Questions.

I see you smile cynically, but try it some time! The secret of its invariable efficacy is simple: everyone – rich and poor, famous and unknown – would rather talk than listen, rather answer than ask, rather entertain than be entertained, rather bore than be bored. Give them the opportunity to do so, and they will always invite you back. With a Robert Browning there is of course no fear of being bored – but the trick works just the same.

'All I meant was that I have no prejudices in religious matters,' I commented. 'My parents brought me up as a Quaker, but I have long since ceased to know what I believe, if anything. But do you not think it possible that a man without any principles might nevertheless exist – at least in principle?'

I underlined my little jest with a smile; but Browning was all high seriousness.

'Never! The idea contains a contradiction. What is a man but a bundle of principles? Poor principles, often, to be sure. Weak principles, wrong principles; mad, sad or bad principles. But principles there must be, all the same – just as this stone, this wood all around us cannot exist without the great Principle which holds its atoms together, binding them irrevocably into the nature of wood or stone. Why, just imagine this . . . ' – he produced a handkerchief from his pocket – 'imagine this little piece of cloth totally released, unpacked and liberated from all restraints! Imagine that hurricane of energy blasting half Florence into instant ruin! The human counterpart of that apocalyptic explosion would be the man without principles. But he cannot appear until the day matter casts off its bonds, and that cannot happen until he appears – and we know when that will be, and who he is: the Anti-Christ! Until then, thank God, we have only mundane wickedness, ignorance and sin to contend with. And we should get on with it, no doubt, instead of philosophising on ultimate things in this fashion.'

I was, in fact, thinking less of what he was saying than of the handkerchief he was waving in front of my eyes. It was of lace, like those the huckster had been selling by the Cathedral the night before. I observed now that a feature of the pattern embroidered on it was a bold letter B in each of the four corners. At first I thought of his own name, then of the maiden name of his wife, and lastly of the pet name by which he calls her: Ba. So the purchase had been innocent enough, after all.

I enquired where we should go to discuss what had happened – half-hoping that he might invite me back to Casa Guidi, which lay at the end of the street, almost in sight of the church. But he merely asked why we should not stay where we were.

'In a church?' I enquired. 'Is it a fit place to speak of such things?'

Browning looked at me keenly.

'Are you afraid we may shock God?' he asked.

VIII

The church was empty but for an old woman praying before the main altar, the constant murmuring of whose weak voice echoed and reverberated monotonously around the nave.

'You remember how puzzled we were by the locket,' Browning began – we were seated side by side on a pew at the very back of the church. 'Puzzled both by the initials engraved on it, and by the fact that according to her maid's testimony Mrs Eakin kept it separately from her other jewellery – kept it hidden, in fact. In fact, of course, these two mysteries cancel each other out. The locket was kept hidden from her husband because it was a love-token, suitably inscribed, which had been given to her by a secret admirer.'

'But who? We have already concluded that there is no one in Florence with those initials.'

Browning pointed to a mosaic in the floor at our feet.

'There is no one in Florence with those initials either – nor ever was!' he retorted.

I realised that my companion must be referring to the letters A.F.V.M., which formed part of the design.

'Those are not initials – the letters stand for *ausculta fili verba magistri*: the opening words of the Rule of St Benedict. As you must know very well,' I concluded lamely, realising that I had been showing off my knowledge to Robert Browning!

'Exactly. And what of the locket? After all, for the lover to identify himself in an offering to a married woman would have been very indiscreet, would it not? It would have given her an excellent pretext, as a woman of good sense, for refusing to accept it. So I sat down last night and started rummaging through the classical mottoes I keep ranged in the most perfect disorder in this head of mine. Love was in the air, so I set down the "A" as standing for *amor*. After that it was simple, for the line is not at all recondite: *Omnia vincit Amor*; "Love conquers

63

all". Virgil continues: *et nos cedamus Amori*: "let us too yield to Love". In other words, the locket was nothing but a *billet-doux* which was sent to Isabel Eakin, inviting her to yield to the irresistible power of love. As we know, she accepted.'

'Accepted what?' I felt obliged to ask. 'The locket, or the proposal?'

Robert Browning looked me steadily in the eye.

'Do you honestly believe it was in Mrs Eakin's power to accept one and not the other?'

Rather than answer this, I remarked that I failed to see how this insight could help us, since we still had no idea who had sent Isabel the locket.

Browning seemed surprised that I had not yet understood.

'It was Cecil DeVere, of course.'

'DeVere!' I cried.

Italians are extremely – some might say excessively – tolerant of noise in their churches, but this last exclamation of mine was so explosive that the old woman at the front turned round and gave us a distinctly un-Christian look. We huddled down in our places on the bare wooden pews, and Browning went on in a whisper.

'Strangely enough, it was your question last night, which left me at such a loss, that set my mind working in the right direction. Strange, the tricks the mind plays on us! You very reasonably asked why DeVere's, of all names, should have popped into my head. Well now, let us try a little experiment. Do you say the very first word that comes into your head when I speak – without a moment's reflection, mind! Ready? Locket.'

'Gold,' I replied at once.

'Knife.'

'Cut.'

'Water.'

'Well.'

'Now then, why do you think just those words, out of all the thousands in the language, were the first to come to your mind?'

'There is no mystery about it. Evidently there is a real connection between the two ideas for which they stand. The locket we have just been speaking of is made of gold, a knife is used to cut, water comes from a well.'

'Precisely. And in the same way, when I mentioned DeVere's

name after receiving a summons to the villa where Mrs Eakin lived, it was because there was a real connection between these two ideas – even though to the best of my belief I was totally ignorant of it. But then, by dint of turning it over in my mind, I remembered that Mr Lytton – a friend of mine – had mentioned in my hearing one evening not long ago, that the lovely young Mrs Eakin was rumoured to have found a romantic distraction to palliate the rigours of her six-month term in the cold old villa which her even colder and older husband had insisted on renting for her. One of the other men present – the company was exclusively male, naturally – chaffed him, saying that he believed that the Lothario in question was none other than Lytton himself. Bob strenuously denied this, and eventually DeVere's name was mentioned – I forget by whom. And that was that. I thought no more about it – I knew neither of the parties concerned, after all. But clearly the connection between DeVere and Mrs Eakin was lodged somewhere in my brain, and on Sunday night it emerged pat, without my even recognising the source.'

Browning had mentioned the strange tricks the mind plays, and it was a further testament to this truth that my thoughts at this juncture were not so much of the shocking and repugnant information which my companion was thus communicating to me in hushed whispers, as the fact that we were there at all, Robert Browning and I, calmly discussing the adulterous loves of Isabel – our Isabel, Prescott! – beneath the chilly echoing vault of the ill-named church of the Holy Felicity.

I had no time to muse, however, for Browning was already plunging relentlessly on. While I lagged behind, cavilling over details, he had got the entire wilderness already mapped out and opened up, and was all set to start trading. In a word, he believed that Cecil DeVere had murdered Isabel and then taken his own life!

The discovery of Isabel's locket at DeVere's apartment, Browning pointed out, was already very strong evidence of his guilt – for who but her assassin could have been in possession of it? As for the scrap of paper which he had removed, this clinched the matter.

'As we know, the knife with Eakin's name was deliberately placed at the villa by the murderer in an attempt to incriminate him. Now you will have remarked, I'm sure, that even educated Italians find foreign names almost impossible to spell correctly. But since this was supposed to be Eakin's own knife, the slightest mistake would of course have given the game away. The existence of this piece of paper' – he produced it from his pocket and smoothed out the creases on his knee – 'might therefore have been logically inferred. It is of course the model which was left for the engraver to copy. Its preservation is no doubt due to characteristic Florentine parsimony: the engraver reused the paper to wrap up the knife when his work was completed and DeVere came to collect it.'

'Admirable! But why was the paper displayed so prominently upon the table? And another thing – why did you take it before the police returned?'

'I'll answer both those questions with one other one: who or what caused DeVere's death? And I fancy the answer, my dear Booth, is that you did!'

I was too amazed by this to attempt any reply whatsoever.

'You are not quite as good at concealing the truth as you may think, I fear,' Mr Browning went on after a moment, with a slight smile. 'When you met DeVere yesterday, I am sure you were convinced that you had completely concealed all our suspicions about the manner of Mrs Eakin's death. But, as blindness sharpens a man's hearing, so guilt hones the moral sensibilities to a fine edge. I'm certain that DeVere observed some alteration in your manner, some slight hesitation, or unwonted reticence. And where another man might have thought nothing of it, he – knowing himself a murderer – was at once beset with horrible doubts. Did everyone believe that Isabel Eakin took her own life, as he wished them to? Or were some of us just *pretending* to believe, the better to take him unawares? These questions urgently demanded answers, but how was he to answer them without giving himself away?

'And so, to probe these fearful suspicions of his, DeVere invented the story of having seen someone prowling about in the garden. If you were convinced that Mrs Eakin's death was a clear case of tragic self-destruction, you would have no interest in tales of an interloper having been seen in the garden some eighteen hours later: some busybody satisfying his morbid curiosity, you would think, and nothing more. But suppose that

66

on the contrary you knew, or at least suspected, that Isabel Eakin had been foully murdered – then the story would become so extremely interesting that you must have been a monster of deviousness not to show it! I am certain you *did* show it, and that DeVere read the truth.

'Consider his position now. Already stricken by guilt and remorse, no doubt, he learns that it is not merely the pangs of conscience which he has to fear, but also the rigours of the law. His crime has been discovered, and it is plainly but a matter of time – and not very much time, at that – before it is known that Mrs Eakin was killed by a secret lover with whom she had an assignation that afternoon, whom she admitted through the garden gate so that he would not be observed – hence her nervousness when Isa Blagden unexpectedly called – and who removed from her body the locket he had given her, lest its presence reveal that she was expecting him at the hour of her death.

'In short, it is but a matter of time before the accusing finger points at *him* – a man whose illicit relations with the victim are already a matter for rumour and speculation. In a flash he seems to see the inevitable arrest, the trial, the shame and scandal, his family's name besmirched for ever! And then, like a blessing, he spies his way clear out of it all, and ends his wretched life – leaving those two pieces of evidence on the table to reveal, to those who could read their cipher, the reasons for his action.

'As for why I removed the paper with Eakin's name, that was a quite possibly unnecessary precaution on my part. I doubt very much if the police would have made anything of it – they do not know about the knife, after all. But it seemed as well to be sure that DeVere's good work would not be undone. The locket is of no importance. On the contrary – they will no doubt assume that some *belle dame sans merci* returned it to DeVere, and that this rejection prompted his tragic plunge into the Arno. Or they will ignore it totally and blame it all on DeVere's tardiness in having his balcony railing repaired. All I know is that they will never suspect the truth now, and that justice is best served so.'

Such was the eloquent manner in which Mr Browning so satisfactorily explained all the many mysteries which have been perplexing us. I complimented him profusely on his achievement, and then turned the subject to his poetry, mentioning the volume of his which I had purchased, and my high opinion of his work.

Unfortunately we were interrupted at this moment by a party of Americans – some resident, some in transit – among whom were several friends of mine. They were bound for the studio of Mr Powers, and had stopped in to admire the astonishing Entombment of Christ by Pontormo which lurks, like some fierce caged animal, behind the railing of a nearby chapel.

I merely nodded and looked away, for I sorely wished to prolong my conversation with Mr Browning. But my friends insisted on coming to speak to me, and thus introductions had to be effected. When one of the visiting ladies discovered that my companion was none other than *the* Mr Browning, the real live husband of her favourite poetess, there was no containing her effusions – indeed, it was only with some difficulty, and a deal of tact, that Browning was able to make her comprehend that the Casa Guidi was not, like the Capponi Chapel, a shrine which could be viewed by tipping the custodian the appropriate sum. And thus our colloquy broke up amid scenes of confusion and near-farce.

As far as these grim events are concerned, there is thankfully little more to add. Despite Browning's idea about the locket suggesting a romantic suicide, DeVere's death – possibly as the result of discreet pressure from the British authorities – has been recorded as due to misadventure. He is to be buried tomorrow. Joseph Eakin has already wound up his affairs here and taken passage from Leghorn to Genoa, whence he continues to New York. Isabel's remains travel with him, and will be interred, I understand, in beautiful Mount Auburn cemetery. The public accounts of her death make no mention of self-violence, and I understand that the Allen family is doing its utmost to sustain the fiction that Isabel was one of the many victims of the influenza epidemic which has swept Italy this winter. The villa stands empty once more, awaiting the arrival of the next wealthy foreigner.

As for Browning's explanation of the mystery, while its logic seems irresistible in its broad outlines, I am unable – or at least do not wish – to believe that it was correct in every detail. In particular, I refuse to accept his implication that Isabel's behaviour towards Cecil DeVere was anything other than unfailingly correct. What *his* may have been towards her is of course quite another matter. The more I think of it, the more that languid Britisher seems to me to have had all the makings of a smooth cunning scoundrel of the worst variety. I can well imagine such a villain unscrupulously taking advantage of the artless and unsophisticated nature of a girl like Isabel, whose candid New England heart had no notion of the devious twists of which the European mind is capable.

I am prepared to grant that DeVere had obtained some hold over her; but we who knew her will surely find it easier to believe that this was based not on any amorous passion, but rather some low and cowardly form of blackmail. It is notorious that DeVere lived beyond his means; how he contrived to do so is not. Various possibilities suggest themselves, but is it not conceivable that he had obtained, through his diplomatic connections, some information about Joseph Eakin which might have seriously compromised that gentleman?

He would of course be too clever to approach Eakin himself. Instead he sneaked to Isabel, insinuating what might happen if he were forced to publish what he knew. And she – yes, this must be it – she agreed to pay in order to shield her husband. But DeVere was insatiable – he demanded more, always more; until on that fatal Sunday Isabel cast caution to the winds and summoned him to the villa. All her native pride and disdain rose up, and she boldly threatened the vile leech with exposure! Now the tables were turned, and it was DeVere's turn to cower! But the heroic woman had risked too much! The stakes were high, and DeVere killed her, the poor defenceless child – killed her brutally, in cold blood!!

It turns my stomach to think that he is to be interred with all due pomp and honour, like a proper Christian, and no one any the wiser. But no doubt it has all turned out for the best, for who stands to gain by having these horrors made public? Our business now must be to bury the dead, to forgive and forget – though it be more than his base heart deserves.

The most important thing is that it is all over, and that now my friendship with Mr Browning – for I believe I can now give it that sacred title; he calls me 'Booth' *tout court*, and takes my arm, and is most free and easy with me – can emerge at last from these shadows which have darkened it right from the beginning.

I look forward to a time when we can meet openly, without this terrible secret between us; when I can be invited back to Casa Guidi, as Mrs Browning plainly wished; when our talk will be not of death and crime and sin but of his work and himself, of Life and Art, Truth and Beauty!

Of his stature both as a man and a writer I have no further doubts. He is the real thing, and in his presence I hope to feel once again that signifying power which can fix the formless flux of being into a lattice as perfectly structured and coherent as a crystal.

That alone can justify my life. And that, alone, can justify it.

Yours most affectionately,

Booth

BOOK TWO

Another Kind of Love

IX

My dear Prescott,

I have so much to tell you I scarcely know where or how to start.
I will therefore begin at the beginning: with those high hopes
which ended my last letter – and which were utterly dashed to
pieces not twenty-four hours later, in a quiet yew-lined alley at
the English Cemetery.

As the Church here will not allow heretics to be buried within
the city walls, the graveyard in question is on a little knoll just
outside the Pinti gate. It is normally a quiet, not to say lonely,
spot; but on the occasion of DeVere's burial service on Saturday
afternoon half Florence seemed to be there, despite the gloomy
weather. The diplomatic corps was of course out in force, to say
nothing of the Grand Duke's personal band, who played a
selection of lugubrious melodies with great relish before un-
wisely attempting 'God Save the Queen', which emerged
sounding like the Grand March from Signor Verdi's latest
extravaganza.

I had wondered whether Mr Browning would attend the
funeral. He had admitted that he did not know DeVere – but
how was he to explain to his wife and Mr Powers that he could
not be bothered to pay his last respects to a man whose word had
been enough to draw him from his hearth on a foul night less
than a week earlier?

At all events, he *was* there, surrounded by all the important
names of Florence: poets, novelists, essayists, artists, diplomats,
critics, and the like. Seizing what I saw as a golden opportunity
to exploit my hard-won intimacy with Mr Browning, I pushed
my way through the throng of eminent personages and greeted
him familiarly.

Never have I been so cruelly reminded that pride comes
before a fall. The change in his manner was painfully perceptible

– and not only to me, which would have been quite bad enough a case, but to all and sundry. I was not only disgraced, but publicly disgraced.

Not that Browning was in the least unpleasant or brusque. The opposite, rather – his expression was laden with that over-solicitude, that excess of polite interest which the English use with people they do not like, or have no interest in, or wish for whatever reason to keep at a distance.

Desperate to get away and hide my shame, I gabbled something about hoping that we could meet again some time soon.

'Ah, yes. Yes indeed,' Browning replied vaguely. 'Yes, we must try to see if we cannot do something of the kind at some time.'

I caught a smile on one of the faceless faces about me, and to wipe it off pursued, 'I am free all next week, for example!'

'Are you indeed? I envy you! But my wife, as you may know, is very poorly at present, and so I must regretfully put the claims of society on one side for the moment – indeed, for the foreseeable future.'

Then, looking about him, he exclaimed suddenly, 'But this will never do, Mr Booth! I am monopolising you most shamefully.'

And he turned gracefully away, and was closed in by a group including young Lytton, the scribbling diplomat he and his wife cultivate. This individual looked at me as they went off, and said something to Browning with what looked most unpleasantly like a smirk. Browning replied – I know not what, nor do I want to know – and Lytton, the puppy, laughed. It was all about as mortifying as can well be imagined.

I made my way home alone, feeling utterly and completely miserable. The light that had flared up and seemed to settle into a steady flame had now been brutally extinguished, leaving me in a darkness even more total than before. I called myself a fool, a credulous idiot, for being so completely mistaken about the nature of Browning's interest in me. So far from our relationship being impeded by his fascination with Isabel's death, it was now clear that it had been that and that alone which had kept it in existence. Now we were like strangers: worse than strangers, indeed, for as strangers we could in time have come to know each other, gradually building an acquaintanceship that might have ripened – given all the goodwill on *my* side, at least – into real friendship.

But from the moment I had unluckily happened to stumble on Browning's secret that night at the villa, everything had changed. The immediate effect was almost miraculous, permitting me to develop what appeared to be a close intimacy with Robert Browning after only a few hours' acquaintance. But like forced fruit, the resulting friendship ripened early and then quickly rotted. The secret which had bound us together then, now split us irrevocably apart. With Isabel and DeVere dead and buried, the mere sight of me could be nothing to Browning but a goad to his conscience, a reminder of whatever guilty knowledge he harbours in his breast. Useless to tell him that I do not care what that secret is! I *know*, and he knows that I know, and that fact now stands between us like the memory of some ancient wrong.

Thus I reasoned, worming myself deeper and deeper into the clinging clayey stuff of despair.

Saturday passed, and Sunday: two days, like most of those which make up a life, so featureless and devoid of incident that they blur into one another, forming one undistinguished lump of time. I lolled around my rooms, stared out of my window, leafed through musty old books, elaborated a thousand impossible schemes, lay on my sofa and gazed up at the ceiling with its elaborate design of concentric circles. I saw no one and no one came to see me. I almost ceased to exist, reduced to a mere licked whimpering spirit hiding in its corner, more than half in love with easeful death.

But such a state could not last, and when Monday dawned bright and clear and sunny I shook off this unhealthy inactivity and determined to escape from the grey walls of Florence and fill my lungs with some country air. There is a stables some little distance from my house, and there I went and hired a gig for a modest sum, and stood in the sunlight and smoked a cigar while the stable lads hitched my vehicle up, allowing myself to be diverted by the sheer vitality of the scene – all the coming and going occasioned by the presence in the same yard of a poultry shop where two frowsy girls stood plucking fowl, a wagon-maker's where a new cart was being painted, a smithy at his bellows, and a cheap inn for the peasantry attached to the stables. All this at the bottom of a well, as it were, with lines of washing strung overhead from one back-balcony to another, and caged canaries chirping away like mad – and through it all a patch of pale delicate blue sky just visible.

It was a week to the day since I had undertaken the journey to Siena to verify Joseph Eakin's alibi, and by dint of brooding upon everything that had happened since then, I found myself taking the same road past the Guidi Palace (I gave it hardly a glance) to the imposing Porta Romana, where as usual I was held up for a lengthy period by the press of bullock-carts laden with vegetables and hides and demijohns of oil and wine, for everything that comes to market here must still pay a stiff tax at the city gate, as in the Middle Ages.

Once outside the walls it is unusual to see another vehicle, and thus I was free to enjoy to the full the beauties of the road, which are considerable even at this time of year. The gentle slopes of reddish-brown soil were superbly offset by the olive trees, with their elusive shade of grey-green – though the mystery, somehow, is as much in the texture of the colour as its shade – which, together with the whole of the pale blue sky I had but glimpsed before, made up a very pleasing composition. It was moreover one of those days when the clarity of the air makes crystal seem murky by comparison. You feel that if only your eyes were good enough you could count the buttons on a shepherd's coat five miles away, or reach out and pick up the team of miniature white buffalo ploughing that distant hillside.

My mood, however, was darkened by the comparison I was bound to make between the last occasion I had driven that way, as Mr Browning's trusted confidant, and my position now. This impression was strengthened when I stopped to eat at the same inn as before, where everything was of course unchanged, as it has been no doubt for the past three hundred years: the same food, the same wine, the same dog, the same peasants. Nothing had altered but my situation. Was there no help for that? Could I find – or make – no way back?

After my stop at the inn I turned off the high road, and headed north and east on little farm-tracks winding over the hills towards the Arno. I was reluctant to return to Florence. Whilst I remained out in the country my fate remained as it were in abeyance, and I sought to frustrate it as long as possible. And so I made my way across the valley by backways and forgotten lanes, right around the city to Fiesole, where I went to watch day turn to night from those immemorial slopes set with villas and long rows of cypresses: a landscape exactly fitted to the human scale, with the wild sublimity of the Apennine peaks behind to put all that barely-achieved perfection in perspective.

The sunset proved to be magnificent – a broad band of brilliant crimson spread right across the valley westward to the sea, cut into by the jagged edges of the coastal hills below, and melting away upwards by infinite gradations into a zone of pure gold which aged to a pale verdigris, and then flowed imperceptibly into the most delicate translucent rose, before cooling to azure which in turn deepened, almost overhead, into a rich indigo canopy flecked with glinting stars and artfully arranged fluffy cloudlets streaked with grey shadows and pink light from the invisible sun. In short, the whole affair was quite in Salvatore Rosa's best manner, and there I stayed, lost in admiration, until it grew dark.

Down in the valley Florence had vanished beneath a thick layer of mist, out of which a few of the taller towers and domes rose up like the remnants of a drowned city. I went downhill towards it as towards the surface of a moonlit lake, and when I reached the shore it was with something like dread that I saw that the road continued down into those grey depths, and that I had no choice but to follow.

I got home safely, however, and was groping my way up the stairs towards my front door, when I heard someone move in the darkness ahead of me. Instantly I stopped, all the hairs on the back of my neck bristling up – a most extraordinary and unpleasant sensation. The next moment a door opened on the next landing up, where a lonely old nobody named Hackwood ekes out a dreary existence with a cat for company. He had opened the door to put this beast out for the night, and it thus remained open only a few seconds – but during that time a shaft of light fell down on to my landing, and reflected back from the toes of two highly-polished black boots standing against the wall near the top of the stairs.

That was all I had time to see before darkness came rushing back, and blind panic seized me. I dashed forward, fumbling with keys that would open any other lock in the universe but my own! Then a hand gripped my arm, and I stifled a scream as a voice whispered, 'Don't be alarmed, Mr Booth! It's only me!' – a voice I recognised with an overwhelming sense of relief as that of Robert Browning.

Somehow the door opened, and we got inside. My nerves were jangling like a pianoforte which some demented virtuoso of the modern school has taken to playing with an axe. Fortunately the lamps were all burning, and in their peaceful light my nightmare terrors were quickly dispelled.

Something in this fact, however, seemed to strike my visitor, who had gone off into a brown study, murmuring 'That's strange!' When I enquired what he meant, he replied, 'The lamps – who lit them?'

'There is no mystery,' I explained. 'My servant left them burning. He knew I would be home shortly, and that I have a horror of the darkness.'

'I do not mean that,' Browning replied. 'I was referring to that night at the villa. Don't you remember? Beatrice – Mrs Eakin's maid – said that when she returned in the evening she found the lamps burning. But Mrs Eakin was dead by five o'clock, when the rain stopped – and at that time it was still light. *So who lit the lamps?*'

I must confess I reacted very impatiently to this belated bit of reasoning.

'What does it matter now?' I protested. 'We know who killed Isabel, and he has paid with his life. I really have no wish to dwell on the topic any further.'

Browning looked at me strangely, and changed the subject, apologising for having startled me. He explained that he had called upon me several times already that day, and on this occasion had been about to give up when I had returned, and he had thus appeared to be lying in wait for me like a foot-pad. He followed this apology with another, much more strongly felt, for his behaviour at the cemetery: it had been but one symptom, he said, of a black reaction which had seized him after the exertions of the previous week.

I nodded politely, and said nothing.

'To tell you the truth, Mr Booth,' he went on, 'I am not near as much enamoured of life in Florence as I once used to be.

Indeed, I should leave for London or Paris tomorrow, if such a thing were possible. But with the state of my wife's health that is of course out of the question, and so I make a virtue of necessity. Which is not very difficult, in a sense: the place has charm, no doubt about it. But after – how long is it now? – almost eight years, it does sometimes all begin to seem a little quiet, a little – dare I say? – *provincial*.

'So you see this bad business, for all its horrors, gave me what I badly needed – a change, a lift, call it what you will. I should not say so, perhaps, but there it is: it diverted me! And when it came, as I thought, to a conclusion, the effect was to plunge me into the blackest depression I have known for many months – and you suffered the consequences, I fear. I do not know if I can do anything to make amends, but since you were kind enough to mention your interest in my work, I have brought you this.'

He handed me a volume, upon whose spine I read the title *Sordello*.

'This piece might aptly be described as an acid test for aspiring admirers of my poetry,' Browning said sardonically. 'Its reception almost broke my heart, for I had the highest hopes of the piece; and although I can now see its faults plainly enough – though not how to remedy them! – I still have a special place in my heart for it, as for a deformed child. Please accept it, with my most humble apologies.'

I was speechless with joy and gratitude. But to my chagrin, instead of continuing to talk thus about his work, Browning turned away – as if to put this matter behind him – and began to pace the floor slowly, hands clasped behind his back.

'And now I have something very serious to tell you,' he went on – as though his poetry were *not* serious! 'Yesterday I was invited to dine by William Bulwer, who was the British Minister here until his retirement recently. In the course of the meal one of the other guests remarked to our host that he was doubly grateful to be there, since his own table was saddened for him by the fact that poor Cecil DeVere had sat at it on that very day a week earlier, the very image of health and enviable good fortune.

'You may imagine with what feelings I listened to this news. I managed to keep my wits about me to the extent of enquiring if it had not been on the same day that Mrs Eakin had yielded to whatever tragic urge had impelled her to self-destruction. This was established, and Bulwer then perorated at some length upon the cruel and unexpected blows which fate deals out, and the whole conversation moved on to an elevated plane – but not before I had ascertained beyond the shadow of a doubt that on Sunday the fifth of February Cecil DeVere had been a guest at a formal dinner, commencing at three o'clock and ending not earlier than half-past six; during the whole of which time he was in the company of eleven illustrious members of the diplomatic community in Florence, and therefore could not by the wildest stretch of the imagination have had anything whatever to do with the death of Isabel Eakin!'

X

Now then, Prescott, a test! How do you think I responded? Rack
your brains and pronounce. Did I gasp and gawp? Hold my
tongue but look volumes? Clutch my temples and fall writhing to
the floor? Invoke the gods?

I did none of these things. I laughed – a fierce, hard, brittle,
convulsive laughter, akin to vomiting. Strangely enough, Browning took this bizarre outburst quite in his stride.

'Oh, you may laugh!' he cried. 'You have my leave. I quite
deserve it. I agree that I look absolutely ridiculous, with all my
fine theories.'

I tried to protest that I was not laughing at *him* – but the fit
shook me so uncontrollably that in the end I had to leave the
room and go and bathe my face with cold water to calm myself.
When I returned I apologised to Browning for my hysterical
outburst, and asked him if there was no possibility of error in
what he said.

'It seems almost impossible that he could be innocent,' I
exclaimed. 'Everything fitted together so perfectly!'

'Indeed. And the irony of it is that evidence has come to light
which appears to confirm my original theory in other respects.
For example, Isabel Eakin and DeVere *were* lovers – of that
there is no further doubt.'

There was no risk of my laughing at this.

'How do you know?'

'It came out over the port. Despite the official line, no one at
the Embassy seems to doubt that DeVere killed himself in
despair at his mistress's death. One of the attachés who was a
close friend of his said that DeVere had bragged to him about it.
He said – but perhaps you would prefer to be spared the details.
Mrs Eakin was a friend of yours.'

'No, no – tell me!'

Browning fell to perusing a small landscape I like to think may
be a Carlo Dolci.

'Well, it seems that DeVere boasted to this friend of having made a conquest of Isabel Eakin. He was that kind of man, apparently – to boast of it, I mean. He even showed him a letter from Mrs Eakin, couched in the most passionate terms. He in turn described her as "frisky". He also – are you quite sure you want me to go on? – mentioned that she had a mole near her right nipple which was extremely sensitive. DeVere further asseverated that he was in the habit of – '

'Stop!' I cried, for I could stand no more. If he had not already been dead, I swear I would have rushed out and killed DeVere there and then.

'Very well!' I went on wildly. 'He is dead, and a good riddance of bad rubbish, say I! What of it?'

'Well there is just the small question of who killed him,' murmured Browning.

'Killed him? But he killed himself, didn't he? You just said as much.'

'No – I said that that was what the Embassy believe. But they do not know about the locket. Only Mrs Eakin's murderer could have had possession of that, and if DeVere did not murder her then the locket must have been left on his table by the person who did, after he also killed DeVere.'

I hid my face in my hands, trying to think.

'But why? It doesn't make sense,' I protested. 'What had DeVere got to do with it?'

'I have given that some thought,' Browning replied, 'and I can see two reasons why the murderer might have wanted to kill DeVere. Firstly, for the same reason that he placed the knife with Eakin's name in the garden of the villa – to divert suspicion from himself. Let us note in passing that he must therefore be someone who would otherwise naturally have come under suspicion. He evidently chose DeVere partly because his known liaison with the dead woman made the latter a convincing suspect.

'But there is another reason, which relates to that story DeVere told you about having seen someone prowling about the Eakins' garden – which we may now presume to be true. You were no doubt not the only person he told about his interesting experience. Suppose, therefore, that amongst others he unwittingly told the murderer himself – who of course had been in the garden that very day, placing the knife where I later found it. Imagine the tremendous resonance of DeVere's words in the vaults of a guilty conscience! Each bland expression seems to imply a wealth of unspoken knowledge; each smile and glance seems to say "I saw you! I know you!"

'Now suppose that the murderer, to find out how much DeVere knows, asks for more details. What did he look like, this intruder in the garden? "Oh, about your height and build," DeVere unwittingly replies – it was true, after all! Now the murderer is sure! DeVere *knows*, and he must silence him at once. He did so the very same night, and when we went to see him in the morning, it was too late.'

I rose from my chair and went over to confront Browning.

'Very well,' I said. 'We have been wrong, despite our best efforts. The time has come to be honest and admit our limitations. This affair has got completely out of hand. Murder is no business for amateurs, and that is all we are. But there can be no doubt now that we are facing a devilishly cool opponent who has already struck twice with complete impunity, and who may even now be planning further outrages. Let us forestall him by going to the police at once and making a clean breast of it! Let us tell them everything we know, everything we suspect, and leave them to decide what action to take. They may be successful or they may not, but we at least shall have done our duty.'

A good speech, I thought it at the time, level-headed and responsible to a fault. Browning's response, to my amazement, was to shake his head slowly.

'To take such a step now would place me in a most awkward position, Mr Booth,' he replied sadly. 'Not that I disagree with you! On the contrary – I wholeheartedly echo your sentiments. Would I had listened to your advice in the first place! But you know the Grand Duke's police – they see plots and conspiracies everywhere. If we go now and tell them that we have kept this matter secret for a week, they will arrest us both on the spot. And the law here is that once arrested you are considered guilty unless you can prove your innocence.'

'But surely you *can* prove your innocence,' I objected. 'You have an alibi for the time of Isabel Eakin's death, have you not?'

Again the shake of the huge head.

'I was out for a walk. Worse, I walked up to Bellosguardo – as I often do. Several people must have seen me there. No, it will look very bad for me, I fear.'

'Why, then let us invent an alibi for you!' I cried enthusiastically. 'I shall simply say that you were with me.'

'No, that will not do either,' Browning pointed out, 'for you really *have* an alibi, proved by Mr Jarves, and plainly there can be no question of dragging him into our conspiracy. No, there is no help for it – I am in a very unenviable position. If the police learn that I have wilfully concealed information from them, and that I have no alibi, then Commissioner Talenti will avenge himself royally for my former intransigence, and this time neither my foreign status nor my friends will be able to save me. I shall be locked up as an accessory after the fact, and what will become of poor Ba then?'

So that was it! Browning's unmanly pusillanimity was explained: it was not for *himself* that he feared, but for his wife, who is utterly dependent upon him. And it is certainly true that once in prison here, it is no easy matter to get out again. One hears terrible tales of men who have spent half their lives in gaol, awaiting trial on some trivial charge (of which, perhaps, they are subsequently found to be innocent). Even commoner is the plight of those who have no relatives or friends to bribe the gaolers and supplement the meagre rations provided, and who almost starve to death. In short, Florence is mediaeval in more than one respect, and the prospect of bringing oneself to the attention of the law is so dismal that one would do almost anything to avoid it.

'In that case let us for God's sake wash our hands of the whole beastly matter!' I implored him. 'The police suspect nothing – still less does anyone else. All we need do is forget what we know – nay, what we *suspect*, for what is it all but mere suspicion, in the end?'

But Browning would not have it.

'That I absolutely cannot do, Mr Booth.'

'Why ever not?'

'Because I am afraid!'

'That is precisely why I am suggesting . . . '

'I do not refer to the police. I am afraid of God! I am afraid that one day I shall be summoned before Him to account for my life – and how should I explain that out of mere cowardice and incapacity I allowed a murderer to go unpunished?'

'But "vengeance is mine, saith the Lord",' I could not help putting in mischievously. 'Will not God punish where punishment is due? How can we judge?'

I immediately regretted this sally, for Browning looked at me sternly.

'Do not trifle,' he replied. 'Is it not as much a judgment to let a murderer go free as to hang him? Either way, we judge him – we *have* to, in this world. His soul is another affair, and there God will set all right. But let us leave this, for I suspect you are not in earnest. I have another reason for declining your convenient proposal, and one which you may well consider to have more urgency.

'Just think: somewhere in this city, at this very instant, someone is sitting thinking how immensely clever he has been! How very cunning, to commit two murders which appear to cancel each other out, leaving – nothing! A work of genius! If you think that I could sit tamely back, knowing that this creature remains alive and free and secure from pursuit, believing that he has fooled us all – well, then you do not know me yet, my friend!'

To this I could only reply, and in all sincerity, that my dearest wish was to know him better; and with that our talk broke up, as Browning was anxious to keep another engagement.

As I saw him to the door, I picked up a letter lying on my doormat, quickly tore it open and scanned the enclosure. My visitor was just taking his hat from the stand. I passed him the single sheet of paper, which ran as follows:

Villa Hibernia
12th February

Dear Mr Booth,
Some exceptionally curious indications have recently come to light concerning the tragic deaths of Mrs Isabel Eakin and Mr Cecil DeVere.

As you know, these two events were not only connected, but the cause of death was in each case very different from that announced by the authorities. However, it now appears that these crimes were but part of a much more ambitious criminal project, whose full scope and extent is only beginning to become evident.

If either you or your associate Mr Robert Browning will be good enough to come to the above address at your earliest convenience, you will have an opportunity of judging for yourselves the truth of this assertion.

Yours ever faithfully,

(p.p.) Maurice Purdy

Browning looked from the letter with a pale face. His hand, I noted, was trembling.

'What devilry is this?' he murmured.

'We must find out without delay,' I replied resolutely.

'Indeed – and let us not make the same mistake as with poor DeVere, but go immediately!' Browning declared.

'But what about your engagement?'

'I can call and make my excuses on the way.'

Now before going any further I should explain that Maurice Purdy is a plump balding little Anglo-Irishman, owner of vast tracts of bogland whose crop of potatoes supports a number of tenant farmers, who in turn support Mr Purdy. When this crop fails – as it did some ten years back, you may remember – a million or so of these Hibernians emigrate to the next world, while an equal number come to try their luck in the New. At other times they remit to Squireen Purdy – well, hardly a million of anything, but enough at any rate for him to live very comfortably here in divinely cheap Florence, indulging his ruling passion for the pleasures of the table.

The man truly lives to eat, and his dinner parties are famous for the quality and quantity of the fare provided. Not that he entirely stints himself in other respects – he has been known to hire a band out to the villa to play symphonies for him. But even then he does not entirely surrender to the muse, but will nibble at some choice delicacy while Spohr or Cherubini warbles.

In short, if we accept Sydney Smith's friend's notion of paradise as eating pâté de foie gras to the sound of trumpets, then Maurice Purdy has undeniably seen heaven's glories shine – but what this utterly inoffensive, slightly comical hedonist could have to do with the mysterious and sinister epistle which had appeared on my mat was a question to which there seemed no possible answer. As Browning said, there was a smell of devilry about it; as though the voice of Evil were to speak through the mouth of a child's doll. How did Purdy know that Isabel's and DeVere's deaths were connected? How did he know that they had not died in the way given out by the police? How did he know that Browning and I had an interest in the matter? Above all, what was the 'much more ambitious criminal project' of which these events were just a part?

We soon found a cab, whose driver – a youngster new to the work, and as keen as mustard – made no fuss about an expedition without the walls, promising to take us to the moon and back if we wished. The initial destination my companion named proved no less interesting, although considerably nearer: Via Dante Alighieri.

I had by no means forgotten the evening when I had followed Browning through the city to this street, where he had disappeared, but the incident had been eclipsed by the more urgent matter which had latterly occupied me. Now it seemed that chance had put the solution to this mystery into my hands.

Our cab drove past the Strozzi palace and through the Old Market, before turning into the street Browning had named.

'This will do!' Browning called up to the driver. 'Please wait for me here, Booth. I shall not be five minutes.'

He was in fact ten. I got out of the cab and strolled back and forth in the misty street. The cab-horse shook its harness and snorted and stamped, while the cabbie essayed a variety of popular Florentine airs.

At length Browning reappeared, full of apologies for the delay. I remarked that it was a very poor and run-down neighbourhood.

He agreed.

Very few foreigners lived in that part of town, I opined.

He agreed.

I myself, I commented, had never set foot in a house in that area.

'It is a charitable duty which I have taken on myself,' Browning replied at last. 'A deserving case to whom it has been possible for me to offer some measure of assistance. And now without further delay let us find out just what Mr Maurice Purdy means by his extraordinary communication!'

XI

Twenty minutes later we rolled in through the open gates of Mr
Purdy's villa, which stands on the hill-slopes to the north of the
city, in the centre of an extensive walled estate. Not only the
gates but also the front door stood open, and lights were burning
in the hall – quite as if a reception had been planned. While we
waited for someone to answer our ring, I remarked on the
absence of the huge wolfhound which Purdy keeps chained up
at the front of the villa, and whose boisterous welcome is
normally such a feature of visits to the house.

Despite the apparent air of welcome, we had to ring three
times before Sergio, the handsome lout whom Purdy for some
reason insists on employing as his factotum, appeared.

'You are the doctor?' he bawled, looking at Browning.

Before either of us had a chance to reply – or even to consider
what we *should* reply – a carriage drew up outside, and a
soberly-dressed gentleman descended. He, it appeared, *was* the
doctor – and was instantly led away into the innermost regions of
the villa by Sergio, whose only response to our enquiries was to
repeat that Signor Purdy was ill and could not see anyone.

This news, of course, merely whetted our curiosity, and we
therefore settled down to await further developments. These
were not long in coming, for the doctor very shortly returned,
with Sergio bustling along self-importantly at his heels. We
introduced ourselves, and enquired whether we could be of
any assistance. The doctor, who proved to be Swiss, shook his
head.

'Everything possible has been done,' he replied gravely. 'Mr
Purdy has been savaged by that hound he keeps, and I am afraid
that he may be most seriously ill.'

More lamps were fetched, and the four of us went to the spot
where the attack had taken place. Here we found the body of the
dog stretched on the gravel. The medical man carefully directed

Sergio and one of the gardeners in the task of wrapping the cadaver in sacking and loading it to his carriage, and he then drove off to examine the beast at his surgery – the implications of this, and of his earlier words, were of course only too evident.

Once the doctor had gone we cornered Sergio and got him to tell us exactly what had happened. I say 'exactly', but in truth the fellow seems to combine the worst of both sexes, being as skittish as a woman and as dull as any peasant – Heaven knows what Purdy sees in him. In the end, however, we managed painfully to cull the following information from the confused and lurid account he provided.

At two o'clock that day, as on every Monday of the year, Purdy had summoned his carriage and had himself driven into Florence to attend the weekly reunion of the Lucullean Club – a select society whose meetings are entirely given over to the consumption of a meal of gargantuan proportions, conversation of any kind being strictly forbidden except between courses, and then only to comment on the fare.

When the gourmets had concluded their deliberations, Sergio drove his master home. On their arrival Purdy got out of the carriage and went over to fondle the wolfhound, as was his invariable habit. The next instant Sergio heard the most terrible scream, together with the muffled barks and growls of a dog and a succession of obscene tearing sounds. Running to see what had happened, he found his master lying motionless on the ground with an enormous black brute of a dog towering over him, its muzzle dripping foam!

The beast immediately tried to attack Sergio as well, but he was just beyond its reach, chained as it was to the wall. He ran into the house and roused one of the gardeners, who brought a gun and – Sergio having decoyed the creature away from Mr Purdy – shot it dead. The master of the house, who had meanwhile fainted, had then been carried inside and put to bed, and the doctor sent for.

'There is one thing I should like to verify before we leave,' Browning remarked, once Sergio had left us to answer a summons from the house. The scene of the tragedy was still brightly illuminated: there was the gravel scuffed up for yards around, and the gun still lying on the ground beside a great pool of blood. But Browning ignored these, directing his attention instead to the chain to which the animal had been attached – or rather to a piece of cheap hemp cord tied to it.

'Does this not strike you as rather curious – and suggestive?' he asked me. But I hardly heard him, my attention having been attracted to something written in fresh white chalk on the dull-red painted plaster wall. It read:

(3) CIACCO

'What do you make of that?' I asked my companion.

He shook his head.

'The word is presumably Italian, but it is not one with which I am familiar.'

At this moment Sergio emerged from the house with the welcome news that Maurice Purdy wished to speak to us.

We found the tubby little epicure in his bedchamber on the second floor of the house – a pale flabby figure cowering in the depths of an enormous featherbed, his features covered in livid scratches. He was in a shocking state of nervous excitement. It seemed that the doctor had administered a sedative, but that this had not yet taken effect; meanwhile Purdy had learned from Sergio of our presence, and had summoned us to commiserate with him on the *injustice* – such was the theme on which he harped – of what had occurred.

'Why me?' he wailed. 'I who have never hurt a fly in my life! Why should Luath do such a thing! I have always given him the best of everything! Why should this happen to me? All I have ever asked is to be let alone to enjoy my innocent pleasures. It isn't fair! What have I done to deserve this? I do declare that it simply is not fair!'

It was a truly affecting scene – the man was almost in tears. Browning and I naturally expressed our horror and sympathy, and in due course I touched on the letter: it was at once clear that Purdy had no idea what I was talking about – he had written me no such letter, nor had he summoned me or anyone else to the villa that evening.

By now the effects of the sedative were beginning to become apparent, and we prepared to take our leave.

At the door Browning suddenly turned.

'Does your dog wear a collar, Mr Purdy?'

'Indeed he does!' Purdy answered in a singsong voice, as though in a trance – with no apparent awareness of the singularity of the query. 'The most beautiful thing, all of local leatherwork, with his name worked in bronze.'

'And this collar is of course attached directly to his chain?'

'Directly, directly! The clasp was made specially for me . . . very good man . . . give you his name . . . tomorrow . . . luncheon . . .'

We slipped silently out of the room. Outside we found Sergio lounging insolently against the wall.

'Ciacco!' called Browning.

Sergio eyes blazed with anger.

'Who are you calling "*ciacco*"?' he demanded indignantly.

'I said Giacomo – that is your name, isn't it?'

'I'm Sergio!'

'My apologies. Why, what does it mean, *ciacco*? Something bad, I'll warrant.'

'It means a pig.'

The long drive back from Purdy's villa to the safety of the city walls seemed still longer because of the stony silence which my companion maintained throughout. I could see that he was both fascinated and terrified by these dramatic new developments: terrified of the magnitude and gravity of this affair he had so lightly got himself involved with, and could not now get out of, but also fascinated – as it were despite himself!

When we reached the city we parted without ceremony, merely agreeing to meet the following afternoon.

'What is happening?' Browning cried suddenly, at the last moment. 'What is this terrible curse which has descended on our little community? A paradise of exiles, Shelley called Italy – is it instead to become an inferno?'

I did not know what to say, for my only thought was of the irony of the situation. My most earnest wish had been granted: I had formed a relationship with a man I believed to be truly great – and we must apparently spend our whole energies discussing these gory and depressing crimes. It is *so* maddening! Imagine being magically transported back to Shakespeare's times – only to discover that you are his lawyer, and he will talk to you of nothing but land values. What of Art? What of Spirit? What of the great ideals that can make human life seem worth the living?

It is on them that I would fain dwell with a soul such as Browning's – instead of which we seem condemned to spend our time contemplating the legs of garden tables, bits of mouldy rope, lamps and pen-knives, and the precise design of dog collars!

And the worst of it is that Browning appears positively to revel in it! It seems that he is in some sense attracted by crime, by diseased and abnormal behaviour of every type, and in the greater detail the better! Indeed, I am very much afraid that there is a danger of his undoubted poetic gifts suffering as a result. In the volume I purchased, for example, I have noticed – despite my enduring enthusiasm for the collection in its entirety – several pieces which display an unseemly fascination with the workings of evil and deranged minds. The one entitled 'My Last Duchess' is a particularly repulsive example of the tendency to which I allude.

There is of course much very fine work in the volume – stirring tales of romance and chivalry, touching lyrics, quaint historical scenes and so on. But there is also this other strain – morbid, dark, introspective, unhealthy – which disturbs me; and what disturbs me still more is that it appears to be of relatively recent origin. *Sordello*, the early work he has given me, appears to be completely free of it. Is this some cancer which threatens to consume his genius? I have no way of answering this question as yet, but I am very apprehensive. Of course a great soul must be able to understand evil and madness – but at a distance, so to speak, without itself being contaminated. Whereas Browning seems to roll in the nastiness he handles, like a pig in mud.

We had arranged to meet at a coffee-shop near the Cathedral after dinner – Browning always leaves Casa Guidi for a walk at this hour, and could thus meet me without any risk of arousing suspicion.

He had already been to visit the doctor who was attending Purdy, and the news was grave indeed, for the dog which had made such a meal of the poor *bon vivant* had proved to be infected with rabies!

Thus poor Purdy's death certificate is in effect already signed, lacking only the date. At some time within the next month or so the hideous symptoms will begin to manifest themselves: the unpredictable shifts from savage excitement to apathetic stupor, culminating in the final death agony lasting for days, in which the throat muscles seize up completely and the sufferer, tormented by extreme hunger and thirst, tries in vain to swallow, unable to bear the sight of food or drink. When I thought of the manner in which Maurice Purdy had lived, this terrible fate put me in mind of some moralistic painting of the Middle Ages. I said as much to Browning, who nodded gravely.

'Indeed. But I fear that something more than just pure coincidence is involved. I inspected the cadaver of the dog which attacked Mr Purdy at the doctor's just now. That beast was no wolfhound – although he had some wolf blood in him, I shouldn't wonder. As for that piece of rope we saw attached to the chain at the villa, the rest of it was still tied roughly round the animal's neck.

'The implication is only too clear. Maurice Purdy has been – or rather is going to be – the victim of a fiendishly cunning murder; a murder which has not yet occurred, but which cannot be prevented. His dog was removed – and no doubt killed – and a rabid animal substituted. In the dark Purdy did not notice the difference until it was too late.'

'And what about the writing on the villa wall? The word "pig" – is that some comment on Purdy's gulosity?'

'Taken in conjunction with the manner in which the victim will die, I think there can be not the slightest doubt of that. It appears to be a classic case of poetic justice, of the punishment fitting the crime. But what disturbs me is the fact that the writing was in Florentine dialect – the word was "*ciacco*", not "*porco*".'

'Are we then dealing with a Florentine murderer? A native? Perhaps some vendetta against the foreign community is intended.'

'Perhaps. But do not forget the letter you received last night. *That* was certainly not written by an Italian, and yet it obliquely foretold the tragedy at Purdy's villa, brought us out to witness its effects, and – most strikingly – linked it to the deaths of Mrs Eakin and DeVere. Now if the attack on Purdy was, as I have suggested, a cold-blooded murder, then it brings the number of such crimes to three; and the number three, you will recall, accompanied the word scrawled at the scene of that attack. In short, a pattern begins to emerge – a pattern which I suspect we may equate with that "more ambitious criminal project whose

93

full scope and extent is only beginning to become apparent"
mentioned in the letter.'

I suggested that the simplest way of verifying this hypothesis
would be to inspect the scenes of the other two crimes which
had occurred, and see whether some sort of inscription was not
also to be found there – and as it transpired that this was
precisely what was in Browning's mind, we set off without more
ado.

XII

As we passed the end of Via Dante Alighieri I thought once again of the strange scene the night before, which the horrors at Purdy's villa had then thrust out of my memory. Of one thing I was sure: Browning's tale of charitable visits had been a shift devised on the spur of the moment to forestall further questions. But why? What is the secret of that house in the meanest area of town, which he visits with such regularity? More and more I am convinced that it is connected in some way with that secret of his which continues to stand between us, despite the superficial familiarity we have resumed as a result of his interest in these murders. I must find it out, and soon! Perhaps if I do so, and then confront him with my knowledge of the truth, then I can exorcise this ghost which, till then, must continue to haunt our friendship.

At length we reached the south end of the Ponte Vecchio, and Browning immediately flung out his hand, pointing.

'Look!'

I could as yet see nothing beyond a white blur on the undressed stone wall outside the house where a few days before the crowd had gathered at the news of a death. But as we drew nearer to the spot I made out the following writing, scrawled up in white chalk on the wall, as at Purdy's:

(5) ARGENTI

' "*Argenti*" – silverware,' mused Browning. 'What possible significance can that have?'

'It might be a reference to DeVere's well-known mania for collecting,' I suggested.

Browning looked happier.

'That's very true. Bravo! I had not thought of that. Yes, indeed. This man had a weakness for *objets d'art*, for precious

95

trinkets. That, then, was his "crime", as greed was Purdy's. Are we dealing with a secret society I wonder? Some nasty little terrorist sect who find Mazzini grown too tepid, the Carbonari too moderate, and mean to hack their way to Liberty with a dagger? But then what of the number? Three for Purdy, but five for DeVere. So much for our theory about *that*.'

I had no idea to suggest, other than to walk up to Bellosguardo, and see whether the inscription at the scene of the first crime – assuming there were one – might not resolve the mystery.

As we walked along, I tried to turn the conversation to something more inspiring than the murky business in hand – in short, to Browning's own work – and mentioned one of the poems in the volume I had purchased. The verse is entitled 'Porphyria's Lover', and is yet another example of that strain which I so strongly deprecate in Browning's work. If I chose to mention it, it was because the story closely resembles his theory about the manner in which Isabel Eakin was murdered.

The poem – as so often in those pieces where Browning exhibits the darker side of his nature – is narrated in the first person, and is set on an evening just like that of Isabel's death, with rain and a high wind. But the position here is reversed; it is the woman, Porphyria, who comes to call upon her lover, who is waiting not in a villa but a humble cottage, situated not upon a hill-top but beside a lake. The inversion is so complete, so striking, as to form an exact mirror-image of the real event.

As there are no servants there, Porphyria sets about making a fire, after which she 'from her form withdrew the dripping cloak and shawl, and laid her soiled gloves by, and let the damp hair fall' – no doubt these lines remind you, as they did me, of Isabel laid out on that cold marble tabletop. She sits beside her lover, who does not answer when she speaks to him. And so the woman does a very natural, womanly thing: 'She put her arm about my waist, and made her smooth white shoulder bare, and all her yellow hair displaced, and, stooping, made my cheek lie there, and spread o'er all her yellow hair'.

We now learn two very interesting things: that Porphyria has come secretly from a dinner party to visit her lover; and that although she loves him, she is not willing to make the final sacrifice, and break the presumably illustrious ties that make their love illicit: 'She too weak, for all her heart's endeavour, to set its struggling passion free from pride, and vainer ties dissever, and give herself to me for ever.' At that moment, however, she loves him; 'happy and proud' – for he too is proud! – 'I knew Porphyria worshipped me.'

What is he to do, her lover? He knows the moment will not, cannot last, for she must return to the realities of her dreary marriage, contracted for base motives, but which she has not the spirit, or the will – call it what you like – to break. ' . . . I debated what to do. That moment she was mine, mine, fair, perfectly pure and good: I found a thing to do, and all her hair in one long yellow string I wound three times her little throat around, and strangled her.'

Is that not disgusting? I find it so – or rather the total lack of any hint of censure on the poet's part. To discuss these things so calmly, so coolly – well, it is beyond me. But there is worse to come, for what does the lover do now? Recoil in horror at the deed he has unthinkingly committed in an instant of frenzy he can never sufficiently regret?

No! On the contrary, like the vilest fiend in existence, he *glories* in the dead body at his side – glories in it equally as it is a beautiful female body, and as it is dead, and therefore will-less, utterly passive and given up to him. What use he makes of his opportunity is left to the reader's imagination, but so heated is the language Mr Browning employs that there can be little doubt as to what is intended: 'As a shut bud that holds a bee I warily oped her lids: again laughed the blue (!) eyes . . . and I untightened next the tress . . . her cheek once more blushed bright beneath my burning kiss . . . '

The almost hysterical alliteration in that last phrase could hardly be clearer in its implications, I think.

But the vilest cut is saved for last, where the 'lover' seeks to possess not merely Porphyria's body but her soul as well. For, all passion spent, he lays her head upon his shoulder – commenting upon how the situation is changed, for now *he* is dominant: 'The smiling rosy little head, so glad it has its utmost will, that all it scorned at once is fled, and I, its love, am gained instead!' In other words, the murderer claims that he was merely fulfilling his victim's 'darling one wish' in killing her. He need not feel guilty! He has no motive for remorse! She wanted to be his, and now she is – for ever. The poem ends chillingly:

> And thus we sit together now,
> And all night long we have not stirred,
> And yet God has not said a word!

To be sure, the piece has a certain power, but of what variety? If it is powerful, it is as a 'penny dreadful' is powerful, and what has that to do with Literature? Could the Shelley or the Keats Browning so admires have ever dreamt of penning such stuff?

My purpose in mentioning it, however, as I said, was not to discuss its literary merits, but rather to elicit Browning's views on the quite extraordinary parallels between this poem of his and the murder of Isabel Eakin.

'I fear it is less interesting than you seem to think,' my companion replied lightly when I drew his attention to the similarities. 'Both, after all, are productions of the same mind.'

I was stunned: for a moment I thought he was confessing to having murdered Isabel!

'That poem was written some twenty years ago, in London,' he went on. 'Nevertheless, when confronted with the evidence that a murder had occurred at the villa – which is just in sight, by the way; look, over the wall there! – I at once dreamed up a theory woven from the same threads: the mad jealous lover alone with his faithful-faithless mistress in the isolated country house. A theory, I might add, which now shows every sign of having been as far removed from reality as the fantasies of poor Porphyria's over-zealous lover.'

'Was the piece based upon an account of an actual crime?' I enquired.

'Not at all. I dreamed it all up.'

'How remarkable.'

'Do I remark a note of disapproval in your voice, Mr Booth?'

I hesitated. Should I risk making my criticisms known to Browning? If I decided to do so, it was not out of any wish to match wits with one so far superior to me in the matters under discussion – for what do my opinions matter? – but rather with that thought again in the back of my mind that I might one day be Robert Browning's Boswell. In that case, I will have to be more than merely sycophantic, agreeable and easy: half the good things of Johnson's we have exist only because Boswell provoked him so, worrying epigrams out of him like a sow rooting for truffles.

'I confess there is an element of perversity in the poem which I find troubling. I understand, of course, that it is intended as a character sketch of an imaginary personage. But there is a sense in which the poem seems to dwell gratuitously upon morbid elements – to take, almost, a kind of pleasure in them. Do you really think that Literature should concern itself with such matters?'

'You pose very large questions, Mr Booth. Tell me – what do *you* think Literature should concern itself with?'

I did not much care for him turning thus on me, in the Socratic manner, but I was ready for him.

'With the True and the Beautiful which Keats said were one and the same.'

Browning shot me a keen look.

'Bravo. Any friend of John Keats is a friend of mine. But the problem with his famous definition – which, incidentally, I most fervently believe to be as true as it is beautiful – is that like all great truths it balances perilously above an abyss of nonsense, where most of those who quote it quite lose their heads. What did Keats mean? That there is a class of things which we call true because they take after their ideal parent, and which you may recognise by their pretty features? Because in that case he was talking nonsense – and cloying, feeble, wishy-washy nonsense at that.

'But I believe he was saying something much stronger and stranger. I believe Keats meant that Truth *is* Beauty: that anything – literally anything – is beautiful, provided only that we are forced to recognise it – at gunpoint, or pen-point! – as *true*. In that moment of recognition the foulest passions, the most loathsome cruelties, the dreariest depths of a madman's soul, assume the quality we call Beauty. Not because they cease to be evil, but because they tell us about what it means to be human— about ourselves.

'Porphyria's lover was mad, of course, but what lover is completely sane? He treated his mistress as a chattel without a soul, a mere object he could dispose of to suit his whims, but do not thousands of husbands treat their wives in exactly the same way? "Aye, but they do not kill them!" you say. I agree – not openly, at any rate, although some might consider a nice quick strangulation merciful compared with the lingering torments of many a conventional marriage. But what matters if the actor rants and raves and overplays his part so long as the things he says are things we have said to ourselves in our innermost hearts, so long as we recognise them as true?

'And that is the only kind of beauty that interests me any longer, Mr Booth. The lyric flights, the exquisite figures, the memorable and the mighty line – all that I renounce to my wife, who as everyone agrees is so much better at them than I. All I claim is my right to sweat away over my ugly little misshapen lump of Truth. And what better place to start than with this grotesque affair we are engaged on? But I fear we are going to be disappointed, for there is no inscription here, so far as I can see.'

We had arrived at the gates of the villa, locked now with a sturdy chain. No inscription was visible on the wall outside the grounds, and since there was no sign of life in the lodge, and no one answered our shouts, there was no way of gaining entrance. It appeared that our journey had been in vain.

We would have gone back then, had I not ventured to suggest that it might be worth our while to inspect the rear of the property as well – and there, on the locked wooden gate leading into the garden, we found the following:

(2) RIMINESE

At Purdy's both the number and the word seemed immediately significant, while at DeVere's the number had puzzled us but the word seemed to make at least a muffled kind of sense. We had therefore hoped for much from the third inscription, and now all our hopes were dashed. *Riminese*, I should explain, is the adjective applied to persons or things appertaining to the town of Rimini, in Romagna on the Adriatic coast over a hundred miles away. What conceivable connection there could be between this place and the death of Isabel Eakin – to say nothing of the significance of the number two – is a question which appears totally insoluble.

Poor Browning! For the second time in forty-eight hours his

theories had collapsed about him in shreds. He had nothing to say, but his features expressed very clearly his mood – one of despondency amounting almost to despair. He plainly had no wish for company now, and in a gruff tone announced that he was going off on a long walk to endeavour to think the whole matter through again.

Well, I shall close now, having no more news to tell you. As I was walking back to my dwelling I chanced to meet the young woman called Beatrice, who used to be poor Isabel's maid. I had not seen her since that memorable night at the villa, when the police official Talenti bullied her so over Browning's supposed connection with her late mistress; and there was no reason why I should have noticed her now, or why, having noticed her, I should have stopped, or, having stopped, should have spoken. There was, I say, no reason why I should have done these things, and every reason (you may think) why I should *not* – but I make too much of it. She gave me a glance as I passed – I must have looked at her too, for she is an attractive girl, as I said – and they have a way of looking at you, these Italian girls, quite different from their Bostonian sisters, as if they know very well what is in your thoughts; so that even though these may in fact have been utterly pure and prosaic, they straight away turn in quite another direction.

But this is mere nonsense and rambling. All I meant to say was that I stopped, she addressed me and I responded, and we talked for a few minutes about this and that – about nothing, really. We certainly did not mention any of the matters which have occupied my attention in these letters – the nearest we came to it was when I asked if she had been successful in finding alternative employment, and she replied that Mr Eakin's parting provision to her had been so ungenerous that she had been obliged to seek a position immediately, and had just found one with an English family.

At length the conversation became desultory, and we parted. Unfortunately I happened to look round almost immediately afterwards, and was most embarrassed to discover that Beatrice had also turned, so that she caught me apparently staring after her. But she did not seem at all put out, but simply smiled. For a moment I thought she was going to say something, but in the end she turned away. There was of course nothing to say.

It just now occurs to me that I should have asked her about the writing on the wall at the villa – perhaps she could have thrown some light on the meaning of that word '*Riminese*'. If only I could find some way of discovering where she lives or works, I might yet be able to do so. I will give the matter some thought.

Ever most affectionately yours

Booth

P.S.

A note has just this moment been delivered, inviting me to a 'spiritualist gathering' to be held tomorrow evening at the house of Miss Edith Chauncey, a noted 'medium'. The purpose of the event, it seems, is to attempt to make contact with Isabel's spirit, and a group of her closest acquaintances here in Florence have been invited to participate.

Now between the two of us, I am inclined to think this spiritualism a great nonsense; but as it is a *sine qua non* of social acceptability in at least some of the most important and sought-after households in Florence, I have been careful to keep my views to myself – unlike Mr Browning, who is a great heretic where the spirit world is concerned, loudly proclaiming it all to be a fraud, its practitioners charlatans and their followers credulous dupes (this despite the fact that his wife is prominent amongst the latter). The result is that I pass for a lukewarm believer, ripe for total conversion to the cause, and it is no doubt to this that I owe my invitation.

I was at first inclined to refuse, for the idea seems to me to be in rather poor taste. But on second thoughts it occurred to me that I should go – if only to see who else has been invited. Who were Isabel's other close friends in Florence? Is it not possible that her murderer is to be found among them? Yes, I think upon the whole that I shall go.

XIII

My dear Prescott,

The above date will be sufficient to indicate that there has been no respite in the storm of events which continues to rage here. Three days, as you see, have yielded enough for another lengthy letter – and yet everything can be traced back in one way or another to the 'séance' to which I was invited by Edith Chauncey, our leading practitioner of the spiritualist art.

It was at eight o'clock on Wednesday evening that I set out for the ancient palace in one of whose remoter nooks and crannies the Misses Chauncey live, as frugally as a pair of Reformed Church mice. The *palazzo* in question is one which really merits the name, which is applied here to any sizeable pile. It dates from the early Fifteenth Century, and originally belonged to a more than usually unpleasant branch of the Strozzi family. This clan having killed themselves off long since, the place is now divided into a multitude of small shops, offices, suites of apartments, storerooms, studios and garrets. In addition to the obligatory private dungeon, the entire structure is rumoured to be a maze of secret passages and concealed doorways, without which no well-appointed residence of the period was deemed complete. In short, the place fairly reeks with 'atmosphere', giving the impression of being packed like a sponge with History – the contents oozing out at the lightest touch of a sympathetic imagination. For anyone with an interest in spirits and 'the other world', no more suitable address could be imagined.

I was welcomed on my arrival by Miss Kate Chauncey, the younger of the two sisters – although 'younger' is very much a comparative term in this case, for neither of them will see fifty again. She stayed in the background for the rest of the evening, as indeed she must have done for the rest of her life; for it is Miss Edith who has 'powers' and 'gifts' and is in short a 'medium' – and one whose reputation is such as to allow her to live, albeit modestly, on the offerings of her followers.

My contacts with this lady had thus far been of the slenderest. I had heard of her – one could not help hearing of her – on every side, for spiritualism is very much the vogue here. How can it fail to be, offering as it does both mystical experiences and practical advantages? It is as though it were discovered that viewing Canova's 'Pauline Bonaparte' by moonlight was a cure for consumption. On the one hand, you are offered beauteous visions from the land of faery, and on the other the chance to commune with your late spouse, or chat to Napoleon. Indeed, I suspect that my resistance to the movement hitherto may in the last resort have amounted to little more than a feeling that it was all rather too good to be true.

However, I never dreamed of mocking the spiritualists to anyone here: they are much too influential for that. There are of course a few die-hard sceptics – notably Mr Browning, who seems to regard spiritualism with a particularly virulent fury, as something not merely untrue but unclean, like a nigger fetish cult. Indeed, his behaviour has apparently been so extreme on some occasions in the past that some spiritualists here regard him as little short of deranged.

The whole movement is of course still at a pre-Nicene stage of indulgent toleration, but despite this, I was extremely surprised to find that the first person I saw on entering the Chauncey's sitting-room was Miss Jessie Tate. This female is really the most extraordinary personage, even by the standards of the Florentine exile community. She is about thirty-five years of age; strong, stocky, almost burly in appearance, with a shock of fiery red hair and an almost violently animated manner; lives alone, smokes the local cigars, and worships Giuseppe Mazzini, whose daggers and bombs she believes will liberate Italy – although who is to liberate it from such liberators she does not say. She talks so hard you seem to hear the tumbrils rolling and the guillotine swish, and although radicalism is rife here – indeed it is as much *de rigueur* as spiritualism in many circles – Miss Tate is generally considered to take things a deal too far. To come upon her there in the Chaunceys' old-maidish parlour was therefore as unexpected a shock as finding a tarantula in one's bed.

Far more disturbing, however, was to learn *why* she was there. The discovery that Jessie Tate is an adherent to the spiritualist cause was not in itself any particular cause for astonishment: spiritualism appeals to all manner of people for all manner of reasons. As far as Miss Tate is concerned it is apparently part of something called 'the wave of the future', which as far as I could gather means that faith in kings and priests is to be replaced by the scientifically demonstrable doctrines of socialism and spiritualism, the latter providing the transcendental ingredient without which the former would become a mere mechanistic materialism incapable of satisfying mankind's higher needs.

This, then, was enough to explain why Jessie Tate was attending a 'séance'; it did nothing to explain why she was attending *that* one. For the intention was apparently to assemble a group of people whose relations with Isabel had been particularly close; since, as Miss Chauncey explained, 'the spirits will only respond if the ectoplasmic vibrations are in harmony': which I take to mean roughly that the inhabitants of the spirit world, like the rest of us, are more likely to accept invitations when the company is agreeable. If close relations with Isabel had been the criterion of inclusion, then what on earth was Miss Jessie Tate doing there?

Well, I was not long in finding out, and the answer left me feeling even more 'streaked' than the discovery that Isabel and DeVere were lovers. For what did I learn but that Miss Tate and Mrs Eakin had been the greatest of friends, and used to meet tête-à-tête at least once a week!

What they found to talk about I find as difficult to imagine as I do what possible attraction Miss Tate's society could have had for a woman like Isabel. The inverse appeal is of course no very great mystery, given Jessie Tate's presumed amorous propensities. I can only suppose that all her talk of a brave new world proved titillating to Mrs Joseph Eakin. After all, she had hooked herself a millionaire and could therefore afford the luxury of cultivating revolutionary blue-stockings. No doubt realising, however, that her ideas would cut precious little ice with Joseph Eakin himself, Miss Tate always took care to visit Isabel in her husband's absence.

The only other person present on my arrival was Seymour Kirkup, a fantastic old gentleman whom I was surprised to see there only in the sense that it seems as remarkable to see him out of his own home as to see a turtle walking about without its shell. To do justice to this extraordinary character I should require Mr Dickens's genius for caricature, combined with the antiquarian charm of a Walter Scott, a touch of Sterne's crankiness, and more than a hint of the outright horror and madness of our own poor Edgar Poe.

Baron Seymour Stocker Kirkup, to give him his full name, seems older than the city itself, whose every stone he knows. He is an accomplished student of Dante, of whose works many rare manuscript versions are to be found in the fabulous library which fills several rooms of the old palace he inhabits. Just for good measure, this building – which overlooks the Arno at the south end of the Ponte Vecchio, a few doors from where Cecil DeVere lived and died – was the Florentine headquarters of the Knights Templar until the brutal suppression of that mysterious order five and a half centuries ago. It contained the chapel of the Holy Sepulchre, whose whereabouts Kirkup claims to have discovered by means of necromancy. He also claims to hold conversations with Dante, who revealed to him the location of his portrait by Giotto, which had been whitewashed over. It is even believed in some quarters that he possesses the secret of the Philosopher's Stone! All in all, then, Kirkup is an eccentric although well-loved member of our little community – and one who enjoys the rare distinction of being notorious among the Florentines, who in general take as much notice of us as cattle of the flies that pester them in summer. Indeed, one reason Kirkup so rarely leaves home is that he is apt to be pursued through the streets by gangs of children yelling '*Stregone*!'. This means a sorcerer, one who exercises power through the agency of evil spirits; which may all seem mere superstitious rubbish in bright breezy Boston, but is still taken very seriously here.

And *his* connection with Isabel? I was ready for anything by now, particularly since I knew that Kirkup is given to recognising spritualistic 'gifts' in pretty young women – one of whom, a former servant, he has installed in his house, where she has subsequently proved to be with child. It turned out that my idea was not very wide of the mark, except that this was no mere senile fancy of Kirkup's: no less an authority than Miss Edith Chauncey herself informed me solemnly that Isabel had had all the makings of a highly-gifted 'medium'. Indeed, Miss Chauncey seemed to regret her 'passing over' almost solely for this reason. In all other respects, she assured me with a rather sickly smile, dear Isabel is so much better off 'on the other side', and once established over there will become a first-rate 'control' (whatever that may be) – indeed, it was for precisely this reason that this initial attempt to 'make contact' had been arranged.

I could not help feeling an instinctive revulsion at all this. There we were, five respectable gentlefolk seated in a primly decorous sitting-room, nibbling Miss Kate's home-made cookies and chatting equably about the great army of the Dead, who it seems have nothing better to do than hang about their former haunts, as ubiquitous and pervasive as some stale odour.

Our company was not yet complete, however. It seems that the number required to initiate an experience of this kind is seven – a figure of considerable mystic significance, according to Kirkup, who treated me to a disquisition on numerical symbolism in Dante which might well have been considerably more protracted but for the arrival of the remaining two guests.

It having been established that these would be people whose relations with Isabel had been particularly intimate, the first thing to strike me about the newcomers was the fact that they were gentlemen. Well, one of them was, at any rate: Charles Nicholas Grant, an Englishman of some fifty years of age, whose family are long-established in the wine importing business. He is blessed with one of those faces which immediately inspire respect and trust, so clearly is it stamped with the great English civic virtues of rectitude and fair-dealing. So what had Isabel and Mr Grant been up to, that he should be invited to help contact her spirit? Well, it seems that Grant's contacts with the Eakins were originally all with Joseph. However, he soon succeeded – as indeed was no matter for surprise, given the charming urbanity of his manner – in ingratiating himself with Isabel, whose passion for art he had helped to gratify by accompanying her on pilgrimages to various galleries, churches and palaces to which her husband, having once paid his respects, declined to return.

I should point out that Joseph Eakin shared the notion, not unknown among our fellow-countrymen, that the Uffizi and Santa Croce are comparable to such domestic points of pilgrimage as, say, Paul Revere's house, or Bunker Hill, in the sense that a decent curiosity to view them may be satisfied by a single visit, and that any desire to go back smacks of excessive enthusiasm. Whereas Mr Jarves remarked to me recently that it was only on the fourth or fifth visit that he began to 'see' a picture at all – as opposed, that is, to seeing his ideas of it, or what other folk had told him they had seen, or what he had read somewhere he should see, and so on. Isabel, apparently, agreed with him – or at least wanted to get out of that glacial villa and down to the life and bustle of the city streets. In either case, Mr Grant served as an escort to whom her husband could not possibly object.

The other person I did not know at all – which you must understand speaks less of me than of him. For without any wish (for indeed I have no need) to brag, anyone that I have not met at least once must exist in some sense upon the fringes of society, unwilling or unable to gain admittance. I have no way of knowing which was the case with the Very Reverend Urizen K. Tinker.

This individual hails, unmistakably, from Illinois, being by his own account one of a veritable tribe of Tinkers begot with what sounds like indecent haste by a Chicago schoolmaster. Urizen K. seemed destined, if his luck held good, for a lowly clerkship in some canal company, when his life was transformed by the first in a series of communications from a source which he terms 'Guard'. These communications concern themselves with the very largest issues: the nature of the universe, the meaning of life, the history and future prospects of the human race, and Mr Tinker's apparently critical role in all three.

As is invariably the case for men of destiny, Tinker's early days were far from easy. He described in colourful terms the pettifogging and obscurantist attitude of various local churches in which he had attempted to have himself ordained, all of whom proved to be tiresomely insistent on the need for a minimum of theological qualifications, and deaf to Tinker's contention that direct revelation – 'a telegraph line to the Deity', as he vividly put it – was worth more than any number of 'bits of paper'. And so, with that spirit of hardy initiative and independence which is said to characterise those who dwell beyond the Catskills, Mr Tinker promptly founded his own church, based on the usual biblical material, supplemented by the so-called 'Prophetic Epics' of one William Blake, a crackpot Cockney mystic – Urizen K.'s father had somehow got his paws on some of this Blake's doggerel, lengthy extracts from which he used to read aloud to all the tiny Tinkers to help while away the long dark cold Chicago winter evenings.

Well, all this was of course ludicrous enough – my only concern was to keep a face straight enough to avoid offending the Very Reverend Tinker, who like most autodidacts is extremely sensitive to slights. What interested me considerably more was the discovery that Tinker's church is supported financially by the bottomless purse of none other than Mr Joseph Eakin! *He* thus sank even lower in my estimation – particularly when I learned that Tinker's relations with Isabel had been encouraged by her husband, and this very much against her own wishes.

I am happy to be able to report that in this matter, at least, Isabel's behaviour was irreproachable. Unlike her fool of a husband – for these tough calculating captains of industry always have their Achilles' heel, which some smart operator will find out – she held that the Very Reverend Urizen K. Tinker was an impostor and a buffoon, and made little or no attempt to disguise the fact. There can be no doubt about this, for I had it from the lips of the prophet himself, who reported his response to have been one of exemplary mildness.

'I turned the other cheek, Mr Booth, sir; and when that would not avail, I turned the first one a-gain! But though meek and lamb-like, very, do not for one single solitary moment permit yourself to imagine that I could be detracted from my plain and bounden dooty. Do not! For you would err, sir, you would err. From that sacred path I would not deviate, nor could not be forced. Back I went to that unhappy female, a-gain and a-gain, in perpetuity and without respite. And but for the fatal catastrophe, I do not scruple to pronounce that the exquisite bliss of inducting a-nother stray sheep into my little flock would once more have been mine. Ah me, the bliss of succouring a lost soul, Mr Booth, sir! Verily I tell you, it is a very u-nique and exceptional grace.'

Hearing the wretched creature thus preen and prattle about having pressed his unwelcome attentions on Isabel, aided and abetted by that credulous pander of a husband, I could cheerfully have strangled him on the spot. Fortunately, Edith Chauncey chose that moment to announce that the proceedings would begin.

XIV

We were led through into a back parlour, hung with tapestries and very sparsely furnished: just a plain sideboard, supporting a single candlestick, and a circular table surrounded by seven high-backed chairs. On the table lay a semi-circular cloth with the letters of the alphabet inscribed around its rim, and two spaces within, marked respectively *Yes* and *No*. Nearby stood the small heart-shaped board mounted on rollers which the spiritualists term a 'planchette'.

When we had taken our places – this operation being supervised by Miss Kate – Miss Chauncey directed us to take the hand of the person sitting to either side of us. I complied with no very great enthusiasm, placed as I was between Miss Jessica Tate and the Very Reverend Tinker. Miss Tate's member proved to be clammy, and given to frequent and presumably involuntary spasms; the man of religion had an almost fiercely positive grasp, which may have been intended to conceal the underlying tremor which I nevertheless detected.

We were now directed to close our eyes, and to concentrate all our thoughts on Isabel. This I duly tried to do, but I found to my consternation that every image came out first as stiff as a waxwork, and then began to melt and run, producing that hideous discoloration and rictus of the corpse I will never be able to forget. To rid myself of these visions I opened my eyes – and was unnerved to find Edith Chauncey, who was sitting opposite, staring fixedly back at me with unblinking insistence, as though inspecting some interesting detail etched on the interior of my skull.

I immediately assumed that I had incurred her displeasure by disturbing the ectoplasmic vibrations, or whatever. A moment later, however, I realised that her stare was *too* intense and unyielding to be a glare of disapproval, however strong. What was disturbing in her expression – as with that of a blind person

– was what was *not* there: direction, focus, intent. Those eyes did not see me, did not see any of us. Edith Chauncey had entered her trance.

Her sister now instructed us to open our eyes, release our hands, and place the index finger of our right hand on the planchette. The little board rolled idly about for a moment or two under the various impulses it received, and was still.

For a few minutes nothing whatever happened. Then, so faintly at first that it was only after hearing it for some time that I understood what it was, a voice became audible in the room: a low resonant voice, unlike any I had heard so far. But I soon realised that it was emanating from Miss Chauncey's throat, although at least an octave deeper than her usual organ.

'Isabel . . . Isabel . . . Isabel . . . ' she intoned, drawing the word out so lengthily that it sounded as though she was about to formulate a question concerning the nature of bells.

My feeling had at first been one of lively interest, coupled with a little natural apprehension. However, as time went by, and Edith Chauncey's trance-voice droned on, repeating Isabel's name over and over again, with intervals of silence during which I became uncomfortably aware of a dull ache in the arm which was extended to touch the planchette, it all began to feel like one of those 'improving' Saturday evenings which my mother and her cronies used to get up for the Boston Women's Guild, when someone would recite half of Southey's 'Vision of Judgement', and you had to sit very very still and try to look as if you didn't care how much longer it went on.

Then, quite suddenly, the planchette, which had been im-mobile all this time, jerked violently first to one side of the cloth and then another. I was far too much amazed at the *way* the thing moved – as though with a will of its own – to consider *where* it was going, but Kate Chauncey kept careful watch, and at length spelled out the word made up of the letters over which the tip of the board rested for an instant at the culmination of each spasm that shook it.

'D,e,v,e,r,e,' she murmured. 'Surely that is the name of the young diplomat who passed over so tragically the other day?'

She went on to mutter something I did not quite catch about 'interference'.

'Where is Isabel?' her sister meanwhile demanded, slightly querulously. 'Come to us, Isabel. Come! Come!'

The board twitched a few times, and then moved to indicate the word *No*.

'Why have *you* come, Mr DeVere?' Miss Chauncey returned – a shade tactlessly I thought, though it is difficult for a novice to know what is or is not acceptable in this novel form of social intercourse. At all events, the spirit did not appear to be offended. Perhaps the dead are above such things.

I speak for Isabel, the planchette spelt out.

'Will Isabel not come herself?'

Not in this way.

Edith Chauncey pondered this cryptic reply for what seemed like a very long time. I took the opportunity to glance quickly around the table: everyone was staring fixedly at the little wooden trolley which had so swiftly established itself as an eighth presence in the room.

'Perhaps the vibrations are not yet in harmony,' Miss Chauncey murmured at last. 'And yet we have made all due preparations. The doors and windows have been locked and bolted, to ensure continuity; the lamps have been dimmed and the circle of hands formed. We are seven, a holy and mystical number: the gifts of the Holy Ghost are seven, Our Lord spoke seven times upon the cross, there are seven phrases in the prayer He taught His disciples, and His Holy Mother had seven joys and seven sorrows, while scholars both Christian and pagan inform us that there are seven saving virtues and seven sins that damn. Why will Isabel then not come?'

Not worthy of her perfect spirit.

'This means of contact is not to her liking?'

With her voice she would speak.

Apparently this all made some sense to Edith Chauncey – to me it seemed merely another example of something I have often observed in published accounts of spirit-conversations, namely that those on 'the other side' seem to be as unwilling as Shakespeare's tiresome Clowns to give a straight answer to any question. My interest was once again beginning to wane. What with the 'stagey' nature of the dialogue – in particular Miss Chauncey's plum speech, clearly got by heart beforehand – I began to feel pretty certain that the whole business was a hoax –

and not a very good one.

'But why have *you* come?' pursued Miss Chauncey.

I bring a message.

'To whom?'

To all and to none.

'And what is your message?'

I died too soon.

At this, as you can imagine, I pricked up my ears.

'Poor spirit!' Edith Chauncey commented. 'Indeed, a tragic accident freed you from the burdens of material existence before your term.'

No accident.

'Was it then your own unhappy hand which removed you from this vale of tears?'

I was murdered.

I looked around at my companions, just visible in the candlelight which stirred up the shadows like shapes underwater. Baron Kirkup sat staring up at nothing in particular, a little smile playing about his lips – whether ironical or merely senile I could not tell. Miss Jessie Tate looked intense, as usual, but also harrowed, and rather furtive. The Reverend Tinker's enormous features were illuminated by a look of beatific benevolence which looked as though it had been obtained wholesale from a five-and-dime emporium in his native city; while Charles Nicholas Grant exuded an air of well-bred embarrassment, as though we were all sitting over dinner and someone had said something faintly indelicate.

'And who did this terrible thing?' continued Miss Chauncey – who did not seem particularly surprised by this development. But the spirit was being coy again.

I cannot say.

'You must say! Both for our sakes and for yours, you must reveal the name of this evil person. For our sakes, because he may strike again. For yours, because until he is brought to justice your spirit will remain blocked by Desire for Revenge, and will be unable to ascend beyond the Fourth Level. Tell us his name, therefore – you who see everything that has been, is, and will be! Who murdered you? What is his name?'

We all stared fixedly at the planchette as though our lives depended on it. The board stirred beneath the seven fingers resting on it, and with a mighty impulse shook off our restraining control and flew clean off the table into the corner of the room – where I for one should not have been particularly surprised to see it scuttle away into the wainscotting like a rat.

Jessie Tate rose.

'We had best stop,' she said curtly. 'Something is wrong. No good can come of this.'

'I've never known such a thing to happen before!' Kate Chauncey replied. 'That poor spirit must be filled with negative energies.'

It seemed as though the 'séance' was at an end, when suddenly the most extraordinary thing happened. I felt a rush, as of air moving in a body; the candle was instantly extinguished, but instead of total darkness there came a weird unearthly glow in the air ... *and all at once I heard Isabel speaking*!

There was no 'like' or 'as if'. It was Isabel herself: that unmistakable, thrilling voice I had never thought to hear again!

'I have come,' she said. 'Not with the spirit board, but with my own voice would I speak. I too have a message for all and for none. I too have been taken from your midst, not by my own sinful act, but cruelly slain by an evil hand!'

Now I am fully aware that these words, set down in black and white and read by you sitting comfortably in your armchair, will appear no less contrived than the earlier utterances I recorded, ascribed to DeVere, which had totally failed to convince me of their authenticity. I must therefore ask you for the moment to take on trust the fact that I did not for one single moment doubt that I was now listening to the real and true voice of Isabel Allen, speaking to me from beyond the grave.

The reason for this sudden access of faith is simply explained: it was the voice itself which convinced me! All the apparatus of spiritualism – the boards and apparitions, turning tables and rapping panels – has always served merely to increase my scepticism. The more complex the machinery, the more easily the effect may be faked. I may not know precisely *how*, any more than I know how a conjuror makes a dozen rabbits appear in his hat, and then changes them into so many doves. But it is of no account: I know the trick can be worked, and clearly perceive the margin where the fudging takes place.

But what margin was there here? There was nothing but a

voice, as unmistakable as a touch or a forgotten scent, coming at you under the skin, behind the brain, circumventing the reason (so easy to deceive with its own cleverness) and breaking straight in upon the spirit to proclaim in accents clear and absolute that Isabel was there among us. Oh, I believed! I had no choice.

But where was it coming from? Had there been some mystery about that I might still have doubted – if I had traced the sound behind some hanging, or inside some piece of furniture, or under the floorboards. Instead, by the strange half-light glimmering down from the lamp-bowl above our heads, I made out quite clearly that it was Edith Chauncey herself who was speaking.

'Aha!' I hear you say, 'so that was the trick!' But no, don't you see? My point is that there *was* no trick – that no attempt was made to disguise or dress up this plain fact, as would have been so easy to do: the usual farce, with the Chaunceys' maid wandering about the room with a white sheet draped round her shoulders. None of that! Just that elderly woman sitting in her place, as majestic and imposing as a Sibyl, through whose throat Isabel spoke to us in her own voice. And if I had still harboured any doubts, *what* she said would have clinched the matter – for it was the terrible truth.

'I too have been the victim of a criminal plot, like that other spirit who spoke to you. But unlike him I am not tied by thoughts of vengeance to this earthly sphere, nor would I obstruct my spirit's passage to the higher realms by dwelling on such unworthy matters. Thanks to my spiritualist training with you, dear Edith, I was already prepared to pass over, and I left my earthly life behind without regrets. But while that unhappy soul is at large, others may be forced to transit before their time. Prepare yourselves, therefore, to learn who took my life. The name will amaze you, yet I speak the truth, for we spirits cannot lie. Know, then, that I was horribly murdered and done to death by – '

All the while Isabel was speaking I had gradually become aware of a strange turbulence – I know not how else to describe it – of the table about which we were all seated. It was as if the thing were afloat, at first upon a sea almost dead calm, with just the slightest swell betraying the mighty potency beneath; then somewhat choppier, frisking on little wavelets; and finally swaying up and dipping down, as though impelled by the passage of long ocean rollers, outriders from the storm that suddenly broke, without warning, cutting off Isabel's final words as the table reared up and crashed down upon the speaker amid the cries and exclamations of all the assembled company.

Well this time of course it *was* the end – for by the time the maid had come running, and the lamps had been lit, and Miss Chauncey had been extricated, and we had assured ourselves that she had sustained no serious injury, there was clearly no possibility of restarting the 'séance' – and precious little desire, either, if most people's expressions were anything to judge by. Even those with considerable acquaintance of supernatural experiences seemed to be badly shaken by what they had witnessed. Seymour Kirkup, for example, was grey and drawn.

'We have indeed had a fortunate escape,' he pronounced in his strange cracked voice. 'There was an evil presence in this room, of that I have not the slightest doubt. Rarely have I sensed the power of Satan more palpably.'

Miss Chauncey appeared at first to be completely ignorant of the astonishing results of her spirtual exertions, but as soon as these had been explained to her she announced her determination to make another attempt to contact Isabel's spirit later that night, and try and learn the identity of her murderer.

Rather to my surprise, both Seymour Kirkup and Miss Jessie Tate went out of their way to try and dissuade her from doing so.

'I really must beg you not to meddle any further with this matter,' Kirkup implored. 'The forces involved are more powerful and more malevolent than you can conceive. Spiritualism is all very well, Miss Chauncey, but we must acknowledge its limitations. Here I sense the presence of Powers of Darkness which can be manipulated only by the exercise of certain esoteric arts of which, forgive me for saying so, you are utterly ignorant.'

But the indignant 'medium' did *not* forgive what she clearly saw as an insult to her skill and professional standing.

'No one is more powerful than the spirits, except for God Himself – and I need not fear Him,' she proclaimed boldly. 'Were all the forces of hell ranged against me, Mr Kirkup, I should not shrink from my duty to Isabel, who spoke of me so kindly just now. Nor do I need to know any heathen spells or mumbo-jumbo filched from musty old books to confront the spirits, who are my friends. We meet together naked, face to face, and know no shame,' she concluded blithely.

Kirkup merely muttered something in a language I did not recognise, and made the sign of the cross. Jessie Tate also tried to persuade her friend not to exert herself any more that night, using more homely arguments – she would over-exert herself and impair her health. But Miss Chauncey remained admirably firm in her resolve, saying only that she would rest for a short while before making a fresh attempt to wrest the name of Isabel's murderer from beyond the grave.

By now, I could quite frankly stand no more. I hardly heard what was going on any longer. My brain was reeling from the knowledge that Isabel had spoken from the dead, that the dead do survive, that death is not just a hole into which we drop and are no more, that there is a meaning and a plan to everything, as Mr Browning plainly believes. Why did this revelation – which I had so often fervently sought and prayed for – now seem more dreadfully depressing than my blackest nihilistic nights had ever been?

Obsessed with these and other matters, I took my leave with almost brutal haste. Social niceties were, however, the last things which anyone was concerned about at that moment, and my perfunctory farewells – indeed, my very departure – passed almost unnoticed.

It would be vain even to attempt to describe my state of mind that night in any detail. If I told the truth I should scarcely believe myself, never mind expect anyone else to do so. Besides, the whole affair was very shortly destined to become the subject of a quite different kind of examination, as you will see, and there is no point in anticipating that event. Let me therefore say only that when I returned home I was so utterly exhausted in both mind and body that I simply fell into bed and passed straight into a fitful sleep, crammed like a bolster with the rags of scrappy dreams.

I was awakened at ten o'clock the next morning by Piero, who – when I asked him angrily why the devil he had ignored his standing orders to leave me undisturbed – replied that there was a policeman at the door with a message for me. Before I had a chance to say anything a burly individual of unpleasing demeanour pushed his way into the room, and informed me, without any over-indulgence in the more rarefied forms of politeness, that my presence was requested at the Bargello – which is the Police Headquarters in Florence.

I felt as though the earth had suddenly and unaccountably been whisked away from beneath my feet. Nevertheless, I attempted to maintain that tone of careless arrogance which the Italians expect from foreigners – not easy to do when one is surprised in one's nightshirt – and enquired coolly if I might know the reason. Imagine my feelings when he replied that I was to be interrogated in connection with the death of an English-woman, by name Edith Chauncey!

XV

A black four-wheeler bearing the Grand-Duke's crest awaited us below. The police constable led me into it, and the vehicle promptly clattered and jolted away through the streets towards the Old Market, where out of a profusion of bizarre and colourful scenes I noticed a showman displaying a crocodile in a tank just large enough for it to thrash about: I felt the strangest affinity with the poor beast, plucked up from its dim familiar surroundings and put on show in an alien land, caged in glass for the diversion of the mob.

When we drove into the mediaeval fortress of the Bargello my spirits sank still farther. As well as being the headquarters of the Chief of Police, or *bargello*, the place also serves as a gaol, and is associated with many sad events in Florence's history. We alighted in the courtyard, flanked by high and gloomy walls, each one of whose stones has a grim tale to tell. I was led up a flight of steps, along a long corridor, down another, through an ante-chamber; and into a large bare room furnished with a desk, two chairs and a portrait of the Grand-Duke Leopold. My escort had not said a word since mentioning Miss Chauncey's name, and he did not break his silence now – merely withdrawing and shutting the door behind him.

Somewhere else in the building someone was crying, or screaming, and my thoughts turned to the rack and the irons and the other instruments which undoubtedly lie mouldering in some corner of the place, as they do in every other Italian prison – even though we are assured that they are no longer in use. The police here are popularly known as the *Buon Governo* – the 'good government': you have to know their ferocious reputation for corruption, inefficiency and brutality to savour fully the almost Dantesque irony of this phrase.

After I had been standing there for a considerable period of time the door opened again, and in walked Commissioner

Antonio Talenti. If anything was calculated to increase my miserable anxiety at this point, it was precisely the appearance of this official. On both the occasions we had met previously the Commissioner had struck me as being possessed of a very sharp mind indeed. Browning's strictures on the police were all very well, but Talenti was Florentine to his bones – and though the Florentines these days may have grown to be windbags, liars, cheats and poltroons, stupidity is no more one of their failings now than it ever has been.

The Commissioner greeted me with mock formality, murmuring that it had been good of me to come. I replied tartly that I had not been aware that I might have declined.

'The manner of the fellow who came to fetch me was such that I might have been under arrest.'

Talenti raised his eyebrows histrionically.

'Under arrest? Why – has some crime been committed?'

I smiled cynically.

'Commissioner, my friend Count Antinori once told me that in this country there are so many laws that everyone has always broken at least one, and thus may be arrested at any moment.'

'You have witty – and eminent – friends, Signor Boot,' Talenti commented – the *th* sound is beyond any Italian's ken, and my name emerged thus throughout. 'But I assure you that you are mistaken. There is no question of an arrest. I simply want to ask you a few questions.'

'Before we go any further,' I said, 'will you please tell me what has happened? I gather Edith Chauncey is dead.'

'All in good time. Please take a seat.'

After a moment's hesitation I did so. Talenti settled down on the other side of the desk.

'Now, before I tell you what you want to know, perhaps you will be good enough to tell *me* what time you arrived at Signorina Chauncey's apartment? You don't deny having been there, I take it?'

'Why should I?'

'Why indeed? Besides, we have plenty of witnesses that you *were* there. At what time did you arrive?'

I might not have been under arrest, but you would never have known it from the official's manner.

'At half-past eight,' I replied promptly.

'How can you be so sure?'

'Because that is the time for which I had been invited.'

The mournful little smile that was never very long absent appeared once again on Talenti's lips.

'How reassuringly English.'

'I am American.'

'It is the same. Were any other guests present?'

I named Miss Tate, Seymour Kirkup, the Reverend Tinker and Mr Grant.

'And had this gathering any particular purpose?' the official continued. It was evident that he knew the answer to this question, as to all the others he had asked.

'Yes. As you must know, we were there for a "séance" – a kind of spiritualist assembly, in the course of which ... '

'Do you believe in spiritualism, Signor Boot?'

I hesitated, sensing a trap which perhaps did not exist.

'I used to. Or at least, I had an open mind on the subject. But after what happened last night ... '

Talenti waited for me to finish. When I did not do so he asked, 'What *did* happen?'

Well, I told him. I altered nothing and held nothing back – I did not dare – but it was not difficult to make the whole proceedings sound like an extremely amateur production of the ghost scene in 'Hamlet'. As I multiplied the details of rushing winds, moving tables, spirit voices and accusations of murder, Talenti's ironical smile reappeared in full blossom.

'So you did not altogether believe in these ... phenomena?'

'How could I, when it was all so crudely done – or over-done? How could anyone?'

'Nevertheless, some of your fellow-guests *did* believe.'

It was my turn to smile.

'Some people will believe anything, Commissioner. Florence has but one Calandrino – with us they breed by the score.'

Calandrino, you must know, is the proverbial credulous simpleton who appears in Florentine folk-tales, as well as in several of Boccaccio's stories. I saw that Antonio Talenti was both amused and flattered by my reference – as I had intended he should be.

'Besides,' I continued, risking a little more now I had established this advantage, 'even if the "séance" had been more convincingly staged, I really fail to see how anyone could take these absurd allegations seriously. There has never been the slightest suggestion that there was any foul play involved in the deaths of Mr DeVere or of Mrs Eakin, has there?'

Talenti stared at me for an unconscionable time. His smile had disappeared.

'As you say, Signor Boot, some people will believe anything,' he said finally. 'And at what time did you leave the Chaunceys'?'

'I'm not sure. I suppose it must have been some time after ten o'clock.'

'You did not see any of the other guests take their departure?'

'How could I? I was the first to leave.'

'Answer my question, please.'

'I saw no one.'

'And you went straight home?'

'Yes.'

'Did anyone see you come in?'

'There is never anyone about at such an hour.'

'What about your servant?'

'He had gone home.'

'So you cannot in fact prove what time you arrived – or indeed that you went home at all?'

I stared at him in some confusion.

'Well no, I suppose not, if you put it that way. But why on earth should I *have* to prove it?'

The Commissioner did not reply. Instead, he lit one of the murderous local cigars, and, after a few moments' puffing, began to tell me what had happened.

The other guests had also left the Chaunceys' almost immediately, although in what order was still a matter of some dispute. Tinker went immediately after my departure, but the testimony of the others was more confused – Kate Chauncey, for example, claimed to have seen Kirkup in the flat long after Mr Grant saw him leave. At all events, there is no doubt that Miss Jessie Tate was the last to go, after which the Chauncey sisters sat up for some time discussing the events of the evening.

'Unlike some of those other guests, Signor Boot, you remained sceptical of the effects you had witnessed – the messages spelt out on the board and spoken by spirit voices. I congratulate you on your perspicuity. I questioned la Caterina' – i.e. Kate

Chauncey – 'for over an hour this morning. She confessed at once that everything that occurred last night, from start to finish, had been carefully prepared in advance by her and her sister – as was invariably the case with their so-called spiritualistic performances.'

I was absolutely aghast. I could not – *would* not – believe it. 'But that voice!' I cried. 'That was Isabel's voice!'

Talenti looked at me curiously, and I suddenly realised that I had blundered: I was not supposed to have believed in the spirits. But as we were speaking Italian, I was able to conceal my slip by pretending that I had simply expressed myself badly.

'I meant to say it was so like Isabel's voice! I was almost taken in.'

Talenti appeared to accept my correction. 'Yes, the Chauncey woman certainly possessed an amazing gift,' he agreed. 'But it was not a supernatural gift – simply a superb talent for mimicry. She could imitate other people's voices – both sexes, and every age – so accurately that even their closest friends could not detect the difference. And when the people concerned were dead, and their friends fervently wished to believe that they were hearing them speak from beyond the grave, then she was never in any danger of exposure.

'It was this, according to her sister, which made la Chauncey's fortune as a "medium". For the rest she relied on the usual trickery involving an accomplice – in this case the maid, who opened a door to create that draught you felt – and such apparatus as wires running under the floorboards, which is how they moved the table. As for the "planchette", that was manipulated by the sisters, working together to guide it towards the letters they had decided upon in advance. As they took care to sit at right angles to one another, the impulse appeared to come from no one person but rather from the board itself.'

A protracted explosion was tearing my soul apart, as all my new-found ideas about the spirit-world and the afterlife blew up in my face. I had to work very hard to keep any trace of this turmoil from showing on my features.

Meanwhile the police official continued with his story. At about eleven o'clock the Chauncey sisters had retired for the night. Before doing so, Miss Kate did the rounds of the premises, as always, checking that all the windows were shuttered and locked and the front door double-bolted from the inside. Edith Chauncey had meanwhile gone straight to her room, situated at the top of a short flight of stairs.

'The only other occupant of the suite was the maid, a girl of fourteen who went to bed the moment her employers had no further need of her, and slept the sleep of total exhaustion which is the only pleasure such poor devils know in this life. She awoke at half-past five, and set about lighting the fires and heating water. As she passed along the central passageway of the suite, she came upon the body of Signorina Chauncey, lying at full-length upon the steps leading down from her room, her head twisted impossibly out of place – turned around like an owl's, the girl said.

'Terrified, she ran and fetched Signorina Caterina, who was still asleep. The moment she set eyes on her sister's corpse Caterina promptly fainted, so the servant ran outside to fetch help. To do so she had to unlock the front door, which was still bolted on the inside. In the street she stopped some peasants on their way to market, and sent one off to call a doctor while she returned to the apartment with the others.

'The doctor arrived some twenty minutes later. His report indicates that the victim fell downstairs and broke her neck about three or four hours before her body was discovered. It would be convenient if la Chauncey had been given to sleep-walking or something of the kind, but this does not seem to have been the case. On the other hand there is no reason to suppose that the victim had an enemy in the world, and any hypothesis that her death was other than accidental seems to raise insoluble problems. If there was a murderer, how did he get in? And if he got in, how did he get out again, leaving the suite as effectively sealed from the outside world as it had been when Signorina Caterina locked up the previous evening?'

Talenti paused, puffing elegantly at his cigar.

'In that case,' I enquired, with a mighty effort to remain civil, 'might I ask why was it thought necessary to drag me out of my bed this morning like a common criminal to answer questions about what was clearly a regrettable accident and nothing more?'

The official smiled his little smile.

'Signor Boot, the English are dying too much just at present! And while in principle I have nothing whatever against that – on the contrary – I should prefer them to do so in their own country, or in France, or at Rome; or in short anywhere in the world but here in Florence, where I have to account for the fact.'

'But what the devil is there to account for?' I demanded.

Talenti took a scrap of paper from a file on the desk and passed it to me.

'Well, this, for example.'

Crudely scrawled upon the paper in red ink, I read the following:

⑧ MANTO

'We found this clenched tight in the dead woman's hand,' I was told. 'Presumably she wrote it just before she died – the paper and ink used were found in her room. Does it mean anything to you?'

'Nothing whatever.'

'You have never seen anything like it before?'

'Never.'

Talenti replaced the paper in the file, and stood up.

'May I now ask you a question, Commissioner?' I enquired respectfully.

'You have already asked several,' he replied shortly. Then, after a few seconds, he went on: 'I do not say I shall answer it, mind.'

I needed no further encouragement.

'It is just this – do you have any notion why the Chauncey sisters should have chosen to invent such an absurd story? Why make themselves look ridiculous, to say nothing of putting their spiritualist pretensions – and therefore their livelihoods – at risk, by making this cock-and-bull claim that DeVere and Mrs Eakin were murdered?'

I was myself taking a sizeable risk, you might well think, in broaching this subject with Talenti. But I simply had to know the answer.

'They made that claim because they believed it to be true,' Talenti replied, savouring the last whiff of his cigar. 'They had been told that it *was* true – that Eakin and DeVere had been murdered.'

Finally I could let my astonishment show.

'Been told? By whom?'

Talenti's smile became openly mocking.

'Can't you guess?'

'I certainly can't!'

'You surprise me. Because the person concerned is a friend of yours.'

I saw that he was trying to trick me into naming Browning, but I refused to be drawn.

'I am fortunate enough to have many friends in Florence, Signor Talenti.'

'I know. I consulted your file before speaking to you this morning, and I find that you are indeed a man with extensive connections. But I am happy to say that none of them – with the exception of this individual, whose acquaintance with you appears to be relatively recent – is such as to excite the interest of this Department. The same, however, cannot be said for *him*, or more especially for his wife. They are considered persons of suspect views – she in particular. And it was in fact from her, according to Caterina, that her late sister learned of this rumour concerning the deaths of DeVere and la Eakin. You will not continue to pretend that you do not know whom I mean, will you?'

I felt it would be decidedly unwise to do so. It was becoming ever plainer that Commissioner Talenti's animus was directed not at me but at Browning. It would benefit neither of us if I were also to get on the wrong side of him.

'I believe that you mean Mrs Browning.'

'Certainly I mean her – a bedridden invalid who amuses herself by writing verses in praise of Liberty and the French Emperor, by criticising our ruler, denigrating our time-honoured institutions and impugning our virility! They make me sick, such people!'

The mask of urbanity had slipped from the police official's face for the first time.

'They come to Florence and lecture us Tuscans on the shortcomings of our government, knowing that we dare not lift a finger against them. I am no radical, Signor Boot. It's my job to see that the laws we have are obeyed. If tomorrow Tuscany becomes a republic, I shall serve my republican masters as faithfully then as I serve the House of Lorraine now, and they, recognising this fact, will retain my services – for you may be sure that if the men I put in prison today put themselves in the Pitti tomorrow, the day after tomorrow there will be others to take their place in prison.

'But them at least I respect, for they play the game like men, for real stakes – their liberty, their lives. But not these Brownings and their like! These foreign intellectuals who blame our government and praise our terrorists! Let them praise and blame their own! I'd like to see them! But of course there's no chance of that, for any disturbance in that quarter just might deprive them of the handsome little stipend which goes so far in thrifty Italy, and which depends on law and order prevailing mightily in rich England. Which it does! Just ask the English Chartists and farm workers! Let them try and better their lot, and straightaway the troops are called out – and meanwhile these so-called liberals look the other way and condescend to pity the poor Hungarians or Poles or Italians. But if a humble Tuscan police official such as myself, having good grounds for suspicion, dares set a man to watch one of these great champions of Liberty, immediately he runs to his friends at the Embassy, and the humble policeman finds himself officially reprimanded by his superiors and warned never to do such a thing again unless he wants to spend the remainder of his career in Leghorn!'

'But what were these grounds you had for suspecting Mr Browning?' I asked, as deferentially as I knew how.

'Ask him yourself!' snorted Talenti contemptuously.

'I did. He wouldn't tell me.'

I did not for a minute think that Talenti would tell me either – I was, after all, prying most fearfully into official secrets. If he did so, it was clearly just to spite the hated Browning!

'The maid, Beatrice Ruffini, deposed in evidence that she had summoned Browning to the villa because he was a friend of the family,' Talenti recited, as though before a court. 'Contradicted by the gate-keeper, who denied that he had ever seen him, she changed her story: the Englishman, she now said, had been a friend of Signora Eakin – the implication was of course that he had been her lover. At this point Browning asked to speak to me alone, and I granted his request. I then asked Browning about the maid's accusation that he had been intimate with la Eakin.'

'Which he denied,' I murmured.

The policeman looked at me with some surprise.

'On the contrary!'

XVI

On some other occasion recently, I believe I compared my
nerves to a pianoforte struck with an axe. On hearing these
words I felt as though the axe had just been buried deep in my
own skull.

'On the contrary,' Talenti continued in an even, unruffled
tone, 'the suspect admitted that he and Signora Eakin used to
meet secretly. She let him in through the garden entrance,
which is why the gate-keeper did not recognise him. He tried,
however, to claim that there was nothing illicit in their relations,
nothing carnal: they were simply friends. They used to sit and
talk. He treated her like a daughter. He just liked to sit and look
at her, to watch her comb her hair. It was all completely pure.

'Naturally I did not believe this for a moment. Men and
women do not behave like that! But then a doubt crept into my
mind. These people – they were English, and the English are
crazy. Their blood is so cold it is a mystery how they ever
manage to breed. So I thought perhaps – just *perhaps* – there was
some truth in this incredible story. Or on the other hand this
Browning might just be arrogant enough to think that a stupid
Tuscan would believe any nonsense if it came from an Englishman's lips. There it was – I didn't know. So I followed the
standard procedure in such cases: I started to make enquiries
about our Signor Browning, and meanwhile set a man to watch
him.'

'But did it really matter whether Browning's relations with
Mrs Eakin had been pure or not?' I asked. 'After all, she was
dead, and by her own hand.'

Talenti smiled.

'I know that now, Signor Boot,' he replied dryly, 'because my
superiors have instructed me that such is the case. But at that
time they had not yet pronounced, and I myself was very far
from being so sure. Suppose for a moment that Signora Eakin
did *not* commit suicide – suppose that she had been murdered.

In that case Signor Browning's relations with the dead woman would have been of vital importance. For who would have killed her, if she had been killed in such a way, at such a time and place? A jealous lover was the obvious answer, and jealousy supposes carnal love – platonic lovers do not murder each other.'

Before I had any time to respond, Talenti's whole demeanour suddenly changed, and he became brisk, efficient and ironical again.

'But why do I bore you with this stale news?' he exclaimed. 'The Eakin case is closed. Indeed, it was never open, any more than the DeVere case – although there again I might have found elements to interest me, had my superiors not determined that his death was of no concern to the Department. And now we have another accidental death! Signorina Chauncey was rather less well-connected than the first two victims, so no decision on the affair has yet been communicated to me – it may even be that I shall have to make up my own mind!

'Who knows? Perhaps the old lady really *did* fall downstairs. I wish you could have helped me with the message we found in her hand, though. Nevertheless, we have had an interesting talk, Signor Boot. Please do not make the mistake of attributing to me any of the things which I have said, or I shall be obliged to deny ever having said anything of the kind – which, as I shall be believed, will have the effect of making you look foolish. Good day!'

And with that he left the room, and a few minutes later the same surly constable who had fetched me led me back to the gate, and vouched for me to the sentry. A moment later I was at liberty!

I am not in the habit of drinking spirits in the morning, but the first thing I did was to enter a café and order a large glass of brandy. Just try to imagine for a moment how you would feel if you were unceremoniously roused from sleep one morning by the police, hauled off to a mediaeval dungeon, and interrogated for an hour about the mysterious death of a 'medium' with whom you had spent the previous evening – whose spirit-show, which had so profoundly affected you at the time, you now learned to have been all sham. And imagine then that you further discovered that the new friend you so admired, and of whom you had hoped to make a high Ideal and a beacon for the future, had been systematically lying to you about his relations with a married woman with whom you had once been in love yourself, and had used his influential connections to foil a police enquiry into the circumstances of her death! Yes, I felt I deserved my glass of brandy.

It was this last, more than anything else that had happened, which struck me with a cruel piquancy. I had been duped, no question about it! By Miss Chauncey, certainly – but she was a professional, and that was to be expected. What was far more disturbing was to find that I had been duped by Robert Browning.

Here was a man whom I had taken to be a very pillar of integrity: one truly great, from whom I had thought to catch – like one in a valley looking longingly up at the far gleaming peaks he no longer aspires to – a little reflected radiance from that sun which had set for ever on my own life. And now not only had this man brutally rejected me once, when he thought my utility was at an end, but I found that in other ways too he was no better than anyone else: another trimmer and drifter whose life was crammed with compromises and secrets – and apparently up to his neck in this whole murky business, into the bargain!

I finished my brandy and wandered back out into the streets, where some sunlight had now contrived to break feebly through the glower overhead, making ghostly shadows on the huge flagstones of the street. As I passed the Badia – an old monastery whose bell-tower is one of the landmarks of the city – I realised with a start that the street on whose corner I was standing was none other than Via Dante Aligheri. Already I could see the house where Browning had called on our way out to Maurice Purdy's – and in another moment I was on my way towards it, determined to find out once and for all the truth behind Browning's lies and evasions.

The building was three tall storeys high, the ground floor being given over in the Italian fashion to stables and storage. I represented myself as being in search of my friend Signor Browning, and uncertain as to which suite he occupied, and by this means I soon discovered that the *piano nobile* was inhabited by a decaying countess, all chattels and no cash, and by various of her relatives – none of whom, clearly, had ever heard the name Browning, or knew any Englishmen, or had any idea what I was talking about.

On the next floor I found three servants of the countess, two squinting seamstresses, a consumptive singing teacher, a German student of art, a bookbinder, and a crazy old man who appeared at his door draped in the flag of the Guelph party. He watched me attentively as I knocked at the one remaining door.

'*Non c'è!*' he cackled – which might have meant either 'he is not there' or 'she is not there'.

'Who lives here?' I asked.

'I don't know.'

'When will (he or she) return?'

'Late. (He or she) works.'

'What work does (he or she) do?'

'I don't know.'

'Very well. I shall return this evening.'

'Gregory returned from Avignon,' the old man responded. 'It is as God wills.'

Thus foiled for the moment, but with high hopes of imminent success, I returned home – where I went back to bed for a few hours. I awoke at four o'clock feeling properly refreshed at last, had a bath, and then read a few cantos of Dante while Piero prepared me a light meal. I was not sure what the evening would hold in store, and I wanted to be ready for anything.

Shortly before seven o'clock, while completing my toilet before leaving, I was informed that Robert Browning was at the door. I had never thought to see the day when this event would find me wishing that I had told Piero to say I was not at home, but such was now the case. After what I had learned that morning I had not the slightest desire to see Browning until I had returned to the house on Via Dante Aligheri and had a clearer idea just exactly what was afoot. His arrival just as I was preparing to go there was therefore extremely awkward.

There he was, however, and I could not very well send him away – although I made the point that I had an important engagement and could spare only a few minutes. Fortunately he was in the same position, which made matters considerably easier.

I gave him a brief account of what had happened the previous evening at the Chaunceys', and its sequel that morning at police headquarters. The point which Browning seized upon was the inscription on the paper found in Edith Chauncey's hand.

'That of course proves that her death was no accident, but the latest in this series of murderous outrages. This time, however, we may at least console ourselves with the thought that the wretched woman brought it upon herself. She had learned the truth about how Mrs Eakin and DeVere died from my wife – who most unfortunately permits herself to be imposed upon by these foul creatures. I had of course told Elizabeth, as I tell her everything.'

Oh, really? I thought. Not *quite* everything, surely!

'Miss Chauncey immediately saw a way to increase her standing in the spiritualist world – to thrust herself up amongst the celebrities of her rotten trade, beside that dung-ball Home. Sooner or later, she must have calculated, the truth about the murders would be revealed – and then everyone would remember how the spirits of Isabel Eakin and Cecil DeVere had said as much, long ago, at one of *her* "séances"! What an advertisement for the spiritualist movement, and for Miss Chauncey in particular! How the number of her followers would have increased, and with it the fees she might command and the donations she might expect! Remember, all this was bread and butter to her – she lived on the vomit she peddled, and would have lived like a queen if this scheme had worked! Instead she is justly hoist with her own petard – which in French, remember, means "to break wind". Miss Muck the "medium" wanted to extinguish the feeble light our reason gives us, like blowing out candles with a breech-blast – only instead she blew herself up!'

This violent and immoderate language surprises, shocks you? But it is *thus* he ever talks of the spiritualist fraternity. His emotion soon spent itself, however, and was replaced by a calmer musing on the problems posed by this new abomination.

'He frightens me, this murderer,' Browning commented. 'He is so clever – so terribly clever!'

'He does not seem very clever to me,' I retorted. 'On the contrary, I believe he has made a mistake which may well prove fatal to him. For by killing Edith Chauncey – evidently to prevent her contacting the spirits of his earlier victims, and thus exposing his identity – he has identified himself in two ways: we know that he must believe in spiritualism and have been present at last night's "séance". That much, surely, is certain!'

'It is just that which terrifies me,' Browning replied quietly. 'As you say, it appears certain – *too* certain! And the more I consider the matter, the more I am tempted to look for our killer in precisely the opposite direction, and figure him to myself as a confirmed sceptic who was nowhere near the Chaunceys' rooms last night.'

'Someone like yourself, in fact!' I quipped.

Browning, to my astonishment, shot me a look of scorn.

'Well as a matter of fact I was hard at hand, visiting a friend who lives on the floor below the Chaunceys' suite – so you are quite wrong about that.'

I could by no means see the logic behind this pronouncement, but I said nothing, for I was impatient to be gone, and said as much to my visitor. We walked downstairs together, and Browning then strode off towards the Cathedral – whilst I cut across Florence to the street where her most famous son, himself an exile, once lived.

I walked quickly, impatient at the thought that this mystery was at last to be resolved, and by the time I reached the house and had run up the four flights of dark stairs I was quite out of breath. When I reached the landing I saw with an indescribable thrill a thin line of yellow light under the door at which I had knocked in vain that morning!

I paused until I had a little recovered my breath before knocking. My heart was thumping madly.

In the event I did not have long to wait. Almost immediately there was a quick scurry of footsteps, and the door was opened by a child I took to be a maid of some sort, dressed in a sort of loose shift, her long raven hair all undone, and on her face as was a look of wonder.

Nevertheless, she recovered her wits first, for she recognised me before I knew that it was Beatrice Ruffini, Isabel's maid, that I was looking at.

We gazed at each other in silence for a long moment. Then she said, 'Ah, you've come.'

'Yes,' I said – I did not know what else to say. Another long moment passed – or so it seemed, although strangely enough I did not feel in the least embarrassed by this bizarre scene.

'I'm glad,' she said at last. 'But I can't see you now.'

'When can I come?' I asked.

'Tomorrow. At the same time. I'll be expecting you.'

She cocked her head slightly on one side. Far below I heard footsteps reverberating in the hallway.

'Go now!' breathed Beatrice. 'I shall expect you tomorrow. Go quickly!'

The door closed, leaving me blinded by the darkness. The footsteps sounded much nearer now, leaping up the shallow steps three at a time towards the first floor. There was no escape that way. I backed into the nearest corner and flattened myself as best I could against the wall, trying to melt into the stone. I felt horribly visible, nevertheless.

The footsteps came up the final flight of steps, and a stocky figure appeared and walked over to the door which had just closed. There was a knock, and a moment later Beatrice opened the door once more. I realised now why I had not immediately recognised her the first time, for she was deliberately 'got up' to seem younger than she was, with a simple one-piece garment, loose hair and face innocent of any paint.

However, I had no difficulty in recognising the dark hair, silvery beard, broad shoulders and strident voice of the caller who stood on the threshold, even though he had his back to me – but then I had parted from him not fifteen minutes earlier.

'Good evening, my dear,' he said. 'And how are you this evening?'

'Very well, thank you,' replied Beatrice sweetly. 'And you?'

'Very well indeed, thank you. May I come in?'

'Of course.'

She moved aside to admit him – and then I saw her start as she caught sight of me crouching there against the wall, plainly exposed. Browning had only to catch her expression, and turn round, and all would have been lost. But the next instant he had walked in, and she had closed the door, leaving me in the darkness again.

There is much I could say – how many notions, fancies, questions and answers fill my teeming brain! But why spin idle words tonight, when tomorrow I will *know*?

Affect. yours

Booth

136

BOOK THREE

The Worst of It

XVII

My dear Prescott,
This business grows more desperate with every day that passes.
All may yet be well, however. True, the murderer has struck
again; but the authorities are now involved, despite all Mr
Browning's efforts to keep them in ignorance – and I, at least,
have managed to get myself clear of the whole foul entangling
affair. Before telling you the how and the why of *that*, however, I
must beg your indulgence to touch a more personal note for a
moment or two.

You will remember with what keen anticipation I had looked
forward to the Saturday evening when I was to call on Beatrice,
Isabel's maid, at the house where Browning was such a regular
visitor. It was an oppressively warm evening. The day had been
airless and overcast, as though the stone walls of Florence had
grown upwards to form a grey dome sealing us off completely
from the outside world. Night came as a welcome respite, the
darkness falling like silence on the eyes. In marked contrast to
the previous evening, I was now not in the slightest hurry, and
savoured to the full the pleasure of walking slowly through the
streets towards my goal.

These Florentine streets, at best narrow, are made to seem
narrower still by the overhanging pent-roofs of the tall houses,
to which extra storeys are continually being added as the
population grows. Because of this, it is a keen pleasure to
emerge into one of the great squares – like drawing a deep
breath! One of the great joys of Florence is the manner in which
one's perception of the space about one is continually being
modified by infinite imperceptible touches as the buildings press
in or fall back, urge their attentions or gracefully withhold them;
so that for richness and subtlety of impression there is really
nothing quite like it in the world.

Nor was the human element missing. Indeed, the entire populace seemed to have quit the dim wretched rooms and dilapidated hovels which appear so quaint to a tourist's eye, and had sallied out into the streets and squares and alleys and courtyards, where every man, woman and child was busily swanking and singing and flirting and talking. An ominous stillness, however, spoke of a storm crouched somewhere in the offing, and thus the gaiety was a little forced.

And so, for the third time, I entered the plain green-shuttered *palazzo* on Via Dante Aligheri. On the first occasion I had knocked at a door where no one was at home; on the second the door had opened, but I had not been admitted. But this time I was greeted, and ushered into a small parlour furnished in a fashion so classically Florentine in every detail that it proclaimed itself quite plainly to be the product of a foreign hand.

Beatrice was wearing a black skirt, a black shawl about her shoulders, and a severe starchy blouse fastened with a plain metalwork brooch; her hair was pinned tightly up. The contrast with her appearance the previous evening was so complete that it was clearly intentional, and I could only assume that in the twenty-four hours since our last meeting she had learned something, presumably from Browning, which had caused her to change her opinion of me.

On the other hand, there I was, visiting her alone in her house at night – surely, if my case had been as bad as all that, she would just have left me standing on the threshold. Instead of which I was invited to take a seat on the divan, while she chose a small and rather uncomfortable-looking stool opposite. On a low table near at hand stood a flask of *vin santo* and a plate of little dry biscuits, hard as rocks, to soak up the delicious honey-tasting wine. This was better, as was Beatrice's manner and way of looking at me – the way I have had occasion to speak of before. I began to feel that I must have misread the portent of her severe appearance.

'You have been lied to,' she said at last, in a low voice, without looking at me. 'I shall not lie to you. You may not believe me – that would be too much to ask, no doubt. Nevertheless, what I tell you will be the truth.'

'Of course I shall believe you!' I cried warmly.

She held up her hands.

'You must not say that yet.'

'Is it so very bad, then?' I asked, half-humorously, for I was in a forgiving vein. Indeed, I rather hoped it *was* bad – I did not want my magnanimity to go to waste.

'No, it is not!' she replied defiantly. 'It is not bad at all. But you won't believe that. It is not your fault. No one could believe it.'

I said nothing. After a moment she went on – speaking very slowly, as though forming each phrase entire in her mind before uttering it. The first thing she said was a blow, although I had already guessed it: the apartment in which we were sitting was paid for by Robert Browning. It was he – the hypocrite! the whited sepulchre! – who had chosen the old books and pictures and hangings and pots and bric-à-brac. And it was he – the respectable and venerated Mr Robert Browning, who has made his marriage into one of the wonders of the world, a modern miracle to whose well-publicised shrine pilgrims flock from every corner of the civilised world – it was *he* who used to come thither every week, whenever the fancy took him, to visit his protégée.

And what, I enquired coldly, was the purpose of these visits? How exactly did the ageing man of letters and the young maid-servant spend their time together?

Beatrice gazed at me imploringly. In her eyes I read a desperate plea for comprehension, coupled with a very lively apprehension as to whether it would be forthcoming. But her reply, when it came, just served to make matters worse – for it was confused and evasive, all shrugs and mumbles and unfinished phrases.

I was merciless. I wanted to know – had to! Then I could walk out of there, search Browning out, and fling his filthy secret in his face. And so I pressed her. Had she not engaged to tell me the truth? Well, now I was calling in that note.

'It's no use – you won't believe me,' the girl repeated bitterly.

Now this intrigued me mightily. Improper or unedifying her revelations might no doubt be – but *unbelievable*? Surely, on the contrary, they promised to be all too drearily predictable! And yet Beatrice apparently remained convinced that I would not believe her. Why, in heaven's name? What hideous tale had she to unfold?

141

Prurient fantasies ran riot in my brain. What barely-mentionable secret lay coiled at the heart of this young woman's relations with Mr Robert Browning? What was so grotesque and unnatural about them? In a word, *what exactly used they to do?*

At length, with an effort that was obvious, she looked me full in the face for the first time.

'Nothing.'

'Nothing?'

Her eyes magnificently flashed.

'You see? I said you would not believe me! Oh, it is too shameful!'

Well, the dam had burst now, and in a flood of words and gestures and tears I had the whole story. My salacious conjectures had been very wide of the mark, it seemed.

According to Beatrice, Browning spent all his time sitting demurely on the sofa, just as I was at that moment (I almost jumped up, as though the cushion had turned red-hot!). She sat beside him, or on the chair opposite, or walked to and fro. She always wore the smock I had seen on the previous evening, and made herself look as young and unsophisticated as possible – to facilitate this Browning would send a note to inform her of his visits in advance. Not of course – save the mark! – that he had stooped to instructing her explicitly how best to gratify his whims; she had learned her lesson as women do, by noting what he praised and criticised.

There they were then, sitting side by side on the sofa. Browning would ask her what had happened to her that day, and she would tell him about any little incident that had occurred – sometimes inventing, for want of matter. Or he would recount a walk he had been on, describing the plants and flowers and birds and animals and insects he had seen, in a grotesque and colourful way that had amused her at first. Sometimes she would sing to him, folksongs which her mother had taught her.

And then, invariably, after about half an hour, he would ask her to comb out her hair for him. Depending on the hints he gave her, she would either stand, or sit, or kneel before him, and set to work – teasing out the individual strands to form a clear untangled stream of hair over her face and bosom, then shaking the shining mass over her shoulders, cascading down her back, or twist it all up into a coil which she then let unwind and fall:

> like a gorgeous snake
> The Roman girls were wont, of old,
> When Rome there was, for coolness' sake
> To let lie curling o'er their bosoms.

I take the liberty of quoting from one of Mr Browning's productions, since he is so much more eloquent upon the topic than I.

And then, after an hour or so, the poet would rise politely and remark that he had to be going. On each visit he would leave a little gift – a scarf, or painted box, or lace handkerchief with her initial embroidered in the corner – which proved to contain, hidden within its folds or recesses, a silver coin.

And that, if Beatrice was to be believed, is all that happened.

'But does he then never so much as touch you?' I enquired incredulously.

'He kisses my brow each time when he leaves. It is like a priest's kiss.'

'Nothing else?'

'Nothing, I swear it! Except that sometimes he touches my hair – hardly touches it, even, but since I have sworn . . . He just brushes it, with his fingertips. I cannot even feel it. But *he* does! It sounds crazy, but it is as if my poor hair is somehow hot, and he had burnt himself.

'I am always afraid then. He struggles for breath like one whose heart troubles him. I do not like to watch him, for my mother died so. But after a while he becomes quite normal again, and goes on talking as if nothing has happened. And that is really all – I swear it by our Holy Mother and all the saints. But you will not believe me.'

Well, Prescott, what say you? What is your impartial verdict? 'Nay but you, who do not love her, did she speak the truth, my mistress?' (Again I take a liberty with Mr Browning's mistress – forgive me, with his verse!)

Well, *I* believed her. A few days earlier I should not have. But incredible as her story might sound, *it was virtually identical to the account Browning had given Talenti of his relations with Isabel.*

In other words, if Beatrice was lying then she had very remarkably happened to choose a lie which corresponded exactly to Browning's own description of his relations with another young woman. Such a coincidence was surely infinitely less probable than the one which I was being asked to accept – especially as the more I turned the whole fantastic business over in my mind, the more it seemed to tally with the shadowy outlines of another, barely-perceived, Browning – one whose figure I had dimly caught sight of stalking through the stanzas of his nastier poems.

So I believed her, and told her so, and a little rim of shining tenderness appeared in her eyes. I had the feeling of having passed a test, and with an air almost proprietary, got up and strode idly about the room, enquiring more generally about Beatrice's circumstances. What of her family? And how had she come to meet Mr Browning?

She replied in the Tuscan manner, frankly and openly. Her mother had died when she was eight, leaving her and her five brothers and sisters to be brought up by an aunt, whose main virtue had been that while she lived she had protected the children from the worst excesses of their father. But with her death the situation of the children became desperate – particularly that of the girls, who were continually subjected to amorous advances on the part of their surviving parent, who had to be kept at bay by the elder brothers.

Beatrice had meanwhile found work in service to an English family, and the contrast between the squalor of her home life and the gracious atmosphere of culture and polite manners which she breathed in the foreign household where she lived, returning home once weekly, made a deep and lasting impression on her. Then her employers suddenly departed, their daughter having lost her struggle with the octopus in her lungs, and poor Beatrice suddenly found herself plunged back once again into the inferno of her own family.

She was desperate to find a new position, and contacted a number of friends of her old employers, including the Brownings, in the hope that one of them might wish to employ her. The Brownings had no need of further staff themselves, but had heard through Mr Powers that a newly-arrived American couple were looking for a pleasant reliable girl who spoke some English. And thus it was that Beatrice came to work for the Eakins.

Deeply grateful, she looked in at Casa Guidi one evening after work to thank her benefactors. When she left, Mr Browning insisted on her taking a cab, for which he paid, and even very gallantly escorted her to it. He asked if everything was satisfactory with her new job, and Beatrice replied that it was, except the post was not 'live-in' – for this was before the Eakins moved to the villa – so that she had still to spend her evenings at home, with all the horrors this entailed.

Mr Browning murmured that something might be done. Could she meet him at a café in a few days' time to discuss the matter further?

'And what exactly did you think Mr Browning meant when he said that something might be done?' I enquired ironically.

'I don't know. I didn't care.'

'You must have had some notion, nevertheless.'

'You sound like that policeman! I tell you I didn't care. If you knew how we lived, all crammed together like puppies, and that disgusting father of mine always trying to touch me – why should I have cared? Anything would have been better than that!'

And so she went to the rendezvous. Prudent Mr Browning, however, did not appear. Instead, the waiter handed Beatrice a note directing her to come to an address in Via Dante Alighieri.

'When I arrived he simply handed me the key and said he would return in a few days to see that all was well. I could hardly believe it. Two rooms all to myself! It was like being in heaven – so much space and air! I told my family the Americans had changed their minds, as foreigners will, and that I was going to live with them. Much they cared! I never see them now, except my sisters sometimes at church. Two days later Mr Browning came, and we sat and talked for three-quarters of an hour, as I said, and when he went he left a coin behind.

'It has been like that ever since. At first I looked forward to his visits. I was a little lonely, for one thing, but also I admired him – truly! I thought it wonderful that any man should be so noble, so pure and selfless, as priests should be but never are. Not ours, at least – your heretic priests may be better. But then, by degrees, all changed. At first I grew bored with this dressing-up. Am I not young enough? Why pretend to be a child? "If this man really sought my good," I thought, "he would not try and make me what I no longer am. He would let me be, let me grow, and take delight in *that*."

'But there was also something else – something more difficult to speak about. This way of his with me – so cool and distant, gossiping like neighbours from one balcony to another – all that was well enough at first, when we were still strangers. But with time it began to trouble me. It is *unnatural*: men do not behave so with women, that much I know! And so what had seemed pure and noble at first came to seem a hideous and shameful secret which I knew I must keep hidden from all the world – just as he keeps me hidden away here. Do you understand what I mean? I blush to say it, but a time came when I almost wished this Browning would use me as my father tried to do. No, do not look like that! I did not love him – never! But that at least would have been a human thing – I could have understood him, and felt that all was well. As it is, I was frightened. I *am* frightened.'

She crossed herself.

'But it will soon be over! He will tire of me – find some younger girl, and turn me out of here. It is terrible to think what will become of me then. My people will have no mercy on me, for I have committed a great sin.'

'But you said there has been no sin!' I exclaimed.

'Of course there has – the worst in Italy! *I have turned my back on my family*! Unless some other foreigner takes me in, I am lost.'

It crossed my mind that it would be extremely unwise of Browning to risk simply 'turning out' Beatrice, in view of the disastrous damage she could do his reputation by telling others what she had just told me.

Then that thought, and its disturbing consequences, was lost in the lingering look Beatrice gave me as she spoke these final words – and at last I felt I understood why she had assumed that prim and proper manner at first. It was not that she had changed her ideas about me. On the contrary, she had been afraid that after what I had seen the previous evening I might have changed *mine* about *her*, and had wished to make it very clear that she was not just some *demi-mondaine* with whom anyone might trifle away a pleasant evening for a price. A marked change had come over her manner since I had accepted that despite appearances this was not what she had been to Browning. Was she now not intimating what she *might* be to me, and I to her?

XVIII

Beatrice may have considered the room which the philanthropic Mr Browning had taken for her to be spacious and airy, as by the standards of the Florentine populace it indeed was; but to my senses it nevertheless appeared distinctly cramped, and on such a night as that, intolerably close and stuffy. I therefore walked over and opened a tall double-door giving on to a small balcony, and stepped outside. It was cooler here; the air was hushed, and from the distance there came a low exploratory rumble, like a kettledrummer trying his instruments quietly in the empty hall before the concert begins.

A few moments later when Beatrice emerged there was barely enough room for us both. As we stood there side by side in the darkness like two conspirators, I realised once again how remarkably at ease I felt in her company, despite the social gulf between us, and the ambiguous nature of our relations. It was no doubt her foreignness which made the thing possible at all – and once possible, it could not but be easy.

I pointed out old Dante's house, fifty yards off on the other side of the street.

'Do you think he chose these rooms because of your name?' I asked playfully.

Beatrice's reply was that characteristic Italian plosive which means that the speaker does not know, does not care, and cannot imagine why any sensible person should do either.

'Who knows what goes on in his head?' she said. 'But I don't want to speak of him.'

I was leaning over the balcony, looking down at the empty street – when I suddenly felt her right arm lightly brush my face, and caught the perfume of her brown skin. The thing might have gone for nothing, had she not looked at me. But that glance, I know not why, bereft me of all reason, and the next instant I had seized her, lowered my face to hers, and was madly kissing her!

Arresting this initial impulse was as hopeless as thinking twice about diving into a deep pool a moment after you have jumped. But another moment later, shocked by the delicious impact, I saw my gesture for what it had been – the unbridled licence of a degenerate, who had basely yielded to his animal instincts and forced his repulsive caresses on a helpless girl, rushing in where poets evidently feared to tread. Desperately I struggled to disengage myself, preparing a speech of fulsome apology.

I *struggled*. But why did I have to struggle with someone who should have been pushing me away with all her feeble strength? The answer, I realised with amazement, was that far from forcing me away, or collapsing flaccidly, a sacrificial victim to my loathsome embraces, Beatrice was responding to my passion with a vehemence that equalled if not exceeded my own. She was kissing as much as kissed, her beautiful live mouth sporting with mine like a creature which had at long last found its fellow, and was glad.

My experience of the female sex – apart from casual encounters with women of the streets – had until that evening been limited to a single experience of love which was illicit, protracted, and as devoid of joy as it was of hope. The object of my desires, when she at length yielded to them, did so in such a way that they were instantly extinguished, and nothing remained but my excitement. This, although of course intense, was entirely superficial. I was excited by the idea of possessing this woman I had so long desired – excited by the idea, not by the act itself, which was in every way brutal, brief and unsatisfactory.

This being so, I was quite unprepared for the very different experience of *that* night – for I did not return home until morning. And it was Beatrice who wished it! You may not believe that, but it is true. I thought I was seducing her, and all the time it was really she who was seducing me! I am convinced she foresaw the whole encounter – indeed that knowledge came to me, quite literally, in a flash.

The flash in question was lightning, and it awoke me out of a profound slumber, with a confused impression of being at sea. I seemed to see an open companion-way, the hatches banging back and forth in a high wind, and a stretch of slippery deck beyond, with squalls of rain driving across it – memories dredged up from those years when my father sent me out on the schooners plying across the gulf to Nova Scotia, to make a man of me. As if to confirm the illusion, the thunder sounded out like ripping calico when a sail splits.

I sat bolt upright, and found myself in a strange bed. On the other side of the room the windows lay swinging open in the wind gusting around the house. The air was filled with the fresh damp smell of rain, and with the sound of it pelting down. Then, suddenly, I made out some sort of shape moving in the darkness. Terror gripped my heart! It had all been too smooth, too convenient and easy. The woman's tales had been lies, just like the man's! I had been decoyed to that house – *his* house – to be made away with!

Then the lightning – as bodiless as moonlight, though far intenser than the sun – suffused the scene again, and I saw that the figure was Beatrice, as naked as Eve. The torrential rain blowing in through the window, which she had gone to shut, had sprayed her shoulders and bosom, and the skin gleamed like polished bronze. It was the most erotic image I had ever seen, and all my fears were swept away as I sprang from the bed and rushed towards her, and found her in the darkness, and embraced her repeatedly.

She *did* plan it, though! She all but admitted as much the next morning as we sat over our coffee. But not for Browning – for herself! She is in love with me, Prescott. Imagine it – Robert Browning's chosen mistress in love with *me*! She scorns him, and calls me a real man – as indeed I am with her.

She does not of course expect me to marry her. Rather I am to replace her previous protector – who will be politely instructed to discontinue his visits forthwith, as his attentions are no longer desired.

'He will ask why,' Beatrice pointed out.

'Then tell him!'

'He will ask your name.'

'Tell him!'

'It's strange! I thought you were his friend.'

'So did I, once,' I replied grimly. But I did not feel grim – on the contrary, I awaited the outcome with the liveliest interest.

So much for this part of my tale. Meanwhile events elsewhere were moving rapidly towards their astonishing climax yesterday. Last Wednesday morning readers of the local news-sheet were startled by a headline in thunderous capitals, reading 'TERRIBLE DEATH OF AN UNKNOWN WRETCH!!!' Here, roughly Englished, is the story which appeared underneath:

'It is early. Sol has not yet shaken his locks above the snowy Apennines, nor will not do so for many hours to come. The city slumbers; each burgher, of whatever rank or station, dreaming of the madcap merrymaking and joyful japes in store at Carnival-tide. The streets are silent, save for the steady reassuring sound of the watchman going his rounds, ever-vigilant in defence of the lives and property of his fellow-citizens.

'As he makes his way along Via di Calimala, near the Old Market, this upright servant of the people perceives a pleasant odour – a perfume redolent of joyful hours around the familial board after Sunday mass, the roast sizzling on the fire. But the zealous watchman straightway thrusts this deceitful vision aside: at hand is a humble palace, once cradle to many generations of Florentines, but which has stood untenanted since Arno in his anger rose two lustra since.

'Wherefore then this olfactory ignis fatuus, this fata morgana of the nostrils, this fragrant will-o'-the-wisp? Such is the question which leaps to the alert constable's mind, and without an instant's delay or a single thought for his own safety the intrepid one irrupts into the edifice – ignoring, in his single-minded dedication to Duty, the directive affixed to its walls by our enlightened civic authorities, warning the citizenry of the perils attendant upon any such ingression.

'Within, the darkness is of Cimmerian intensity – a very abyss of impenetrable obscurity which threatens to extinguish by its overwhelming preponderance the feeble rays of the watch's lantern.

'But stay! What is this other light? What this weird luminance which seems to emanate from the very walls themselves? And what, ah God! say, what is that fiery portal gaping there like the very maw of our Dante's celebrated Inferno?

'What a terrible scene! A citizen of Lucca, sure, would straightway turn and fly from such an awful apparition! Never would a faint-hearted Siennese or braggart Pistoian have stood his ground – nay, though it were broad daylight and they in five or ten, as one would they have turned and fled!!

'No daylight here. No cheering companions. It is the witching-hour, when hell-hags roam. Our man is all alone. *But in his breast there beats a Florentine heart*!!! Unmoved, he boldly advances upon the terrific vision – which shrinks – dwindles – fades before his unquailing orbs, into another horror, no less ghastly for being of this world. Too much so!

'Within the wall he discovers a capacious oven, relic of those happier times when the fruits of Ceres were elaborated here for distribution to the populace. Once again a fire glows within, as when the baker plied his life-sustaining art.

'But what dreadful sight is this? With what unnatural cargo is the oven now freighted? Not with bread, nor yet a fragrant pot of beans, but with a HUMAN BODY!!!! An unrecognisable and loathsome mass of carbonised flesh and bone! Whose unconsumed extremities appear more frightful still by contrast with the ruin of the rest!'

It was in fact by those 'unconsumed extremities' – which included a large hand sporting several unusual rings, one of them bearing the seal of his Church – that the authorities succeeded in identifying the victim, the Reverend Urizen K. Tinker.

The unfortunate ecclesiastic was apparently lured to his death by means of a note which his wife – for, unlikely as it may seem, Tinker proved to possess an uxorial appendage – told the police had been delivered to their rooms at about ten o'clock the previous evening, but which had subsequently been burned by its recipient. Tinker had then left home, without tendering any explanation to his wife, who in turn had not dared request one.

The official theory at present appears to be that Tinker was murdered late on Tuesday night, presumably by the author of the note: there is no indication of his identity, nor of the motive for the crime – the public prints made no mention of any puzzling inscription having been found at the scene, so there was no reason to think that it formed a part of the series of which only Browning and I were as yet aware.

The assassin is supposed to have attempted to conceal the outrage by incinerating the corpse in a disused baker's oven –

which, however, does not explain why he failed to take the elementary precaution of removing the highly distinctive rings his victim was wearing. Indeed, it seems more likely that one hand had been left dangling out of the oven precisely so that Tinker's identity *would* be established. But in that case why was any attempt made to burn the body at all? The thing appeared a fathomless mystery.

I had not seen or heard from Browning since the Friday night when I had crouched in the darkness at the head of the stairs outside Beatrice's rooms, praying that he would not catch sight of me. However, the morning following the discovery of Tinker's corpse I received the following note:

Dear Booth,

Heureka! The secret of the inscriptions is mine! Eleven o'clock tomorrow morning, at the gate to the Boboli Gdns. *'Recover* hope, all ye who enter!'

R.B.

Of the many thoughts which streamed through my mind as I scanned these lines, the uppermost was simply a sense of shock at the realisation that Browning still had not the slightest inkling of what had happened. Here he was, dashing me off a hasty summons, quite as though he could dispose of my time and person in the same old free and easy way as ever; as though I were still his acolyte, to be ordered to appointments when it suited him, and then dismissed and scorned and sniggered at by his high-class friends when the situation changed!

Well, he was mistaken, very much so – and the time had come to let him know, to make him feel it. For a moment I was tempted to return a delicately wounding letter in reply – as short and pointed as a stiletto.

But I soon thought better of it. Not that I wished to spare his feelings – had he spared *mine*? – but rather I saw that I had to deliver much more than just a smart rejoinder, a neat snub. There was too much at stake for that. I had to cut all my involvement with Mr Robert Browning, to disassociate myself from his 'investigations' before it was too late.

Playing the amateur police detective had seemed a worth-while price to pay for sharing Browning's company, back in the

days when that had been the *summum bonum* of my existence –
and when the truth behind poor Isabel's death had been the sole
object of our quest. How long ago and far away all that seemed
now! My idol had proved to have feet not just of clay but of
mud and grime and every sort of filth; while the jealous lover
we had originally sought had swollen up, as in a dream,
out of all proportion, and become a homicidal maniac whose
atrocities were turning 'our' Florence into a slaughter-house.

It was high time to withdraw, to get out from under – while I
still could! And to do that – to make Browning understand that I
was in earnest, and would not be swayed – I should have to see
him one last time in person.

I took a leaf out of Beatrice's book, and arrived for our
appointment dressed in my most sombre and formal apparel. If I
hoped Mr Browning might be given pause for thought and
reflection by this, I was quickly disappointed, for he just hailed
me with all his characteristic gusto, and thrust his pass – a
privilege which comes of living in the Guidi Palace – under the
nose of the guard, who duly admitted us into the Grand-Duke's
domain.

It soon became clear that Browning was in his most energetic
form. He hurried me along a promenade, between massive shiny
evergreen hedges, so fast that I thought there must be something he wished to show me at the end. Once we got there,
however, he merely turned down another alley – this one
covered in trellises, where in a few months the vines will bud
and leaf – and I began to realise that my companion's haste was
an index not of any urgency in our goal, but of his state of
nervous excitement. And so we went on, circumnavigating the
magnificent gardens at a cracking pace, passing the bold vistas
and romantic prospects so artfully arranged to catch the eye
without so much as a glance, while Browning talked, and talked,
and talked.

I found it extremely odd to be trotting along beside the man,
knowing what I knew; and odder still to think how recently I
used to idolise him, and to dread nothing so much as the one
thing I now sought above all: to be rid of him and his
never-ending talk full of allusions in half a dozen languages I do
not know to half a hundred books I have never read and do not
wish to read.

How his self-indulgent verbosity used to inspire me when I thought he was the real right thing I had found at last! And how it disgusts me now I know what manner of thing he is. Listen:

'It was the word "*manto*" first set me thinking. The Italian of course means a coat, from the Latin *mantellum*, cognate with the familiar "mantle". Greek, on the other hand, has *mantis*: a prophet or soothsayer, whence all our compounds that terminate in "–mancy". 'By your necromancy you have disturbed him, and raised his ghost' and so on – this of course being just what the late Miss Edith Chauncey was at when she met with her unfortunate accident. It is however unlikely, despite her fame, that our local soothsayer will have a city named after her – as was the case with the daughter of blind Tiresias, one of her predecessors. The city in question is *Mantova Gloriosa*, the birthplace of the Mantuan Swan sung by Cowper ... '

And so on, and so on. But do not fear – I shall spare you any more of the facetious riddles and learned references and pedantic explications I had to suffer, and bring you immediately where he in the end came out.

'Does not this garden, on such a day as this, seem a vision of paradise?' Browning rhetorically enquired. 'And yet, in that note I sent you, I suggested it might bear a slightly-adapted motto from a celebrated account of another place. You took the hint, I trust? There is no need for me to explain further. No?'

I did not speak.

'Why, man, that's the key!' Browning cried impatiently. 'Old Dante and his Inferno!'

XIX

Browning stood gazing triumphantly at me, his chest pushed out and hands working away in his capacious pockets – the very image of a provincial shopkeeper who has backed the Derby winner. What an odious little man, I thought. Him, great? Him, a genius? Never, plainly, had I been further from the mark than when I had somehow contrived to persuade myself of *that*.

'Dante!' he repeated enthusiastically, when I failed to respond. 'The thing is so plain now that it seems hardly possible I did not see it long ago – but who would have thought to look for such a freakish association? There is no longer the slightest doubt about it, however. Take Chauncey, for example. She was found, you remember, with a broken neck. The maid – a lass of imagination, evidently; I should like to meet her! – described her mistress's head as having been turned around like an owl's. Dante put it more prosaically:

> *Come 'l viso mi scese in lor più basso,*
> *mirabilmente apparve esser travolto*
> *ciascun tra 'l mento e 'l principio del casso*

' "As on them more direct mine eye descends, each wonderously seem'd to be reversed at the neck-bone . . . ": such is the poet's terrifying vision of the soothsayers, who are punished in the eighth circle of his hell. The leader of this pack was a woman – Manto.

'The correspondence is clear. Miss Chauncey pretended to be what Manto was: one who seeks to push aside the curtain of mortality, to see further than God judges proper for His creatures – what Dante would have called *un'indovina*. The poet imaged such people grotesquely mutilated as a fit punishment for their temerity, their heads so wrenched out of place that they, who presumed to scan the secrets of futurity, could not even see where they were walking. Those who scorned man's limits, mercifully imposed by a just and loving God to shield us from knowledge we are not strong enough to bear, are denied in eternity even that degree of foresight which is proper to man.

'But now – and here's the true devilry of the thing – what Dante imagined and wrote, someone in Florence is putting into practice! Thus Edith Chauncey is found dead, her neck broken like Manto's, and a piece of paper thrust into her hand like the sign hung about the neck of an executed felon, spelling out the nature of her offence. On it appears the name of her archetype in Dante's poem – MANTO – and the number of the circle in which that personage is to be found – 8.

'Once I had found this key, unlocking the remaining inscriptions was of course child's play, and each served to confirm the pattern until all possibility of doubt was extinguished. Thus at the spot where Maurice Purdy was savaged by an enormous rabid dog we found the figure 3 and the word CIACCO. We were told that this means a pig, as indeed it does. But Dante employs it not as a noun but a name – it was the nickname of a notorious Florentine glutton, who also features in Boccaccio's *Decameron*. In the third circle of hell the poet saw him punished "*per la dannosa colpa de la gola*", "for the pernicious vice of gluttony" – but how much better those yawning Tuscan vowels draw the gorging craw ever calling for more and more! There lay Ciacco, wallowing in the mud, his flesh ripped and flayed by the Hound of Hell itself – "red of eye and slimy black of pelt, his paunch distended and cruelly hooked his claws". I think you will agree that the hydrophobic beast that savaged Purdy made a very acceptable Cerberus, all things considered. As for his victim, belly-worship was his religion – he lived to eat, and died eaten.

'Cecil DeVere, on the other hand, devoted himself not to the inner but the outer man – a fact which did not escape the murderer's ferocious irony. "Argenti", he called him, "Silver" – the nickname of one Filippo de' Cavicciuli, whose ostentatious extravagance was such that he had his horse shod with silver shoes: "*equum ferris argenti ferrari fecit*", as the old chronicle says. DeVere, of course, did not go quite so far, but it cannot be denied that he spent a considerable amount of time and money on his appearance. Argenti ended up immersed in the mire of a dead channel in the fifth circle of Dante's Hell; DeVere in the filthy slime of the Arno.'

'I was not aware that dandyism was either a mortal sin or a justification for murder,' I put in tartly.

'It is of course neither,' returned Browning, shooting me a look of some surprise. 'As regards the author of these crimes, it is surely superfluous to state that we are dealing with a totally deranged mind, for whom the merest peccadillo can be used to justify any abomination. In that he is the opposite – or, better, the negative – of his model. Dante hated not the sinners but the sin – the wickedness which shuts out that pure love-drenched intellectual light he sings in the *Paradiso*. He was a great hater because he was a great lover, and knew that a man cannot be one without the other.'

'A great lover – him!' I exclaimed contemptuously.

'His work is full of love.'

'It is full of the *word*, certainly,' I retorted. 'But to know what manner of lover a man is, ask his mistress! I think I know what *she* would say. "He, a great lover? Oh yes, to be sure! One always glowering alone in the corner at a party, with never a word to say for himself; or lurking in the street outside my house, writhing in spiritual ecstasy – ready to swoon if I happen to notice him, and lock himself up in his room half-dead with grief if not. One whose secret wish is just to touch my hair, and kiss my brow – and nothing more! A great lover, him? Yes! Of himself!" *That*, depend upon it, is what Beatrice would say.'

I had allowed myself to say far more than I had meant to, and had spoken with undue warmth. Browning gave me a long thoughtful look. I knew that he had not yet been to call on Beatrice, and thus could have no notion of what awaited him there, or of how his secret had been betrayed. But however he explained them to himself, my words had plainly struck home.

'I'm not sure that I am very interested in what Beatrice would say,' he replied with distaste. 'Who was she, after all? A vulgar merchant's daughter who married a banker and died young. It may be that she would have been rash enough to speak of the poet in the fashion you suggest, although give me leave to doubt it. But if he had not singled her out from all the other pretty children, no one today would have the slightest interest in what she had to say about anything. One might hope she would remember *that* before she opened her mouth to mock her benefactor.'

I judged it expedient to bring these giddy conversational acrobatics down to earth.

'I'm not sure that I see why Beatrice Portinari would have had any cause to consider Dante her benefactor. But let us leave Literature on one side, Mr Browning, for there at least I am no match for you. Tell me, what of the inscription we found at the Eakins' villa? *Riminese* was the word, but who or what is of Rimini?'

'Francesca,' replied Browning shortly.

I did not pretend not to understand this reference to the most famous canto in the entire *Inferno*: the tragic and moving tale of Francesca da Rimini, murdered by her deformed husband when he found her in his brother's bed. She and her lover appear in the second circle, where

> the stormy blast of hell
> With restless fury drives the spirits on,
> Whirl'd round and dash'd amain with sore annoy.

The reference irresistibly brought to mind the memory of how the long white shape which had proved to be Isabel's body had been pushed and pulled about by the storm wind in the garden of the villa. She then, had been adjudged one òf those carnal sinners 'in whom reason by lust is swayed'.

I murmured some expression of appreciation for Browning's achievement in deciphering these enigmatic graffiti which had so sorely perplexed us hitherto. But somehow the triumph was quite gone from my companion's manner: he did not seem to care about the inscriptions any more, or his cleverness in deciphering them. When I enquired – as I was bound to do – about the fate of the hapless Tinker, knocked down in a slum and stuffed into a baker's oven to roast, Browning once again contented himself with the briefest possibly reply.

'Farinata.'

'Sorry?'

'One of the heresiarchs tormented in red-hot tombs in Dante's sixth circle.'

'And the inscription?'

'Was written up on the wall of the bakery, in the usual fashion.'

'It is strange, then, that neither appeared in any reports of the crime. Are the authorities perhaps attempting to conceal the enormity of this murderous conspiracy, to forestall any panic among the foreign community?'

'No, they are merely ignorant of its existence – just as they were of the marks left by the garden table beneath Mrs Eakin's body, which no one but I remarked.'

Mrs Eakin? I thought – need you be so formal when speaking of your former mistress?

'I found *them* because I was looking for them,' Browning went on, 'and I found the inscription in the bakery for the same reason. Among the painted list of items for sale, still visible on the plaster, was the word for flour: *farina*. Someone had added two letters in white chalk and a circled figure six.'

Browning was visibly regaining confidence as he recounted these further examples of his cleverness. It was time to prick the balloon again.

'Very well,' I commented wearily. 'So we understand the messages this maniac leaves at the scene of his outrages. As an intellectual achievement this is no doubt something upon which you are to be congratulated. But forgive me please if I look at things from a more practical point of view. "The English in Florence are dying too much," the police official told me. What hope is there of halting this process? Your discovery is very interesting, but what use is it? Where, in other words, does it get us? What are we to *do*?'

We had all this while been walking up the great central avenue which leads from the lily pond at the south-western end of the gardens, near the Porta Romana, to the famous terrace in front of the fortress of the Belvedere, where we had just arrived. This commands the most striking and extensive view of the city, and thus Browning was able to parry my question with an urbane ' "Do", Mr Booth? Why, with such a prospect as this before us I hope we shall not be vulgar enough to dream of "doing" anything – anything that is but just rest our arms on this railing and our eyes on one of the great achieved miracles of the human spirit'.

It is true that the view *is* miraculous, and ir nothing more than the way it obstinately continues to survive the worst that journalists, diarists, essayists, belletrists, aquarellists, hacks, sketchers and daubers of every nationality and either sex, professional and genteel, have been able to do to render it trite, familiar and hateful. There it was again, as fresh and satisfying and perfect as the first time I set eyes on it – all those tiled roofs catching the light at every conceivable angle, showing up as hard and abrasive as sandpaper here, there as soft and plush as velvet. This warm wash of russet, together with the walls in infinite varieties of umber, buff, fawn and burnt sienna, is then punctuated by the three slim towers of the Badia, the Bargello and the Palazzo Vecchio; by the massive rectangular bulk of the Strozzi and Antinori palaces; by the buxom comfortable domes of Santa Maria Novella, San Lorenzo, Santa Croce; and by half a hundred monuments, antiquities, towers and turrets whose names even now I hardly know. All this, good as it is (as who should say!), is lifted, made perfect, unique and whole by the presence at its heart: Brunelleschi's great cupola rising massively weightless over the Cathedral Church of St John, superbly dominating and pulling together the entire composition.

Legions had stood where I was standing, gazing like Keats's stout Cortez. What their wild surmises may have been I do not know, but I am sure I was the first to look out there and feel that the Florentines had done right to exile Dante!

To be sure, this nightmare inferno whose geography Browning was exploring with such excitement was but a parody of the poet's vision. Nevertheless, a man who occupied his life with the creation of an all-embracing minutely-organised vicarious universe in which he was exalted and his enemies made to suffer atrocious and degrading torments – what had he to do with the genius of this place whose finest monument was just this scene before my eyes: not the obsessively organised masterpiece of some lonely exile, but the splendid product of evolution, chance, history, and a dozen different hands?

Browning had also been actively contemplating the scene.

'How often I have stood up here,' he pronounced, 'or on the brow of Bellosguardo, or at Fiesole, looking down on Florence! There it stands, like a theatre after everyone has gone home. How noble the verses must have been! And how the actors must have moved like kings, and spoken like gods. What we but dream of and play at, they *performed*. But where are they now? Vanished without trace!'

A desire to shine was almost embarrassingly evident in my companion's words and manner. The thought which flashed into my mind, rightly or wrongly, was that he had sensed that I had withdrawn my admiration, and was waxing brilliant in order to try and win me back. If so, his efforts were wasted.

'Until now!' he added, giving me a significant look. 'Now that power and scope of conception and execution have surfaced once again, albeit in an evil guise. But let us admit it – there is grandeur, there is genius, in the thing! No petty crime this! No nasty tale of a lover's spite, as at first I thought. No – nothing less than to re-create Dante Alighieri's Inferno here on earth, bang in the middle of the nineteenth century, punishing the heirs of the poet's sinners in ways which parallel those which he described. This is evil on a scale worthy of this setting! Tell me honestly, Booth, do you not feel some slight admiration for the man?'

'Not the slightest,' I replied coldly. 'Indeed, I am afraid I must say that I most strongly deprecate the views you have just expressed. Unlike you, I do not find evil and crime amusing or inspiring, but dreary, dark and desolate. You ask me to be honest: let me therefore tell you that if I agreed to our meeting today, it was solely for the purpose of announcing my fixed intention of withdrawing from any further involvement in this affair.

'As you must remember, I have on several occasions urged you to place such information as you possess in the hands of the authorities. You have until now succeeded in convincing me that this would be a mistake. In the wake of recent events I am no longer convinced. You, of course, must do as your conscience directs. But please be clear that I shall henceforth disassociate myself entirely from any further private investigations into these crimes.'

Browning stood staring, his bottom lip hanging down, for all the world like a little boy trying not to cry. I almost felt sorry for him – until I recalled how he had treated me that day at the English Cemetery.

'But *why?*' he wailed. 'You used to be so eager to help me!

What has happened to change you? What are these "recent events" you speak of?'

This was too bad. I had thought he would be angry and stalk off, but by showing his hurt so plainly, Browning was managing to make me feel at fault. Was I never to be in the right with the man? There was, however, no turning back now.

'Yes, I *have* changed,' I told him. 'We have been speaking of Dante. He said that his life began again the day he met the woman you have described as a vulgar merchant's daughter. Well, I too have met Beatrice.'

Our looks met with an almost audible chink.

'Very well, Mr Booth,' Browning said – and his voice was hard and full of menace. 'In that case I need detain you no longer.'

And now, at last, he turned on his heel and strode off – too late! My victory rang hollow, and I felt I had blundered badly, perhaps fatally.

XX

I set off for home, only to get lost in a maze of alleys and paths of
that over-elaborately calculated landscape. One spot in particular returned continually to haunt me: the path curved invitingly
away downhill in what seemed the right direction, only to come
to an abrupt end against a high stone wall in a close airless
dead-end where I could hardly breathe.

As I found myself back there for the third or fourth time, and
stopped to try and get my bearings, I heard laughter close
behind me. I whirled round, but there was no one there. The air
suddenly felt chilly, and I shivered as though someone had
walked across my grave.

Then there was a rustle in the bushes, and I took to my heels!
Had Browning been right, then? Was this garden hell itself,
from which there was no escape? Would I always find myself
back at that same spot where the path went wrong, listening to
that mocking laughter, for all eternity?

Strangely, however, in my blind and stupid panic – for the
gardens were now rapidly filling with people, and it had been
some innocent laugh I must have heard, from another alley
beyond the hedge – I somehow managed to find the exit which
had eluded me before, and in a few minutes was out of the
gardens of the Pitti Palace and back in the noise and turmoil of
the streets.

When I had met Charles Nicholas Grant at Miss Chauncey's
ill-fated 'séance', he had told me that he was staying with the
Ricasoli family, and urged me to call on him, and as my way
home took me directly past the Ricasoli palace I took this
opportunity of doing so. Mr Grant received me kindly, and sent
the footman for a bottle of wine – which his firm imports, he
informed me with a smile and a wink, to add substance to their
claret in poor years.

Mr Grant proved to be a rather different quantity tête-à-tête
than he had been in company. The urbanity and the polished

charm were rather less in evidence, and a bluff boisterous high spirits considerably more. In particular I found him as thrilled as a schoolboy at the prospect of the poor old Florentine Carnival, which he evidently envisaged as a spanking new edition of the Roman Saturnalia, with all its original excesses intact and a variety of modern ones superadded. His manner became frankly conspiratorial as he intimated that one as long resident in the city as myself must surely know all those special places and times when the flame of Carnival burned most intensely, and a good time was to be had by all.

I agreed that I might possibly be able to furnish him with certain indications, and even offered to accompany him if he so desired. He said he could wish for nothing better. I then described some of the traditions of the Carnival, including the opportunity it presented to indulge in masquerade.

At this the staid merchant's eyes lit up. Nothing would do but we must immediately repair to an outfitter who specialised in this kind of apparel, and look out something suitable – or rather *unsuitable*. After much reflection, Grant settled for a suit of jester's motley, complete with cap and bells – and of course a mask to conceal his identity, lest his respectable acquaintances here catch him thus playing the fool. This costume was duly ordered to be made up in time for the Saturday, when the festivities commence in earnest, continuing without respite until the climax of the grand procession on Shrove Tuesday – on which day Grant and I made our arrangements to meet and sally forth together in quest of adventure.

Meanwhile I at last heard from Beatrice's lips the news I had longed for – that Browning had been to visit her, and she had severed her relations with him.

'I said that I was grateful for all he had done for me, but that his visits had become inconvenient, since I had lately been the subject of the attentions of another gentleman, who had proposed marriage to me. I thought it better to say so' – she went on quickly, having caught the look I gave her.

'Did he ask who he was, this gentleman?'

'No.'

'What *did* he say?' I asked in some exasperation. I had expected something more satisfying than this.

'Nothing, at first. He just looked at me very long and very

hard. Then he shrugged, like one who wishes to pretend that he does not care. "Very well," he said. "But you'll be sorry!" '

'Was it a threat?' I asked.

'I don't know. Perhaps. Or a prophecy.'

A dark cloud seemed to settle on her face, normally so serene, and I made haste to dissipate it with renewed demonstrations of affection.

'At all events,' I pursued, 'the important thing is that he is out of your life – out of both our lives. Why should we mind what he says? He cannot harm us!'

But Beatrice remained doubtful.

'For my sake, be careful!' she urged. 'He is clever, and has powerful friends. Such men are always dangerous.'

The rest of the weekend and the Monday passed without further incident, and shortly before ten o'clock on the morning of Shrove Tuesday, in accordance with our arrangement, I presented myself at Mr Grant's suite. I found that former pillar of the City of London already fully attired in the costume he had ordered, and as excited as a girl on the eve of her first ball. We accordingly wasted no further time in joining the merry throng in the streets, where everyone in Florence – rich or poor, young or old, foreign or native – was out savouring the intoxicating atmosphere of light-hearted revelry.

It must be admitted that much of the entertainment on offer is of a distinctly juvenile variety: bags full of lime and flour are carried, and liberal quantities of both distributed indiscriminately in all directions, and dropped on to the heads of the passers-by from balconies and windows – all to the accompaniment of loud squeals and giggles. Missiles far more dangerous are the *confetti*. These were originally sweetmeats, but are now more usually plaster imitations, rock-hard, which are flung with merciless force at any unsuspecting or distracted bystander, the more venerable or respected the better. Indeed, this aspect of Carnival epitomises life in Italy, where there are no bystanders, and the highest possible tax is levied on anyone who allows his attention to be distracted for a single moment from his immediate surroundings.

My masked companion and I proceeded at a leisurely pace through the streets and piazzas, where Mr Grant attracted much attention. But the Florentines are above all an articulate race –

from a jester they expect jests, and finding my companion unable to satisfy this want, despite his fetching costume, they soon deserted us to admire some other prodigy. But these fickle folk were immediately replaced by fresh admirers, so that upon the whole Mr Grant had no reason to feel that his efforts had been wasted.

The fresh air soon gave us an appetite, and as Grant wished everything that day to be as typically Florentine and as different from his usual life as possible, I took him where no foreigner would normally dream of going – to a little cook-shop near Santa Croce, where we dined off the modest local fare – slices of fried polenta, artichoke fritters, chestnut dumplings and river fish, with a flask of the new wine to take off the taste of the old oil. Mr Grant enjoyed himself hugely, making a considerable impression both on the other clients of the establishment and on our flask of wine, which in turn made a considerable impression on him.

Midday had struck when we at length arrived in the great square before the Franciscans' basilica, where the procession was already forming up. By and by it moved off amid the clacking of hooves and the rumble of wheels. As the leading coach-and-six lumbered by we caught a glimpse of the Grand-Duke Leopold himself, waving mechanically to the crowd. He is an utterly inoffensive and insignificant person, who would do very well as Governor of Rhode Island. His sole wish in life – to be spared any trouble whatsoever – is one which he is unlikely to be granted, the times being what they are. But it cannot be denied that he has done far better by his subjects than many Italian sovereigns, and it is a measure of how exaggerated some reports of their discontent have been that he is able to appear in public protected by no more than a couple of lackeys and an ornamental cuirassier or two. As for the notorious Austrians, they were nowhere to be seen – having no doubt realised that whatever pleasure they might extract from the spectacle would hardly compensate for the twitting and the taunts they would have to endure.

After the horse guards, looking as operatic as such characters generally do south of the Alps, came another equipage enshrining the Grand-Duchess – a much more formidable proposition; one of the Neapolitan Bourbons of the grand old 'Let them eat cake!' stock – and then a long train of more or less decrepit carriages filled with the nobility of Florence.

I now suggested to Mr Grant that we might to advantage cross town and watch the *défilé* pass down Via Tornabuoni to the Piazza Santa Trinità, where the quality and the foreign community most thickly gather. Here, I hinted, my companion might take advantage of the licence of Carnival to play a prank or two upon some of his friends. We accordingly set off through the heart of the old city towards the river. The streets, as I had expected, were eerily deserted, their inhabitants having taken themselves off to enjoy the gratuitous entertainment.

I was more than a little worried about the time, but when I finally emerged in the Trinity square the procession – which makes a long detour by way of the Cathedral – was not yet in sight. I accordingly took a turn up and down the street, accompanied at a slight distance by my masked companion. I was recognised and hailed by a number of friends and acquaintances, and thus the time passed very agreeably. The only slightly discordant note was struck by the very large number of uniformed police to be seen about the square – a show of force which no one to whom I spoke seemed able to explain.

At length I fell in with a company which included Mr Hiram Powers and Dr Harding, a local physician. The conversation turned upon the terrible slaughter in the Crimea, where Harding has a son serving – this is indeed the modern way of sending our fellow-creatures to the next world, Prescott! A thousand here, a thousand there: a whole nation of the dead raised at one fell swoop. It makes the efforts of our murderer here in Florence seem as much of an anachronism as Cellini's salt-cellar beside the serried ranks of the standard Birmingham model!

Suddenly I caught sight of the slight figure of Commissioner Antonio Talenti moving slowly and watchfully through the crowd. I immediately extricated myself from the discussion on the war in the East, and went to greet him.

'Are you alone, Signor Boot?' the police official remarked, with that insinuating smile of his.

'No, I am with Mr Grant,' I replied, indicating the figure in motley who was busily jingling his bells at some attractive young ladies.

'And Mr Browning? Where is he today?' Talenti pursued.

'I have not the slightest idea, I am afraid. I have severed all connections with Mr Browning.'

The Commissioner gave me an appreciative glance.

'Really? You have done well, Signor Boot.'

'I trust that you are not expecting anything in the nature of a disturbance?' I asked the police official, who never ceased peering alertly this way and that the whole time we were talking.

'I received a note this morning, hinting that some attempt might be made to disrupt the Carnival as it passed along Via Tornabuoni,' he murmured. 'It is most likely a hoax, but I am bound to take every precaution.'

Since Talenti appeared to be in a confiding mood, I asked him if any further progress had been made in apprehending those responsible for the murder of Mr Tinker. But it appeared that the police were baffled, principally because of the apparent absence of any motive for the crime.

'Motive is what always traps the criminal in the end, Signor Boot!' the official told me. '*Cui bono*? as our ancestors put it. Find that out, and ten to one you have your man. But in this case there appears to be no answer to this question, and so for the moment we remain in the dark.'

While we had been talking the procession had come in sight at the end of the street, along which it proceeded towards us at crawling pace, at length rolling past to some rather desultory cheers. To the Commissioner's evident relief no incident occurred, and the crowd began to disperse to seek further diversion at one of the many public and private functions which enliven the final evening of the Carnival.

I looked around, but could not see the figure of the portly jester anywhere, although until then he had been as conspicuous as a circus elephant. Talenti had already taken his leave of me and was walking away, but I went after him and asked if he had noticed Mr Grant leaving; he had not. My companion seemed to have been there one moment and gone the next.

Then, suddenly, one of the constables came running up to Talenti and gabbled out some news so quickly that I could catch only two words. But that was enough, for the words were 'terrible' and 'murder'!

I was of course quite forgotten as the Commissioner barked orders at his men and ran off down an ancient street leading off into the slum quarters. I followed as fast as I could, but what with one thing and another it was five minutes before I caught sight of a knot of people huddled about the entrance to a little courtyard. I pushed my way forward, and by dint of much ruthless elbowing and peering over shoulders was able to make out what they were looking at.

The yard was occupied by a workshop where boats are brought from the nearby Arno to be repaired and recaulked. Several of these vessels lay about, together with a prodigious quantity of timber – and an enormous cauldron of pitch, with a fire of wood-shavings smouldering underneath it, on which all attention was fixed. Or rather not on the kettle itself, but on the pair of legs that were hanging over the side of it.

Two constables were endeavouring manfully, but without apparent success, to raise the remainder of the body out of the molten pitch in which it was entirely submerged. But neither I nor Commissioner Talenti – who was seemingly engaged in a heated altercation with one of the bystanders – needed any further clue as to the identity of the victim. Those dangling shanks told their own pathetic tale, clad as they were in tight-fitting gaily-coloured jester's motley.

Suddenly I heard my name called out – and realised in the same instant that the man quarrelling with Talenti was none other than Robert Browning.

'There he is!' cried Browning. 'God be praised – it is the man himself! Mr Booth, kindly explain to this overbearing official that you did indeed write me that letter! Come, all will soon be clear!'

Talenti motioned to me to come forward. Browning, I was told, claimed to have received a letter from me, urging him at all costs to meet me that afternoon just a few steps from where we were standing. It was for that reason that he had been at the spot where the police had arrrested him a few minutes before.

'Well, Signor Boot?' Talenti demanded. '*Did* you send this man such a letter?'

Browning was looking at me with the calm confidence of one who is about to be vindicated at last.

'I am sorry, Browning,' I said to him. 'I cannot continue to lie to the police.'

Then, turning to the Commissioner: 'I know nothing of any

letter, and certainly did not ask this man, or anyone else, to meet me here this afternoon.'

'That will do!' cried Talenti in a voice of triumph. And he directed his constables to take Browning away.

My former associate, for his part, shot me a look of infinite contempt.

'You will be sorry for this!' he hissed. 'Both of you!'

The formula was the same – deliberately so, I felt – as he had used to Beatrice. But while she had been in some doubt as to whether or not it had been meant as a threat, I was left in none whatsoever. I did not make any atttempt to respond, however, contenting myself with maintaining a dignified silence.

Of course, it was easier for me to be gracious, for it was not I who was being hauled off to the Bargello like a common criminal this time! On the contrary, if there is one person in Florence other than the Grand-Duke himself who is utterly above suspicion in this affair, then it is your correspondent. How could it be otherwise, when during the entire time from Grant's disappearance in Via Tornabuoni to the discovery of his corpse in the courtyard I was engaged in conversation with Police Commissioner Antonio Talenti himself! A finer alibi could not be wished for, I think.

Before leaving the scene, I could not help remarking the attention being given by spectators and police alike to an inscription in chalk upon the hull of a nearby wherry. It read:

⑧ BONTURO

I might of course leave you to puzzle this out yourself, but to save you hunting out your Dante let me remind you that Bonturo Dati of Lucca was the most notorious of the corrupt public officials who are punished in a lake of boiling pitch in the eighth circle of the *Inferno*. What this crime has to do with Mr Grant is by no means immediately clear – unless indeed there proves to be any substance in the rumour I have heard that his sojourn on the Continent was not undertaken entirely voluntarily, and that an air of scandal surrounds his period of office as an alderman in the City. But people love to talk ill of their neighbours, and we exiles more than most. On the other hand, he admitted cutting his claret with chianti, and a man who is capable of that is surely capable of anything.

For the rest, I need tell you only the two facts which have emerged in the hours since yesterday's tremendous events. First of all, most important, Mr Browning was released later the same day, after being questioned. There seems to be no evidence to connect him with the death of Mr Grant other than his having been found near the body. Were he an Italian, that might be enough, but as it is, not only must the letter of the law be observed, but all its dashes and dots as well. But truth, like murder, will out, and thus we live in daily expectation of some clamorous announcement.

The other snip of news is just that a second body was discovered soon afterwards, in an alley some distance away. At first this promised to shed new light upon Grant's death, but the victim has since proved to be one Giuseppe Petacco – a notorious ne'er-do-well who has been in police hands more than once. It is thought that he most likely met his death in some brawl or act of vengeance unconnected with the atrocious fate of poor Grant.

All may yet be well, as I said at the beginning of this letter, but I do not by any means deceive myself that the danger is past. Nor could I, while my relations with Beatrice continue to be as intimate as they are at present; for she in particular continues to be in a state of morbid anxiety, sure that some calamity is about to befall us. All my attempts to laugh or reason her out of this delusion are to no avail – so much so that I begin to think it may be best for us to leave Florence until this affair is over.

I have accordingly urged Beatrice to give up her post and go south with me – we could take a cottage on Capri or Ischia and live there as happily as Adam and Eve until the summer comes. But she, like a true Florentine, is loth to leave her native city. It is odd that I should care so – why do not I simply go myself, and leave her? That is what I ask myself, and find no answer. All I know is that I have not gone, and will not go without her. For myself, indeed, I scarcely care any longer, but if anything were to happen to this Italian girl I should never forgive myself. Is it not odd?

Yours ever most affectionately,

Booth

171

XXI

My dear, dear friend,

You cannot guess what pains it costs me to write. My muscles have all turned traitor, and my body become an Iron Maiden for the poor scrap of spirit which still unwillingly inhabits it – yet still worse is the *mental* effort, to remember what I have told you and what not, what you know and what you do not know – to say nothing of what you may have guessed. I am terribly afraid I may lose my grip on the story before I finish, at moments everything quivers and shimmers so. Was there not some philosopher – you will know who I mean – who held that the material world is only sustained by God's attention, and that if that failed for a split second the whole universe would start to curl at the edges, smouldering and shrivelling up like a sketch tossed on the fire?

But I *shall* finish – I must! This at least I shall achieve, though nothing else.

The week following Grant's death was like one of those great calms which sailors fear worse than the fiercest storm, when nothing stirs and the very air seems all to have been sucked away, leaving a breathless vacuum beneath which the ocean lies so flat and bland you fancy you could dance quadrilles on it. So it was that week. There was an oppressive absence of event: the police investigation once again came to nothing; Mr Browning made no attempt to make good his threats.

I had by now convinced Beatrice to leave Florence with me, but she would not quit her post without giving due notice; and while she worked out her time I lay abed, or on the sofa, or at the balcony door, dreaming of those azure depths, the rocky coves, wind-battered centenarian olives, the sky a flawless sheet of polished lapis-lazuli . . .

Every evening, when she returned, I ordered up supper from the *trattoria*: first some rounds of fire-charred bread rubbed raw with garlic, salt-sprinkled and drenched in olive oil as green and cloudy as glass on a beach; then a mess of hand-rolled noodles soaking up some rich dark sauce of hare and wild mushrooms; and then a chicken roast on a wood fire, and some fruit, and a flagon of wine.

And so time passed, until it was Friday the 3rd of March, and the last day of her service.

That evening I sat in the room at Via Dante Aligheri awaiting my mistress's return as usual. A bottle of champagne stood on the table beside a huge bouquet of flowers. I waited, and I waited. The wine grew warm, the flowers began to wilt, and still Beatrice did not come. At length, when ten o'clock sounded without any sign of her, I grew so anxious I could sit there no longer. It was unheard of for her to be so late.

My mind ran riot with unpleasant speculations, which I could do nothing to allay – it was of course out of the question for me to enquire of the family for whom she had been working. I nevertheless left the house and walked to where they lived, to see if I could catch any sight of her, half-hoping to meet her on the way. I knew not what I hoped, or feared – but in the event I saw nothing and nobody.

My next impulse was to return home, in case there might be some message for me there. As I hastened through the dark and empty streets my heart was full of evil forebodings, and I seemed to see the final look Browning had given me, and to hear him say, 'You'll be sorry for this – both of you!' That 'both' had puzzled me at the time – had he intended Talenti, who had been present, or Beatrice?

When I opened my front door I looked at once at the silver salver where Piero puts any letters which have been delivered in my absence. There was a long envelope there, bearing my name in a hand I recognised. I tore it open and scanned the contents in a flash. This, word for poisonous word, is what it said:

Dear Mr Booth,

I took the liberty of calling on you this evening, at an hour when I knew you would be from home, to discuss this brave New Life of yours. Your manservant was about to leave, but before doing so was good enough to let me in to await your return, which I gave him to understand was imminent.

I fear I misled him, though, for of course you were

wandering 'pensive as a pilgrim', as the bard has it: dreaming about everything save that which was under your nose (I quote from memory: consult the original for further details).

R.B.

I walked through to my living-room with this extraordinary composition in my hand – and stopped dead. Books, papers, clothes, and household articles of every description lay strewn about the floor in the most complete disorder. My first thought was that I had been the object of a burglar's attentions, until I caught sight of several valuable objects which should in that case have been taken. What then? A wanton explosion of destructive energy appeared to have reduced my home to a diabolic shambles, as completely and impartially as a bomb.

Then I remembered the letter. Browning claimed that my servant had left him alone in the suite – was this his revenge? That he sought revenge was no longer in doubt – that much, at least, I could understand from his cryptic letter. But was it credible that *this* childish tantrum was all a mind as cunning as his could dream up to torment me?

I picked up the letter once again. That it was crammed full of secret significance I did not for a moment doubt. That my future happiness, and quite possibly my survival, depended upon my understanding it was no less evident. *What did it all mean?*

I strode restlessly back and forth, picking my way between the volumes which lay singly, in piles, precarious heaps and fallen rows all over the floor, alternately picking up the malicious text and then throwing it down again in despair – a process I repeated half a hundred times as the night wore on.

The Dominicans' chimes had sounded two o'clock before I got my first glimpse of its hidden meanings. I had initially assumed that the phrase 'this brave New Life of yours' was a mocking echo of Miranda's naïve exclamation in Shakespeare's *Tempest*: 'O brave new world, that has such people in it!' The irony of *that* was evident, if Browning knew – as he presumably did – about my relations with his former mistress. But why 'Life' for 'world'? Why were only the two words capitalised? Why capitals at all, for that matter?

The truth came to me, as it will, in a flash. The 'New Life' of course referred to the collection of verses which Dante pub-

174

lished in celebration of Beatrice – the *Vita Nuova*. Having
understood that, it took me very little longer to recognise
'wandering pensive as a pilgrim' and the rest of it as the
paraphrase of the opening of the famous sonnet on the death of
Beatrice: *Deh peregrini che pensosi andate.*

On the death of Beatrice! A chill ran down my spine. 'Consult
the original for further details.' I ran to the case where I keep my
Italian classics – and gave out a howl of fury when I realised that
it too had been wrenched off the wall and the books hurled to all
four corners of the room. Like a beast, I scrabbled desperately
on all fours among the volumes which lay strewn about the floor,
seizing each in turn and flinging it away like the rubbish they all
were now – all except that one I sought, and could not find.

Dear God, I found everything else that night! Books I had
forgotten about, books I did not know I had, books I did not
know existed: everything from Browning's own *Sordello*, which
he had given me to make up for his gaffe at DeVere's funeral, to
a broadsheet singing the exploits of the Monster of Modena, a
berserk butcher who terrorised that Dukedom early last century,
turning his victims into the large spiced boiling sausages for
which the region is famous. Everything but Dante's posy for his
dead love!

At last I gave it up, staggered to the table, sat down and
poured myself a glass of brandy – and there was the volume I
had been seeking in vain, 'under my nose', as the letter had
fruitlessly hinted. Feverishly I snatched it up, hunting out the
sonnet in question. Ignoring a piece of paper which fluttered to
the table as I found the page, I skimmed the first twelve lines,
and found this: *Ell'ha perduta la sua beatrice.*

Now Dante meant by this that Florence had lost the person
who had made her blessed, the source of her beatitude (with a
quibble on Beatrice's name). There is, however, a simpler way
of reading the Italian, and it was this, I knew, that Browning had
intended: 'You have lost your Beatrice'. He had made away with
the poor girl – killed or kidnapped or God knew what! I was
beside myself with anger and remorse. Let him do his worst with
me, but why should *she* suffer, poor child?

Then I noticed the scrap of paper which had fallen to the
table when I found the correct page of the *Vita Nuova*. It had
writing on it, I saw, and picked it up, and read:

Since you have been kind enough to act as my guide through hell, I thought it only fair to treat you to a little tour of purgatory. You have been my Virgil. What shall I be to you?

I heard half past three strike, and still I sat there, my brain swarming with a hellish brew of thoughts and dreams all stirred up and simmering together, poring over the opaque message before me. 'You have been kind enough to act as my guide through hell'; 'You have been my Virgil'. That was clear enough – a reference to our joint investigation into the murders based on the *Inferno*. 'I thought it only fair to treat you to a little tour of purgatory'; 'What shall I be to you?'

Who had been Dante's guide in purgatory? In the *Inferno*, as every schoolboy knows, the poet was guided by the spirit of Virgil; in the *Paradiso* by that of Beatrice. But in the *Purgatorio*?

I had to find my copy of the *Divine Comedy* to answer this, and that cost me another three-quarters of an hour of frenzied searching through the ruins of my library – for this time it had not been conveniently left on the table for me. When I finally located it, however, I felt that my time had been well spent, for I discovered that Dante had been guided through purgatory by the most celebrated of the Italian troubadours – Sordello!

I could hardly be in any doubt what Browning intended me to do next: the reference was plainly to his long poem dedicated to this personage, which had been in my hands earlier. But my subsequent searches had created so much fresh disorder that it took me almost an hour to find it again; and when I had I realised that I had not the slightest idea what to do with it.

I picked the volume up by the spine and shook it – and out fell another piece of paper with some lines of writing on it. I gathered it up, and read:

> Speaking of your servant, are you still missing some of your personal possessions? I trust not. It might prove embarrassing if the police had to be informed. But no doubt you can locate them first. How about this, for example?

> Select your prey,
> Waiting (the ....-....... in the way
> Strewing this very bench)

At the scene of the last murder. You have until dusk tomorrow.

I read this through, at first, with a sense that Browning must have taken leave of his senses. The comment about my servant, in particular, seemed utterly nonsensical, for while Piero may be a vain unprepossessing little squirt, he has never presumed to try and steal so much as one of my fallen hairs. So what was Browning getting at?

'It might prove embarrassing if the police had to be informed. But no doubt you can locate them first.'

Then a very nasty suspicion peered over the rim of my mind, like the forelegs of a big blotchy spider crouched beneath the floorboards. A moment later it crawled boldly out and showed itself. *Browning had stolen some of my personal effects and hidden them at the scene of the murders in an attempt to incriminate me!*

I leapt up, already making for the door. Then I stopped in my tracks. What had he taken? Without knowing that I could not be sure I had recovered everything before the police were informed that evening – as the note clearly threatened.

Now I realised why my premises had been ransacked. It was precisely to prevent me taking a rapid inventory of my possessions and noting what was missing. Browning wished to force me to work it out the hard way: by solving the riddle written in the letter. Three lines of poetry, with a word left blank. Clearly the only solution was to identify the poem from which it had been taken, and read through it to find the missing word. But what was the poem?

With a shudder of horror I realised that it must be Browning's own *Sordello*!

Now I saw the whole game to which Browning was challenging me. To save myself from imminent arrest on the false evidence he had planted, I had to try and track down and recover each of the items in turn. To know what to look for I had to find the words missing from the quotation supplied. And to do that I had to read *Sordello*.

Do you realise what this meant? *Sordello* is the poem which all but destroyed Robert Browning's promising reputation overnight, and established him in the one he presently enjoys – of being the most tedious, pretentious and obscure poetaster in existence. If it had merely sunk into oblivion the case would not be so bad, but although barely one hundred and fifty copies have been sold, the poem is notorious and the stories concerning it are legion. One man thought his mind had gone because he could not understand two consecutive lines. Mr Carlyle – one of Browning's supporters, mind! – did not even trouble to read the piece, his wife having read it through without having any idea whether Sordello was a man, a city or a book. The present Poet Laureate, so his brother informed me when I mentioned the piece, claimed to have understood only the first and last lines, both of which, he said, were lies: 'Who will may hear Sordello's story told' and 'Who would has heard Sordello's story told'.

In short, the thing is a *bête noire*, a monstrous abortion of some six thousand lines, each both incomprehensible in itself and lacking any evident relationship to those immediately preceding and following it. And it was *this* which Browning was forcing me to read, literally to save my life – knowing full well that no lesser incentive would be sufficient. This was revenge, indeed!

But for all his cleverness, I might well have called his bluff, and gone to bed – had it not been for Beatrice. For myself I would have risked it, but I could not rest easy until I knew she was safe. To do that I had to find Browning, and I had no hopes of finding him at home. No, he would be hiding at the centre of this maze he had constructed for me, and to locate him I should have to find my way through it – of that I was convinced. And so I set to work.

Five o'clock rang as I leafed through the hateful volume, wondering where to start – hoping the pages might have been marked, or that my eye would magically light on the right passage. No such luck!

One thing, however, did soon occur to me. *Sordello* is divided into six Books, and six was the number of murders which had recently taken place in Florence. The note instructed me to start at the scene of the *last* murder, so might the quotation before me not prove to be from the last of the six Books?

It seemed worth starting there, at any rate. And so, eyes aching and brain awash, I began to pore over the bad print of that damned volume. When I had scanned all eight hundred and eighty-two lines of the final Book, I knew that unless I had been nodding somewhere – which was all too probable, and the fear of it was part of what made all that followed one long purgatory indeed – the lines in Browning's note did not appear in that section.

I was in despair – a furious raging despair, for Browning had out-thought me. But there was no time to lose: if the lines did not appear in the Sixth Book then they presumably appeared in the First; and there, sure enough, after reading another three hundred lines of meaningless rigmarole, I found what I was looking for:

> . . . select your prey,
> Waiting (the slaughter-weapons in the way
> Strewing this very bench) . . .

The slaughter-weapons! Hardly had I found the words than I had snatched up a lantern and my travelling-pistol, stuffed *Sordello* into my pocket, and was gone!

XXII

It was still pitch dark, and very cold. The streets were empty and every house tightly shuttered. I ran along the cobbles which were still greasy from the rain which had fallen earlier in the night – ran, and fell painfully, bruising my hip and almost shattering the lantern. Thereafter I continued at a more moderate pace into Via Tornabuoni and down towards the river. At the Trinity square I turned left, and in another minute was standing outside the boatyard where Grant's body had been found.

The gate was shut, and the lock – forced open by the murderer – had been replaced. But with some little difficulty I was able to climb over, lit my lantern and started to search. After spending half an hour at my task – shifting heavy balks of wood with a jeweller's care, to avoid making the slightest noise, fearing every minute that the watchman would take me – I had to admit defeat. If anything had been hidden in that courtyard, it had been done so well that I could not find it. But surely Browning could not have intended to make it so difficult, I thought. He must have meant to give me a fair chance at least, or where was his sport?

Then an intriguing thought occurred to me. The note had not spoken of Grant's murder, but of 'the last murder'. Now the *last* murder which had taken place, strictly speaking, was not that of Grant but of the ruffian Petacco. True, this was not supposed to have anything to do with the crimes we had been investigating, but it seemed worth at least having a look there.

The instant I stuck my lantern into the mews where the Italian had been found stabbed, I beheld a writing chalked up on the wall which told me, even before I looked any further, that I had found the place. It read:

> A poor gnome that, cloistered up
> In some rock-chamber with his agate cup

His topaz rod, his ....-....., in these few
And their arrangement finds enough to do.

A few seconds later I had found 'the slaughter-weapons' – a lead-weighted stick given to me by my father when I set out for Europe, with my name and address in Boston inscribed on a plate; and the other a knife on the Bowie pattern, with my initials engraved on the blade.

So far, so good; but what further tests lay ahead? Had I known, I think I might have turned that Bowie-blade against my own heart, and ended the torment then and there. How Robert Browning would have laughed to see me – huddled in the doorway of a slum tenement, an hour before dawn on a freezing winter's morning, straining my bleary eyes over his most arrant piece of incomprehensible nonsense by the light of a lantern, at the raw end of a sleepless night!

Well, I shall not make you live the horror with me – in the end I found the quotation, and knew the thing I sought was a seed-pearl, tiny and inconspicuous, mounted on a tie-pin. This was an ornament which I am given to wearing on important occasions, and many people in Florence would have been able to identify it as mine. I cursed Browning roundly in Italian and English as I picked my way through the old centre of Florence towards Via di Calimala, where Tinker died.

The old bakery was not difficult to identify, even in the dark, with its wooden buttresses built across the street outside to shore it up, and posters warning that the building was in a dangerous condition. But where to look for that confounded pin? I blundered about the ruin, scaring a pack of rats that seethed about the floor. I could make out Browning's inscription on the wall easily enough, but I did not trouble to read it yet: it would be time enough for that when I had found the pin.

In the end there was only one place left to look – the most obvious, logical, and dreadful. And there I saw the tiny gem, gleaming in the lamplight against the charred stones at the very back of the oven, far out of reach. There was no help for it – I would have to crawl in and retrieve it.

The horror of it, Prescott! For think – I had to enter that terrible cavity *head first*! There was barely enough room for my shoulders, and voices screamed in my head that I should get stuck, wedged there for ever; or that the building would collapse, as the notices threatened, pinning me there, my mouth full of Tinker's ashes, while the rats came to feast on me.

Well, I survived – but the man who crawled out of that hell-hole, pearl tie-pin in hand, was but a shadow of the one who had gone in two minutes earlier. Already Browning's devilish plan was working.

Upon the wall, by the light of my quivering lantern, I read the following:

> We watch construct,
> In short, an ......

The clues were getting shorter and more difficult, I noted sourly.

By now, though, despite everything, I felt I was ahead of the game. I had already solved two of the six riddles Browning had set me, and had the entire day to meet the challenge of the other four. For a moment I was even tempted to return home and sleep – sleep! How sweet the word sounded, lulling my ears with its insidious music.

But I soon saw how foolish this would be. After all, I had no notion of how much harder my task was likely to become. Would not my tormentor deliberately have made the first tests easier than those which came after, so as to encourage me to continue? Such, after all, is the essence of purgatory. In hell all hope must be abandoned, but is there not a kind of peace in that?

When my thoughts turned to the scene of the next crime – that ancient palace in the Borgo Pinti where the Chauncey sisters had used to receive spirits, and the faithful – I at once realised that this presented a problem quite different from any encountered so far. For Edith Chauncey had been murdered *inside* her home. How then had Browning been able to place any of my belongings at the scene? And how would I be able to get in to retrieve them?

First, at any rate, I had to know what I was looking for. I betook myself to a café which had just opened and flopped down at a table, drinking five coffees one after another in a vain attempt to sting my brain into some semblance of activity. Then

182

I settled down to read through another slab of the unspeakable *Sordello*.

People came and went – street-sweepers, market porters, servants on their way to work, travelling salesmen, soldiers, priests, layabouts and ruffians of every description. Sordello himself might have entered and sung a lay or two without attracting more than a casual glance from me. Eight hundred and forty lines were my lot this time, before I found that the missing word was the unhelpful 'engine'. The next ten lines made matters clearer: 'A kernel of strange wheelwork . . . grows into shape by quarters and by halves; remark this tooth's spring . . . ' Very good, Mr Browning, I thought – you have stolen my watch. I settled my bill and set out for the Chaunceys' home.

The door was opened to me by a strange girl, who very quickly apprised me of the fact that Miss Kate Chauncey no longer lived there, that a German family had moved in, that no Englishman had called recently, nor had any packets or parcels been delivered – and then shut the door ungently in my face.

I stood dumbfounded on the step. Was the game to break down so soon, then? Had Browning not foreseen this check? Perhaps he was not so clever after all.

I was on my way downstairs when the horrible thought struck me – and the rock-like building itself seemed to move as in an earthquake. I ran quickly upstairs again, past the floor where the Chaunceys used to live, up to the landing above. And there, scrawled in chalk upon the wall, I read the hateful message:

From the wet heap of .... where they burned.

In the corner stood a large earthenware pot, and inside this I found my half-hunter. I now knew that I had at all costs to go on to the very bitter end – and how bitter that end was bound to be.

I stalked the streets like a revenant till I saw a cab, and commanded the driver to take me to my destination with such a baleful glare he did not even haggle about the fare. Inside the musty vehicle I sat and tried to hold the book steady enough to hear another thousand lines of Sordello's dreary story told. But I would grow cunning, I thought: instead of wading through pages of dead verbiage to find the quotation, which usually seemed to be near the end, I would work my way back. But once again Browning had out-guessed me, unless it was just my bad luck. At all events, the line was but fourteen from the *beginning*, this time, and the word 'rubbish' – whatever that might mean. I seemed to hear Browning's sardonic laughter echo about me, as that day in the Boboli Gardens. I was very tired by now, and subject to mild hallucinations.

When I reached Purdy's villa I found that in this case there was not the slightest difficulty about gaining access to the property. The gate stood open, and I was able to walk in and look around to my heart's content. The snag was that there seemed to be nothing to be found: no inscription, no 'rubbish' – nothing. I searched for an hour or more in vain, and then at last sat down to rest my bones for a moment amid the fragrance of rosemary and thyme in the little herb garden on the sheltered south side of the villa.

I awoke, with a start, to find a dead man staring down at me. At first I thought I was dreaming, but then the corpse moved closer, growling fearfully, and I knew it was no dream. I crawled backwards, trying to distance myself from the thing. There was foam on its lips, I saw – and I knew it then for what had once been a man named Maurice Purdy.

Suddenly it sprang! I knew that death was on its mouth and in its touch. With an energy I did not know I possessed, I leapt clear of its attack and ran screaming from that place, and did not stop until I was out of sight of the villa.

That effort, and the terrible shock of seeing a man I had believed to be dead and buried – and very soon would be – standing there before me, utterly dissipated any beneficial effects of my long sleep. And it *had* been long, I discovered, for it was now past noon, and since my cabbie had long given me up I should have to walk the four miles back to Florence. And all without having recovered the object of my quest – or even knowing what it was.

As I trudged despondently along, I caught sight of some chalk writing on the low stone wall which bordered the lane, and the next moment read, with a thrill, this line:

As in his ...... she felt her tresses twitch.

Scattered all over the verge, I found scraps of paper, calling cards, letters, accounts from tradesmen, and such like stuff – each with my name figuring prominently. This, then, was the 'rubbish'. I gathered it all up and stuffed it into my pocket. It had of course been here, I realised, that Purdy's giant wolf-hound had been discovered the morning after the attack on its master, stretched lifeless beside the road with its brains blown out.

As I continued my forced march back to Florence, more than one innocent peasant who saw me striding along – dishevelled, wide-eyed, an open volume of verse clutched in my hands – no doubt thought that he had seen a mad poet. 'Mad perhaps, but no poet!' I felt like shouting. 'Spare me that, at least!'

Meanwhile *Sordello* drummed inexorably into my brain, five steps to each line of that damned pentameter, until I thought I would go deaf or crazy or both. But in the end I found the line, and knew it was a pair of gloves I had to try and recover from Cecil DeVere's apartment.

The bells were striking half-past two when I finally reached the cypress-shaded mound to which most of those on whom I was presently calling had moved, and passed through the Porta a' Pinti and back within the walls of Florence. My legs were aching fiercely, but I had to keep up my relentless pace as far as the Cathedral, where I found a cab at last, and drove the rest of the way to the Borgo San Jacopo.

By applying to the porter's lodge, I soon discovered that DeVere's suite had not yet been re-let, and on representing myself as interested in taking it I was able to have myself shown around the premises. A sad sight they were, now that all their late occupier's possessions had been crated and shipped back to his family home: bare plaster walls, a few lost-looking pieces of furniture, the floor one gleaming bleak expanse of marble. For the first time I was struck by the melancholy of murder – not the thrills and horror of the hunt, but just the dreary reality of empty homes, of grief, and a way of life destroyed.

As soon as the porter showed me out on to the terrace I saw what I was looking for: the chamois pair with my initials stitched on a tag inside the wrist, draped over the newly-repaired railing at the very spot where DeVere had fallen to his death. Unfortunately the porter had seen them too.

'Ah, the gentleman who came this morning has forgotten his gloves!' he cried. 'I will keep them until he returns for them.'

I had to think quickly.

'I know the man! He is a friend of mine. He came to look the premises over for me – it is on his recommendation that I have come. I shall take the gloves and give them to him this evening at dinner.'

I added a brief description of Browning, which convinced the porter that I was speaking the truth, took possession of the gloves, and left.

It was by now the dead slack part of the afternoon, and I might have known that it would prove impossible to find a cab to take me up to Bellosguardo. Nevertheless I stood waiting for almost half an hour in the sun opposite the axe-like wedge of the Palazzo Guidi, trying to force my eyes to follow my shaking finger across page after page of Book the Sixth of *Sordello*: A Poem in Six Books; by Robert Browning Esq.; London: Edward Moxon & Son, 172, Fleet St; 9, Capel St, Dublin; & Derby MDCCCXL (his dad paid the costs, he told me) in search of the teasing reference I had found neatly penned on a slip of paper inserted into the right hand glove:

Quench thirst at this, then seek next ....-......

When at length I found the missing word it was like a needle through my heart, confirming all my fears. But at least I had done with Browning's damned drivel for ever – and with a great hoot of glee kicked the volume like a punctured football about the courtyard of the Pitti Palace, till I woke the guard, who shouted at me to desist. Then I set off almost at a run through the slums of the Oltrarno round the Santo Spirito and Carmine churches, towards the San Frediano gate.

As I passed down a narrow street near the latter church, I heard an unearthly wailing, and the strange chant of many voices united in a barbaric rhythm, and the next moment six tall figures masked in black appeared, their faces hidden, trailing sable robes behind them and carrying a heavily draped coffin. I staggered back into a doorway and covered my eyes to keep the awful spectacle away – although I knew very well it was only the Fraternity of the Misericordia on their way to bury some pauper.

Yet I felt that it was also a bad omen, and wished I knew some spell to keep its baneful breath at bay.

Long, hard, steep and hot was the lane that winds up to the pleasant villas of Bellosguardo that day; still and silent as a tomb between the high stone walls which seemed to shimmer like veils in the heat. Four o'clock struck from a church somewhere as I neared the massive iron gates at the front of the villa, which I found ostentatiously locked with a length of heavy chain secured with several padlocks. I hardly paused in my step, but turned down the lane which skirts the villa to the north. The garden gate was also locked, but I soon found the key in its niche where lizards sport in summer, and let myself in.

The word I had finally found in the last Book of *Sordello* had been 'well-spring'. This had puzzled me at first, for the words thus far had named the objects I had to seek, while this referred to a place. I knew it, though, and made my way without delay through the scattered trees and shrubbery of the wilderness at the end of the garden, across a lawn bordered by flowerbeds, and around the screen of box hedging to the corner where the well was to be found.

I peered down into the dank depths, without being able to make out anything of interest other than the fact that the mouldy green rope hung limp, the bucket which normally hung from it having been removed. Then, without the slightest warning, my ankles were grasped and raised and my whole body tipped forward and held helplessly poised above those horrid depths!

Of all the shocks I had sustained so far that day this was by far the worst – I seemed to hang there like a man above the gallows-trap, with the noose about his neck. Oh, I fought, of course – just as those about to be hanged do. I kicked, I screamed, I struggled – but all along I knew that if my assailant chose to tip me forward, head first down that narrow stone chute into the water far below, then I was doomed!

How long I remained thus I know not – merciful time had been abolished, as it is in hell. Then I was hauled up again, and released, and fell to the ground. I already knew, of course, who I would find standing there behind me.

XXIII

'Please forgive me!' cried Browning, with a slightly hysterical laugh. 'How often we used to play such pranks at Eton! Such jolly fun! Of course it would sometimes go too far. One fellow fell thirty feet into the quad. Landed on his head, luckily, so it didn't do him any harm. He's an eminent member of the Cabinet now.'

'You were never at Eton,' I returned coldly, when I could trust myself to speak. 'You told me you had a private tutor.'

'Did I? Did I? Well, well – I must have imagined it all. But why waste time here in one of the least conspicuous and attractive parts of the garden, when from the belvedere we may enjoy the fabled view as the sun sets? It is this way – but of course you know that!'

Thus burbling, thus chirruping, Browning led the way across the garden. It occurs to me now that I might have blown his head off there and then. But there was something so irresistibly easy and unsuspicious about his manner – whoever would have thought that such a man intended any harm?

The sun was by now low in the sky, bathing the fluted columns of the Classical summer-house in a warm pink glow. Before us stretched the famous prospect over the Arno valley, where little Florence lies dense and compact within its walls amid the isolated farmsteads and winding tracks of the plain. The belvedere itself was completely bare of furniture at that season – a mere empty shell. The only extraneous object stood near the foot of one of the columns. It was a large bucket, brim full of water; the well-bucket, in fact. For a moment I felt a stab of alarm. But what possible threat could a bucket of water, of all things, pose?

Browning turned to me.

'Do you know why I have brought you here?' he asked. 'It is to hear my confession, before I do away with my worthless self. I have sinned greatly, Booth. I killed them all, of course. I admit it. That's why I did not want the police involved. Yes, I duped you cruelly in more ways than one, I fear. I am the murderer we have sought for so long! Not only that – my poems are all written by my wife! I am a nothing! Worse than nothing: a dream, a nightmare . . .'

No, of course he did not say that. He did not say anything at all, in fact, but just stood there admiring the view, for all the world like a man without a thought on his mind or a care in the world.

'Where is Beatrice?' I demanded at last.

'She is in a safe place, in good hands.'

'What have you done with her?'

'She is in the keeping of the sisters of the convent of Santa Maria Maddalena delle Convertite at Pistoia. They make a speciality of caring for fallen women.'

'You sanctimonious bastard!'

I reached into my pocket – and Browning threw himself at me, like a football player. Taken utterly by surprise, I fell awkwardly, hurting the hip I had already bruised that morning and striking my head on the base of one of the pillars of the belvedere.

I have no notion how long I lay there on the marble, dazed from the blow. Then something struck me like a whiplash, and I sat up to find myself drenched in cold water. Browning stood over me, carefully shaking the last drops out of the bucket he had just emptied all over my recumbent form.

He produced a large revolver from his coat pocket.

'I have this from Powers,' he explained. 'He is under the impression that I wish to shoot rabbits with it. I did not disabuse him, although I should not dream of doing anything of the sort. He mentioned that it was the product of a certain Colonel Cold or Colt – the name means nothing to me, but may perhaps to you. Apparently the shells it emits, being of an unsually large calibre, inflict such extensive damage to anything they strike that even a glancing wound is quite likely to prove fatal. I therefore advise you to make no rash movements.'

I listened in silence. The water ran down my neck and throat in little rivulets, and was soaking through the clothing on my chest and side, where it had already penetrated to the skin in several places.

'Put your hand into your pocket and empty out everything in it,' Browning went on. I did so, and my travelling-pistol fell to the floor with a clatter. Browning directed me to push it across towards him, and he picked it up and pocketed it.

'As I was saying,' he continued discursively, 'Beatrice is in very good hands. It is true that she was somewhat unwilling to see reason at first. But when it was made clear to her that she had a choice between the convent and the police she came quietly enough.'

'She has committed no crime,' I croaked.

'What!' cried Browning. 'A girl of nineteen who lies to her family, runs away from home, and allows herself to be maintained by a man – and a foreigner, at that! She would have been gaoled for five years at least. The convent is no luxury hotel, it is true, but it is a great deal better than a cell in the Murate.'

'You blackguard!' I spat out.

'I – a blackguard!' he replied indignantly. '*I* did not seduce the poor child! All I wished to do was to save her from abuse at the hands of her unspeakable father! This I did – and was scrupulously careful always to treat her with the greatest possible respect. It was *you* who brought about her ruin, Booth. You!'

'She loved me! She told me so!'

'Then you are the more culpable, in having exploited her tender emotions in order to gratify your own vile cravings.'

'They were *her* cravings too.'

'Enough!' he almost screamed. 'Do not provoke me with any more of these filthy insinuations! I will not be responsible for my actions! Why should I listen to your putrid drivel? You – who destroyed the purest and loveliest friendship of my life! You – who turned that sweet girl-child against me! You . . . You . . . '

Browning had been getting more and more excited as we spoke, until he burst out in one of those paroxysms of rage to which he is notoriously liable whenever one of his pet bugbears – spiritualism, or loose morals – is mentioned. Now, in the course of an expansive gesture illustrative of his utter contempt for me, the heavy revolver which he was holding slipped from his hand and went flying through the air. It struck a column, chipping the stone, and deflected to crash to the floor within easy reach of my hand.

For a moment neither of us moved, so stunningly sudden had been this reversal of fortunes. Then I quickly bent to grasp the weapon, and turned it on my adversary – who was staring at it in absolute horror, as though he had just witnessed something impossible.

Slowly, painfully, carefully, I got to my knees, and then stood up.

'So, Mr Browning! "God's in His heaven and all's right with the world", eh? Are you still so very sure of that? No second thoughts? All's still for the best, is it?'

To do him justice, he returned my stare unflinchingly.

'You have the advantage now, Mr Booth,' he replied. 'Very well – use it! Add me to your list of victims. But do not presume to mock my beliefs.'

'Ah, so you *had* guessed my little secret! I thought so. You should not have put my knife and life-preserver on Petacco's body, or my watch on the wrong landing – that rather gave the game away.'

'On the contrary,' replied Browning, with a contemptuous laugh, 'that was the whole point! You haven't been so clever after all – only lucky. My "game", as you call it, was a test, carefully calculated to appeal to a mind like yours, to prove that my suspicions about you were correct. Who but the murderer would have thought of looking for his murder weapons at the spot where his accomplice got his reward – the accomplice who had sported in jester's motley on Via Tornabuoni to give you the perfect alibi while the real Grant lay already dead in the vat of pitch? I checked with the shop that made up Grant's costume, and they confirmed that a man answering your description had ordered an identical one in a slightly different size that same afternoon.

'Who but Edith Chauncey's killer would dream of looking for his watch on the landing *above* her suite – the landing where he had hidden while the maid ran for help that morning? Since no one could have got into the suite that night I knew the murderer must have been there all along – and who more likely than the man who left first, his departure almost unnoticed by the others?

'But the clinching proof was the third – have you noticed how everything in this affair seems to go by threes? I wonder how many visitors to this villa have any notion of the existence of a well in the garden, let alone its exact location. But *you* knew, just as you knew where to find the key which opens the garden gate. And that proved what I suspected: that you were Isabel Eakin's secret lover, who murdered her on this spot one month ago, and then wet the body with water from the well – which is where you found the rope too, of course – to make it seem your mistress had died hours before, while it was still light and you were dining with Mr Jarves.'

'She was *your* mistress too, God rot you!' I cried furiously. 'Talenti told me everything!'

'Then he told you nothing but the lies I made up on the spot to conceal my friendship with Beatrice, which I feared might have been misconstrued and rebounded on her, poor child. *That* was why she summoned me here that night, you fool! I never knew Isabel Eakin – never met her or her husband!'

'That's not what Talenti believes, and *he* is no fool!'

'He may not have been a fool,' Browning retorted, 'but he allowed his hatred of me – a hatred I do not know what I had done to deserve – to blind him to the truth.'

'Why do you speak of him in the past? Is he dead?'

'In a sense. Certain of my friends here, appalled by his treatment of me, made representations to the Grand Duke. As a result, Commissioner Talenti has been transferred to Grosseto.'

It was brave humour, I was forced to admit, from a man facing his own imminent death. The sun had now disappeared below the edge of the hill behind us, and the air was getting chillier every moment. The water had by now completely penetrated my clothing, and unless I got warm and dry very quickly I greatly feared that the result would be a fever.

'You seem to have won all the battles so far, Mr Browning,' I muttered, grasping the revolver in both hands. 'Too bad you are going to lose the war. Why did you pour this damned water over me, anyway?'

Browning suddenly looked weary, old and frightened. I think he had just realised for the first time that he was about to die. 'What does it matter?' he murmured, and I was glad to see that his voice trembled.

I should have liked to prolong his torment, but there was no time to lose. I steadied the butt of the gun in both hands, as we were taught in the militia, and began to pull the trigger.

It moved about a quarter of an inch, and then stopped.

'Go on, then!' Browning shouted. 'Fire, damn you!'

'I assure you that I am most earnestly endeavouring to do so!'

I was now openly wrestling with the trigger, which had evidently been damaged when the revolver fell.

Browning smiled – horribly! – and put his hand into his pocket, and took out my travelling-pistol, and aimed it at me.

'I'll warrant this one works, though!' he crowed.

My whole life seemed to swim before my eyes in that instant – a life of disappointments, of bad luck, and of hopes raised only the more ruthlessly to be crushed – and in a fit of sheer misery, frustration and despair I hurled my useless weapon to the ground.

There was a deafening report. Something whizzed through the air between Browning and me, and the revolver shot off across the marble floor under the impulse of its own recoil, fetching up under a bush in the garden. Frightened fowl rose into the dusk, squawking madly.

'Well!' said Browning, when the silence of the evening had settled once again, 'I think it is high time to bring this reciprocal demonstration of incompetence to an end, and leave you to face the verdict of One who does not err. Before we part – for ever, in all probability – please answer just one question. *Why*, Booth? In God's name, *why*?'

I hardly heard the question, for what Browning had said before had struck a chill, more piercing than any I had felt yet, clean through my sodden garments and shivering flesh to the very innermost core of my being. After scrutinising me in silence for a long time, Browning finally shrugged his shoulders.

'If you will not speak, I cannot make you do so. Let me make it clear, however, that you have nothing to gain by your silence: you are going to die in any case, that much is virtually certain. In a few moments I shall leave, as I arrived, by the garden gate – the owners very kindly provided a key for an anonymous foreign visitor who wished to admire the celebrated view from the belvedere. That reminds me, by the way – you had best give me the key *you* used to get in.'

I tossed a heavy metal key at Browning's feet. He gathered it up.

'All exits from the grounds are securely locked, as is the villa itself, and the lodge-keeper is away until tomorrow visiting his son-in-law in the city. The night threatens to be clear and very cold – yet you apparently plan to spend it out of doors, and in wet clothing too! Most unwise, Mr Booth!'

'What about your Christian mercy and forgiveness?' I cried. 'I am penitent, truly penitent! I have begun a new life, as you jested in your note. I will go away – anything – only let me live! Sweet Christ, do not murder me!'

'Very touching, Mr Booth. I wish I could believe you. But it would make no difference. Since you once feigned an interest in my work, you will perhaps permit me to quote from one of my plays: "It is because I avow myself a very worm, sinful beyond measure, that I reject what you ask. Shall I proceed a-pardoning – I who have no symptom of reason to assume that aught less than my strenuousest efforts will keep *myself* out of mortal sin, much less keep others out? No – I do trespass, but I will not double that by allowing you to trespass." '

'God rot you and your work, you hypocritical scab! I hope your wife dies in agony this very night!'

Well, *that* got home! Indeed, I had almost overplayed my hand – for a moment I was afraid he would shoot me in cold blood. But in the end he contented himself with spitting saliva rather than lead, turned on his heel and walked off without another word.

The sound of his footsteps receded, ever more faintly, through the garden. A distant gate opened, closed, and was locked.

XXIV

I hurried down the steps of the belvedere as fast as my shaking limbs would carry me. The garden was quite silent and almost completely dark. I scurried along the path like a dead man issued from his grave.

A reciprocal demonstration of incompetence, was it? Not *quite* reciprocal, I thought. I had achieved my first aim, at least – to get Browning so worked up that he did not think to try the key I had given him in the lock of the garden gate. If he had, he would have found that it did not fit, for the simple reason that the one that *did* was still in my pocket.

I opened the gate cautiously and stepped out into the lane, a free man. Scrambling over the low wall opposite, I dropped into the field which adjoins the lane and started down the steep slope as fast as I could. Browning's natural route home was by the same road as I had taken that afternoon, which curves around the hillsides to the church of San Francesco di Paola lying somewhere in the darkness below me. By cutting across the field I could reach the church before him and be lurking there in its shadow when he passed, my Bowie-knife at the ready. Then we would see who was incompetent.

One thing was clear – Browning had told no one of his suspicions, which were in any case no more than that. So when the poet's body was found in a lonely lane outside the city walls – minus watch, pocket-book, cufflinks and wedding ring – the crime would be ascribed to some footpad. 'Poor Mr Browning!' people would say. 'He *would* go for those long walks alone at night. We always did think it rather imprudent.'

Only Talenti knew enough to have suspected something, and thanks to Browning and his influential friends Talenti had been exiled to the malarial swamps of the Maremma! It all seemed deliciously ironical.

But first I had to reach the church before my enemy, who was a notoriously fast walker. The hillside was very steep, and cultivated in the traditional Tuscan manner, with rows of vines strung between olive trees running across the slope. I was therefore forced to follow one row of vines right across the field to the far edge, and then run straight downhill as fast as I dared. The moon had not yet risen, and it was a wild and perilous course I ran, falling half a dozen times, but always leaping to my feet again, eager to continue.

I had completed well over half the distance when I tripped on an olive branch, went flying forward, and fell heavily on my left ankle, which turned over. Even then I did not give up, but hobbled on somehow, supporting myself on the branch which had tripped me. But to no avail. Twice, three times I passed out from the intense pain – and when I came to the last time I heard eight o'clock chiming from the church I had hoped to reach. I had been unconscious for several hours, and Browning had long reached the safety of his home. All my hopes were dead, and I seemed destined to join them very shortly.

I shall not attempt to describe that night. Dante's poem is a work of genius, but no one can read it now as he meant it to be read – as a Baedecker to hell. How luxuriously his damned souls seem to us to suffer, mangled by ingenious cosmic machinery, designed expressly to inflict the specific punishment prescribed for their sin, no expense spared! One might write a very different account of *our* hell – but no one would wish to read it, any more than you would wish to read about the night I spent shivering uncontrollably in that naked ditch beneath the bright, distant, indifferent stars.

As I lay there I thought over Browning's final question to me: why? And I bitterly regretted not having told him to his face that the fault was all *his*. For Isabel's death is the only crime I take upon myself, and that was a *crime passionnel* if ever there was such a thing!

Ah Prescott, what a joyful turbulence possessed my soul when I saw her again that summer day at Bagni di Lucca! How my heart cried out in mingled agony and joy, like a healed lung which starts to breathe again after years of clogged suffocation! I waxed sentimental; she was kind. I became bolder; she smiled. I made love to her; she encouraged me. What bliss!

It could not last, of course. Her idle spoilt passions changed as quickly as they came, and before long I was made aware that a rival had supplanted me in her affections. I had no idea that it was DeVere – she might be still living if I had, for contempt would surely have quenched every other emotion. But I thought she had thrown me over for some great figure from our Florentine Pantheon; for someone like Browning, in fact!

I had drunk heavily that Sunday at Jarves's, and when I reached the villa at dusk I was in an ugly temper. Isabel was waiting for me in the large salon, softly lit by lamplight. She was in a dumpish mood; she said she wanted to return to America – she was sick of Florence, sick of Italy, sick of Europe. What? I cried – and leave *me*?

All my smouldering resentment burst into flame. I flung accusations at her wildly, not caring what I said so long as it hurt. I called her faithless, vile, impure; she responded in like manner, laughing in my face and calling me a bumptious empty failure, a creeping conceited nothing unworthy to lick her husband's boots. In the end I could not endure her frightful voice a moment longer, and so I put my hands around that squawking throat, and silenced it.

Forgive me for not telling you all this before now, my friend, but it would not have done, would it? I have at least told you nothing *untrue* – and I am sure I have hidden the truth away somewhere, despite myself, in a description of a street-scene or something of the sort.

So Isabel was dead. Very well – but I did not intend to swing for her, after those things she had said. No, instead she should swing for me! It took very little time to think it out. I fetched rope and water from the well, carried the table over, and strung her up. No one had seen me come, and no one saw me go – and if Browning had not stuck his interfering snout in where it had no earthly business to be, the whole unseemly matter would have been passed over in a decent silence, and all the innocent people who have died since would be alive and well today. That being so I think I can justly say that it is on his shoulders, not on mine, that the responsibility for their deaths ultimately rests. *I fail to see how any impartial person can possibly deny that.*

When I found that my charade had been exposed, I at first hoped to avoid any further unpleasantness by leaving that knife engraved with Eakin's name in the garden on my way to Siena.

With his alibi that scheme went for nothing, but when DeVere asked me what I had been doing in the garden that morning, I realised that he would do very well as my scapegoat. I went to see him that evening, and applied a heavy seventeenth-century silver candlestick – over whose acquisition he had invited me to exult with him – to the base of his skull. When I discovered later that it was *he* who had been Isabel's latest attachment justice seemed doubly served.

Then that Saturday, at DeVere's inhumation, came the terrible and decisive shock of realising that my new 'friend' Browning was treating me just as Isabel had – as a plaything to pick up and throw down as the whim took him. Was I so boring, then? Well, I would make myself interesting!

That Sunday, as I lay around my flat, I picked up the *Divine Comedy*. The volume happened to fall open at the Argenti episode in Canto VIII, and I was struck with the resemblance to the discovery of DeVere's body in the Arno that morning – the more striking given the similarity in their characters.

I toyed idly with the idea, purely as an abstract notion at first. What about Isabel? At once the famous description of Francesca da Rimini and her lover, eternally restless and wind-whipped, suggested itself. Isabel, then, would be punished as Lustful – as was just. Not that she was a raging Messalina in her desires – on the contrary! But she *was* a prey to her shallow passions, as Dante intended: someone vain, light, inconstant, worthless. My idea appeared more satisfactory the longer I thought about it. Yes, I would make myself interesting all right – *and* divert suspicion from myself for Isabel's death for ever.

The remainder of the weekend I spent planning the attack on Maurice Purdy, and on the Monday I returned to the inn where I had eaten on my way to Siena. Posing as a doctor studying hydrophobia, I bought the mad dog I had observed there and carted it in a wicker basket to Fiesole, and then after dark to Purdy's villa. Here I put a bullet through the wolfhound's brain, scribbled the Dante reference up on the wall and released the rabid beast to greet Mr Purdy on his return from feeding with his fat friends.

I would have been content to stop there. What happened at the Chaunceys' was totally unpremeditated – the spirtualist's hocus-pocus so convinced me that I decided that she had to be silenced that very night, before Isabel or DeVere could use her powers to take revenge on me from beyond the grave. Instead of going to the front door when I left, I therefore hid in a little glory-hole used to store cleaning utensils. In the middle of the night I crept out, and smothered the old lady first with a pillow, to avoid using violence to a woman – a thing I deplore. I then dislocated her neck, and arranged the corpse at the foot of the stairs with a suitable inscription clasped in its hand. In the morning, when the maid went off for help, I slipped out of the apartment and up the stairs to the next landing, where I waited until she had returned and the door was shut again before going home – only to be awakened a few hours later by the police, which I can assure you was a very unpleasant shock.

At the Bargello I learned that all my pains – and it was no joy sitting there on a cold hard stone floor, knowing that if anything went wrong I was caught like a rat in a trap – had been wasted: Miss Chauncey had been a harmless fraud. But I was in up to my neck now, and my only thought was to keep my head above water. So when Tinker let me know that he had fathomed my secret I had no choice but to get out my well-thumbed copy of Dante again.

I willingly admit that I underestimated the 'Reverend' Tinker. Because the man was a patent confidence-trickster, I marked him down as a fool – but I was mistaken. He was the second person to leave the Chaunceys' that night, so when he reached the front door and found it still locked and bolted for the 'séance', he was puzzled. When he heard about the mysterious death of the 'medium', he put two and two together with remarkable celerity. This was the limit of his cleverness, however; for instead of informing the police – which would have been the end of me – he gave me a few days to think that I had got away with it, and then called to see me and explained frankly what he knew, what he had guessed, and what he wanted. The answer was cash, in quite considerable amounts.

I agreed, of course – what else could I do? But I told him it would take a little time to have the sum he requested sent from America. He made no objection to this, and we parted very amicably. Tinker therefore had no particular reason for suspicion when he received a note the following evening from a very attractive lady whom I knew he had met shortly before. She had been 'deeply impressed', she said, with his 'forceful and fascinating personality', and urged him to come to her that evening at an address in Via Calimala and relieve the spiritual crisis which was so sorely tormenting her. Tinker was no fool, as I have said, but we all have our weak spot; mine is Literature, his was the fair sex. And so he came, and I was waiting for him, the oven already nicely glowing.

By now I had discovered the truth about Browning's relations with Beatrice, and my interest in him was at an end. It was moreover becoming urgent to escape from the juggernaut I had set rolling before it crushed me. For this, one further victim was required; and after mature consideration I chose Mr Grant.

His death was my masterpiece, if I do say so myself. It was worked with a double, of course, as Browning finally realised. Petacco had been the porter at one of my previous dwellings in Florence; I looked him up, explained that I wished to play a Carnival prank on some friends, and offered him a coin of a value he had not seen for some time if he would assist me. He agreed readily enough to dress up in the costume I gave him and to wait for me in an alley behind Piazza Santa Trinitá.

Having got Grant more than slightly inebriated, it was no problem to lead him into the boatyard, knock him down with my lead-weighted stick and tip his body into the cauldron of pitch. I then proceeded to the alley where Petacco was awaiting my arrival and we then made ourselves as conspicuous as possible in the Trinity square. As I had hoped, Talenti was there – I had sent him an anonymous threat in hopes of bringing him in person to secure my alibi – and I made sure we stayed together until Grant's death had been reported, after which I hurried to the alley where Petacco was waiting to be paid. Having used the Bowie-knife on him, I stripped off his Carnival glad rags, which I threw down a sewer on my way to the scene of Grant's death. The letter to Mr Browning had been very much a shot in the dark, and I was delighted to find that it succeeded better than I had dared hope. I thought it a particularly fine touch to sign the counterfeit with my *own* name!

And it all worked perfectly – except that Browning, with his accursed shopkeeper's fascination with petty facts and dreary details, somehow found me out. But how much more a poet, how much greater an artist, am I! The bold conception, the reach, the range – these are mine, and mine alone. But such things count for nothing in this world, and so he wins.

Or rather, does not win! For though I should have died that night, I did not. In the morning I was awakened by a dog which barked over me until its master, an old peasant, came to see what was the matter. He fetched his son, and the two of them laid me on a ladder and carried me to the farm, where I was washed and put to bed by the woman of the house.

For the next week or so I lay in the grip of the most tremendous fever, which set my lungs aflame worse than they have ever been. By the time it subsided, the tell-tale clots of bright red had begun to appear in the matter I coughed up, and I gave myself up for lost. The peasant's wife, however, forced me to drink certain foul-tasting infusions, which miraculously cured me. What they contained I have no idea – and would rather not know! – but in due course I was able to sit up in bed and take solid nourishment, and within a week or two I was not just well again, but feeling younger and more alive than I have for twenty years or more! Once I had recovered fully I slipped away to the place from which I presently write, on the coast, at the edge of a line of high cliffs, overlooking the sea.

I spend my days peacefully planning my future. With so much time before me, and my youth and health completely restored, my only problem is *which* future to choose! Meanwhile I lie gazing down at the waves breaking on the rocks far below, and the limitless expanse of open ocean stretching away to the horizon, and beyond.

This may well be the last letter you will ever receive from me, my dear friend. For who knows how reliable the postal facilities may prove to be in those lands for which I am bound? At all events, I have little more to say, except that . . .

XXV

Piazza S Maria Novella 23
Florence
Tuscany
March 11th 1855

Dear Sir,

Although Mr Booth did not directly instruct me to do so, I have no hesitation in forwarding the enclosed letter to the person for whom it was evidently destined. I say this without having glanced at its contents; my reason being simply that owing to his poor health I have carried all Mr Booth's mail to the Post Office this last six months, and with one exception, of a commercial nature, it was all addressed to you.

Your name was familiar to me from my conversations with Mr Booth. He was extremely proud of his friendship with you, and displayed to me on more than one occasion his signed copy of your work on Theoretical and Practical Ethics. I am conscious that I have the advantage of you here, for there is no reason to suppose that Mr Booth has ever mentioned my name in his letters. Nor have I any wish to bring myself to your attention now; if I now take the liberty of doing so, it is solely in order to explain why it has fallen to my lot to break these painful tidings to you.

As you must know, Mr Booth's health had been steadily deteriorating for some considerable time; indeed, the pulmonary consumption from which he suffered was, I understand, diagnosed before he left America. While the progress of the disease was to some extent retarded, and its effects mitigated, by the favourable climate here, the outcome was never in the slightest doubt.

Mr Booth and I had been neighbours for several years, but lacking an occasion to speak, we remained strangers until my cat found her way into Mr Booth's suite on the floor below mine one day last year. This trivial event gave rise to an acquaintance which gradually ripened into something like friendship as we came to know each other better – and as Mr Booth's failing strength caused him to depend more and more upon my assistance.

Although it was only in the last few months that he became completely bed-ridden, he scarcely ever went out, and never received company, even during the period when this remained a possibility for him, preferring to immerse himself in his beloved books. I doubt whether he knew half a dozen people here, all told. It must be said, indeed, with all due respect, that he could be a difficult man. I do not believe that I am abnormally sensitive, but on more than one occasion I have been sorely tempted to break off our relations, so deliberately offensive and wounding have I felt his behaviour to be. This is the more puzzling, in that he was extremely touchy and proud himself. If in the end I always relented, it was simply because I could not bear the thought of him sitting all alone downstairs, knowing he was dying.

It often happens that chronic maladies appear to take a turn for the better shortly before they run their course; such was the case with Mr Booth's. This illusory improvement coincided with, and may even have been occasioned by, the arrival in Florence of Mr Joseph Eakin, the Philadelphia steel magnate. He and his wife were very much the talk of the town last season, and their comings and goings were reported in all the prints. Very much to my surprise, Mr Booth intimated that he knew one or both of these persons, whose social orbit nevertheless appeared so very different from his own. When I enquired why in that case he had not been to call on them, he replied that he would do so directly his health had improved further – for he still cherished hopes of a complete recovery.

But that day unfortunately never arrived. The young Mrs Eakin succumbed to a fever, and shortly afterwards Mr Booth's own health went into a rapid and irreversible decline, and from that moment on he was confined entirely to his room. An Italian girl was hired to nurse him, while I myself called upon him several times each day.

Late last night I heard him coughing and moaning aloud in a way that greatly distressed me; I therefore dressed and went to see if I could assist in any way. I will always be glad that I did, for I found that the nurse who should have been with him was unaccountably absent, and the bed was in a frightful state, pulled about by poor Booth's tormented writhings, the sheets and pillows stained with blood he had brought up in his struggle to breathe.

I stayed with him until the fit passed, and then did my best to make him comfortable. But as I was about to retire, his hand suddenly shot out of the covers and gripped my arm, and with a cry of terror he begged me not to go. I therefore fetched a chair, and sat down by the bed to keep him company.

After a time his hand grasped my arm again, but gently this time; pulling me towards him. When I was quite close, he whispered, 'I *have* been happy!' The manner in which he said this was extremely singular: as though it formed part of a conversation in the course of which someone had ventured to affirm the contrary.

I hastened to assure him that I believed what he had said. He did not seem to hear me, however, only repeating, in the same way, 'I *have* been happy! I *have*!'.

He died almost immediately afterwards.

> I have the honour, Sir, to remain,
> Most respectfully yours
>
> Edward Hackwood